Praise for Lisa

'Lisa Timoney's debut has all the elements of a fabulous family drama . . . it kept me turning the pages from beginning to end!'
Kerry Fisher

'Heartbreaking and life affirming.'
Emma Robinson

'A warm-hearted, page-turning read.'
Ali Mercer

'A thoughtful family drama about a tangle of past secrets.'
Jill Childs

'A gripping story of family secrets, love and past tragedy that kept me hooked from beginning to end. A seriously impressive debut.'
Annie Lyons

'An assured debut about family, loyalty and secrets.'
Laura Pearson

HER MOTHER'S LIES

Lisa started her career teaching English and Drama, and when she had her family, combined all three to write novels about family drama. Originally from Yorkshire, she now lives in a London suburb with her husband and two teenage daughters, so expects there's plenty more drama to come.

By the same author:

Her Daughter's Secret

Her
Mother's
Lies

LISA TIMONEY

avon.

Published by AVON
A division of HarperCollins*Publishers*
1 London Bridge Street
London SE1 9GF

www.harpercollins.co.uk

HarperCollins*Publishers*
Macken House, 39/40 Mayor Street Upper,
Dublin 1 D01 C9W8
Ireland

A Paperback Original 2023

1

First published in Great Britain by HarperCollins*Publishers* 2023

A catalogue copy of this book is available from the British Library.

ISBN: 978-0-00-855318-0

Typeset in Sabon by Palimpsest Book Production Ltd, Falkirk, Stirlingshire
Printed and bound in the UK using 100% renewable electricity
at CPI Group (UK) Ltd

For John.
I love you.
Thank you for showing me how to strive.

Chapter One

Bonnie

Present Day

Should I stay or should I go? The Clash song looped in Bonnie's head as she turned over in bed, the dust and chemical smell of the new duvet reminding her she wasn't at home. As if she needed reminding.

She couldn't stop the song repeating any more than she could stop all the other thoughts crashing into her mind and causing havoc. The familiar dread wanted to pin her to the mattress, but she forced herself to sit up and drop her feet onto the floor. She tapped her toes on the carpet and glowered at the still-full packing boxes by the door, her brain screaming the last line of the song. It was a question she'd asked herself over and over again during her first sleepless night in this strange room: Should I stay, or should I go?

She tied her dressing gown cord firmly around her middle and went through to the sitting-room, stopping at a pile of canvases propped against the furthest wall. The prospect of unwrapping them made her stomach churn. They'd never been hung. She'd lugged them from the tiny studio where she'd painted them – desperate to transfer her overwhelming emotions onto the canvas – to the beautiful stone villa in Glasgow, to here; this featureless new-build in a town where she didn't know a soul.

She took a sharp breath, then forced her fingers to work quickly. The bubble wrap protecting the first canvas came away easily and fell to the floor. She twisted the painting around and let it wind her. The significance of those dark blue brushstrokes leading to the glowing light in the centre tightened her chest. She leaned it against the back of the sofa, stepping away to view it properly, the polythene film crackling in tiny eruptions under her bare feet.

Freeing the rest of the canvases, she balanced them on the sofa and armchair. She sliced open box after box, rummaging until she found picture hooks, a tape measure, and a claw hammer. Not allowing herself to stop and think, she measured the walls, making ghost-pale pencil marks on the paintwork, then tapped hooks into the plaster.

She hung the blue painting first.

Next was an orange picture of two figures holding hands, walking towards a golden glow. Concentrating on the exact position of the hook, Bonnie bashed the hammer harder than she intended and it flew from her grasp into the air. She grabbed for it as it smashed into a box, shattering a glass photo frame just as she thrust her hand inside.

She sat, watching the blood from her glass-punctured thumb trickle across the faces in the photograph, whispering, 'I'm sorry. I'm going to stay here until I've put things right. I'm so, so sorry.'

* * *

By five o'clock she couldn't force her heavy limbs to do any more so she slumped on the sofa and dragged the pink throw over her. With bare feet, she kicked a box aside, sipping the weak gin and tonic she'd made because it felt like it was the sort of thing a single woman living alone should do. It was supposed to feel decadent. At the very least it should be relaxing, but the bitter drink did nothing to stop dark thoughts finding corners of her mind to burrow in.

Through the balcony doors, she watched a painted barge make its way along the canal. She waited for the beauty of the view to lift her, but the boost she used to feel when her eyes caught something enchanting failed to materialise. She stared until the patterns on the boat pranced, then blurred. She blinked tears away. What was she doing, drinking alone and crying like a middle-aged Bridget Jones? If she carried on like this, she'd have to get a cat.

Her stomach rumbled and she shoved off the throw, feeling the chill of the room. Her head spun when she stood. *That's what you get for forgetting to eat*, she thought. *Idiot*. She took the glass through to the kitchen and poured the contents down the sink before opening the fridge door. The salad she'd intended to have for dinner drooped in its bag, the grilled chicken pale and corpse-like. She couldn't face it. Right now, she needed salt, fat, and sugar.

She scurried through the car park towards the main road, zipping her biker jacket against the wind. Turning towards the high street, she pushed her long fringe behind her ears, but it was pointless as the wind just blew it back into her eyes.

Before she reached the junction leading to the town's main shopping street, the sight of a huge brick building set back from the road made her stop abruptly. Behind a car park with bays numbered in yellow was a ramp with an iron railing, leading up to a surprisingly ornate red brick frontage. A tatty sign held by ropes at each corner said 'Bocks' in large letters, with 'For All Your Storage Needs' in smaller type underneath. It hung limply over the ugly blue doors, like a smile that didn't reach the eyes.

Her feet crossed the tarmac and before she knew it, she was pressing the buzzer to the left of the blue doors. A camera spied on her from next to the sign, which strained against its ropes in the wind. Looking at her watch, she saw it was 6 p.m., probably not a good time to view a storage facility. She was turning to leave when there was a loud click and the door opened a crack.

She stepped into an atrium that reminded her of her old junior school, with high ceilings and shiny white walls. She shuddered at the spectres of spelling tests and times tables that the sight conjured. Did people who were taller than her five-feet also feel like children out of place in an adult world? She put her shoulders back and practised her best grown-up face.

Beginning to think she'd been let into the eerily quiet reception by accident, she was turning to leave when the unmistakable clack of heels on laminate flooring made her jump. The red door on the other side of the hall opened.

'Can I help you?' asked a tall woman with short, high-lighted hair and a pinched face. She kept her hand on the door. One foot, in patent shoes, remained on the other side of it, giving the indication she would only tolerate the briefest of interruptions.

'Sorry, yes,' Bonnie blustered. 'I was wondering about storage.'

'What kind? Domestic, commercial?'

4

Bonnie swallowed. 'Sorry, yes, erm, domestic. Not much, just some . . .' She stopped, partly because she already felt stupid for babbling and partly because she had no idea what she would store in this big, cold building.

The woman marched forwards, the door slamming behind her. Lifting a portion of the wooden reception desk, she stepped to the other side and let it fall again. She rummaged among heaps of untidy papers.

'I'll give you a price list' – she tutted – 'if I can find one in this lot.' She gave an unconvincing smile and took a pair of glasses from where they nestled in her hair, balancing them on her nose as she glared at one leaflet after another.

'Ah, here. This has the unit sizes and costings.' She thrust a sheet of paper at Bonnie. The woman had the air of a stern school mistress and Bonnie had to resist the urge to say, *Thanks, Miss*, and ask if she might be excused while sticking two fingers up behind her back.

'Very kind,' she said, in the voice she usually saved for wealthy clients in her old life. Why did she let people intimidate her so easily? She smiled brightly and was about to turn to leave when another of the leaflets caught her eye. It said: *Part-Time Receptionist Wanted*.

'Excuse me.'

The woman looked over her glasses and Bonnie noticed there were dark circles under her eyes. 'Yes?'

'Are you looking for a receptionist?' She glanced around the room, noting the ancient computer and hooks behind the desk holding plastic packets of padlocks

'Umm?'

'Because I'm new to the area and was thinking about looking for a part-time job.' Bonnie spoke quickly. She knew if she didn't blurt it out, she'd overthink and end up saying nothing. She straightened her spine, directing her gaze six inches up to meet the woman's eyes.

The woman's shoulders visibly dropped, as though she was giving up on a fight. 'Right, well, I suppose you should take one of these.' She picked up another leaflet with a manicured hand and passed it to Bonnie who was suddenly aware of her bitten-down nails and the grubby plaster on her thumb. 'All the details are on there, along with my daughter's phone number. She's the one who's pushing for this.'

Bonnie took the leaflet and stared at the name and phone number.

The woman cleared her throat. 'Was there anything else?'

'No, thank you . . . sorry, I didn't catch your name?' She paused, head tilted to one side.

'Alice Egerton.'

Bonnie gave her warmest smile. 'Nice to meet you, Alice. I'm Bonnie Lombard.' She tucked the papers into her bag. 'I'll be in touch.'

As she trotted down the road towards the Chinese takeaway, there was a new lightness in her chest. The wind cooled her face and blew out her hair like a fan on a film set. She was Bonnie Lombard, successful interior designer. She'd recently sold her business for an enormous amount of money. She would never need to work again, but more than anything in the world right now, she desperately wanted this job.

Chapter Two

Alice

Present Day

Alice sat on the hard chair, clasping her hands together and pushing them into the fabric of her tailored trousers. Her reflection in the glass behind the desk looked haunted, her eye sockets hollow and dark. She tried to unclench her jaw and relax the deep line between her eyebrows. The shadow of someone's reflection behind her in the bank's partitioned pseudo-office made her turn. Her jaw tightened again when she saw it was a barely-adult in a suit.

He held out his hand and she shook it, aware her palm was clammy. She tried not to stare at the shaving cut under his bottom lip. She wasn't sure why he'd bothered shaving. From the softness of his cheeks, it looked like it would take him a week to muster stubble.

'Thank you for coming in, Mrs Egerton.'

'My pleasure.' The words came out crinkled. She coughed to loosen her voice and repeated, more assuredly, 'My pleasure.'

He didn't introduce himself, but Alice could see from the laminated badge on his lapel that his name was Sam Logan. Should she call him Mr Logan? That would feel absurd; he looked about twenty-four, the same age as her daughter. The voices of the bank tellers and customers in the main room were clearly audible from this pretend office. Was she really meant to discuss her humiliating financial situation behind this flimsy screen?

'Since the business account and the mortgage are joint names, I had hoped Mr Egerton would be joining us today.'

Alice shifted in her seat. 'My husband is unwell. He has a heart condition and has been told he needs to rest as much as possible. I run the business and have done for the last three years.' She didn't add that she'd worked hard to ensure Richard was oblivious to the fact the business account was overdrawn and they'd missed two mortgage payments on the house. The stress might kill him.

Sam tapped on the keyboard on the desk, squinting at the small computer screen. He turned it to Alice. 'This is the balance of the account.'

Alice took her glasses from where they perched in her hair and put them on. She looked at the screen and winced. 'Yes.'

'So, you can see why we needed this meeting.'

'As I informed you in my email, this is only a temporary situation. When the storage facility plot is sold, we'll be able to repay the overdraft and settle the mortgage. It will sell for considerably more than it's worth as a business. It's only a matter of time.'

'I wish it was as simple as that.' He swung the screen back towards himself. 'Am I right in thinking the planning application has been turned down once? And it failed the appeal?'

8

'Yes, but—' She wished she could undo the bow tied neatly at the neck of her blouse to release the heat crawling up her body.

'I'm afraid we have to work with how things stand now. Not how they might look if a gamble pays off.'

Sweat dribbled down Alice's back. 'It is not a gamble. It's a process. Bureaucracy.'

'A process that has already failed twice.'

Did he think she didn't know that, that it didn't keep her up at night? 'We have amended the plans to ameliorate many of the objections.'

'Still—'

'Our house has equity. A lot of equity.'

He rubbed at a red patch under the collar of his shirt. Alice saw he was almost as uncomfortable as she was, which somehow made it worse.

'But, unfortunately, now you are in arrears on your mortgage.'

His pitying smile made her look down at her hands. 'How long?' she asked.

'Sorry?'

She swallowed and looked directly into his eyes. 'How long will the bank give us before it forecloses?'

'Well, as you say, the house is worth considerably more than the mortgage, so if you put it on the market now . . .'

'No. I can't sell the house. Give me nine months.'

He sat back in his chair. 'That's not really—'

Alice pushed words past the lump in her throat. 'Six? If you allow me six months from now to get planning permission, then I can sell the plot and I will have more than enough money to pay off the overdraft and the mortgage. The new plans are almost ready. That's where a lot of the money has gone. Architects cost the—'

Sam sighed. 'But—'

'If permission is refused, I will sell my house and pay both debts in full. You have my word.'

'I'm afraid we work on figures, not words, Mrs Egerton.'

The sound of chattering voices beyond the screen seemed to amplify. She talked over the noise. 'Please. Let me try. My husband is ill. My daughter wants . . . It's our home . . .' She dug her nails into her palms. 'Let me try.' She leaned forwards, pointing at the screen. 'Do the figures. Please. Work out what I need to get us through the next six months. I'm sure it will be far less than the equity in the house.'

He didn't meet her eye when he shook his head. 'We can't offer you any more because your income doesn't cover what you already owe.'

'But—' Tears stung the corners of her eyes.

'I'm sorry, Mrs Egerton. I wish it was better news.'

'I understand. I'll arrange . . . something. A payment plan, or . . .' Alice stood, knocking her thigh hard on the desk as she quickly shook Sam Logan's hand and left before she humiliated herself even more.

She rushed back in the direction of Bocks, hoping nobody had called by and found it closed. On the way, she passed a run-down parade of shops at the shabby end of the high street. A scuffed black sign by a doorbell next to a kebab shop said, 'Financial Adviser: Loans, Mortgages and Investments.' Alice paused briefly, before pressing the bell.

* * *

She wasn't proud of the fact she waited until Richard's sleeping tablet made him drowsy before giving him the documents to sign that evening. After the bank refused to help her, her only option was the dodgy financial adviser. If Richard had seen how much they would have to pay in interest on the sub-prime loan she'd taken out against the house, there was no way he'd have signed.

The only thing she could buy now, was time. She had six months to make it work.

Chapter Three

Alice

Alice closed her front door behind her then stooped to release her feet from her shoes and rubbed at her aching soles, the nude tights wrinkling under her fingers. She should probably start wearing flats to work since her back twinged with sciatica most days, but that would feel like giving up and she was not a quitter. She put on her slippers. Straightening, she rolled her shoulders to release the tension that built from the moment she walked into that bloody storage facility to the minute she returned home and poured herself a glass of Malbec in her favourite crystal glass.

'Richard,' she shouted, her voice loud in the cavernous hallway. 'Where are you?'

'In the sitting-room. Good day?'

She kneaded a knotted muscle in her neck and pushed open the door to the sitting-room. She didn't know why she asked where he was when she got home from work

13

because Richard was always exactly where he should be; in his chair, paper on his lap, and wire-rimmed glasses balanced midway down his nose. His beige jumper and grey trousers melted into the neutral tones of the room, the light brown sofa, and tasteful prints arranged symmetrically on the cream walls. She leaned down to kiss his forehead.

He squeezed her hand. 'Any news from the front line?'

She imagined guerrilla fighters, head to toe in combat gear, hiding in the narrow corridors behind the cardboard boxes, wielding staple guns. 'No, nothing to report. Did you take your tablet?'

'Yes.' He smiled. 'I remembered today.'

Was she meant to pat him on the head for remembering all on his own to take the tablets that thinned his blood enough to get through his clogged arteries? She imagined adding it to the list in her head along with every other thing that kept their small family from combusting. The muscles in her cheeks twitched as she caught herself and clamped her teeth together. This was not Richard's fault. She needed to remember that.

She patted his shoulder and stepped back into the hall, standing under the chandelier that dripped from the landing ceiling to the centre of the impressive atrium.

'Laura!'

A voice replied distantly from upstairs.

'Laura? I can't hear you!'

Footsteps thudded along the landing, and a face appeared over the white banister. 'That's because we're not in the same room, Mother.' Her tone was exasperated. 'If you came to my bedroom instead of summoning me from the hall, you'd be able to hear me. I'm not a child who hasn't done as they're told, for god's sake.'

14

'But I want you to come here.' Was she supposed to run upstairs to speak to her daughter now, as well as everything else?

A huge sigh could be heard as the head dipped out of sight, then reappeared at the top of the staircase.

'Oh, god. I'd forgotten about your hair.'

'Let it go.' Laura trotted down the stairs and marched past Alice, who followed her into the kitchen, the sting of the pinched nerve in her back making her breath catch.

Sighing, she lifted a mug that one of them had left on the granite island and put it in the dishwasher, then wiped away the ring it had left on the black surface. 'But why have you left it dark at the roots? If you've got to have candyfloss-pink hair, why not do the whole lot? Roots used to be a bad thing in my day.'

'I'm twenty-four years old.' Laura turned sharply. 'You need to let me do what I want with my own sodding hair. I wish I'd gone for fuchsia now, instead of this tasteful pale pink.' She inspected a strand, twirling it around her finger.

Alice groaned. 'Tasteful? We'll have to agree to disagree on that.'

'Nothing new there.'

Alice wasn't about to rise to the bait. 'Anyway, why are you so touchy this evening? I'm the one who's been in the misery maze all day. My back's killing me.' She lifted a bottle of red wine from the island's built-in rack and tipped it, raising her eyebrows to her daughter, who nodded. She reached into the glass-fronted cupboard near the sink and plucked out three glasses with slender stems.

'I'm trying to finish that application for my MA. I haven't got half the experience I need.' She watched Alice

15

pour the red liquid and then took a sip. 'I bet nobody else applying for an MA in Fine Art did a BSC in boring Business.'

'What's the phrase? Let it go?' Alice poured a third, smaller glass, and took it through to the sitting-room, Laura following.

'What are we letting go?' Richard took his glass and smiled at his wife, folding his paper and putting it on the coffee table.

'Her silly ideas, hopefully.' Alice sat, laying her head on the back of the sofa, and exhaling deeply.

'Oh, for the love of . . .' Laura balled her fists. 'Doing an MA is not a silly idea. You make it sound like I'm planning to give away all my worldly possessions and go and live in a Kibbutz.'

'You haven't got any worldly possessions.'

'And why's that?'

'Let's not do this again. I'm tired.' Alice pulled her head upright with an enormous effort. 'I'm just saying that now might not be the best time to take something like that on.'

'The best time for who?' Laura stalked from the room before Alice could reply.

'Whom,' Alice whispered. She stuck her tongue out at a frowning Richard.

'That went well,' he said, blowing into his cheeks and letting the air out slowly.

'She's stubborn. I don't know where she gets it from.'

'That much is true.'

Alice closed her eyes and took another drink, concentrating on the rich flavour, the feel of it on her tongue, an infinitesimal burn of alcohol at the back of her throat and up into her nose. The loosening of her muscles would come soon, she hoped. 'I only called her down to help with dinner, and now she's gone again.'

'Anything I can do?'

She looked at her husband. His thin face had aged ten years in the last three. Now the deep laughter lines were less visible than the worry lines carved across his forehead. 'It's fine, it's only a salmon tray bake. I'm sure I can manage.'

She pushed her hands against the sofa cushion, feeling her elbows creak as she levered herself from the seat.

Laura was leaning against the island in the centre of the kitchen scrolling through her phone when Alice entered. 'Could you give me a hand with dinner?'

'I would've made dinner while you were at work, if you'd let me.'

Alice groaned. 'I don't want to argue, I just want a bit of help.'

'Yep, that's what I do isn't it? Help.'

Alice's shoulders slumped. 'What do you mean by that?'

'I help out at home. I help with the business. It's time I did something for myself.'

Alice quietly closed the kitchen door, leaning her back against the wood. 'Your point is?'

Laura pulled out a stool from under the lip of the island and sat. 'All my friends have lives of their own. They've got flats and boyfriends. What have I got?'

The temptation to point out all the ways her own life had changed in the last three years almost overwhelmed Alice. She hadn't planned to be working long hours in a business she had no interest in just to keep their house from being repossessed. She shouldn't have to take out an extortionate loan against her beautiful home. She should be looking forward to a comfortable retirement, flicking

17

through brochures for Caribbean cruises, not manning the desk at a shabby storage centre.

'You're not exactly suffering, are you?' Alice gestured around the large kitchen with its full fridge and wine rack, expensive tiled floor, and marble dining table. 'And you've got a degree and a job. When I was your age—'

'No.' Laura put her flat palm in the air. 'I'm not listening to how you and Dad worked your way up from nothing again. I know you worked hard.' Her eyes flashed with a fire Alice recognised. 'But I'm sick of living like I'm some kind of add-on to your life. I need to do something for myself.'

Alice pushed herself away from the door and sat on a stool close to Laura. She spoke quietly. 'It won't be forever, just until we get planning permission on the plot. When we've sold it, everything will change.'

Laura gripped the edge of the granite. 'No, it won't. There's always something that means you need me to stay.'

'That's not fair. Everything I've done is to make things better for all of us, for all our futures.'

'That's my point. For the future. But what about now? The plans might never be agreed. We both know that. Even if they are, can you honestly say there won't be another reason for me to hang around here and see *what the future brings*?' She did air quotes with her fingers and Alice wanted to slap her hands. She had no idea of the lengths Alice was going to, to make their futures secure. One day they'd look back and be grateful, and that day couldn't come soon enough.

'It's already been three years since I moved back home.' Laura gave a short laugh. 'Three years, Mum. Am I meant to put all my plans on hold on the off-chance things might work out for you?'

Alice whispered, 'It's not just for me. It's for all of us and for your dad. You know how bad he feels about everything going wrong.' She looked back at the door to make sure it was still closed. 'If we can keep the units going until the council sees sense, then at least he'll have something to look forward to. He needs to think everything is going smoothly so he doesn't worry. And I'm trying to give you what you want. Honestly, I am. It's just taking longer than I thought.'

Laura stared down at her hands, releasing her grip on the island, and picking at flecks of what looked like red paint. Alice became conscious of the humming of the fridge, trying to think of something to say to bridge the gap between herself and her only child.

'A woman came in yesterday and took one of your leaflets.'

Laura looked up, her brown eyes bright. 'You put them out?'

Alice shrugged. 'Not *out* exactly, but they were on the desk and she asked about the job. She took one away with her.'

Laura spoke quickly. 'What was she like? Do you think she was interested?'

Alice pursed her lips. She shouldn't have mentioned it. What was she thinking? 'I have no idea. She said she was new to the area, so I don't imagine we'll be the only place she's looking.' She lifted herself from the stool and opened the fridge, taking out the salmon, peppers, and mange tout, and dropping them on the island. She silently totted up how much this meal cost, wincing at the thought. 'I wouldn't get your hopes up.'

'But if she does apply, and she's suitable, then I'll have the time to do my course.'

Alice turned and put her hand over Laura's, then lifted it quickly. 'Let's not get carried away. She hasn't even applied yet and she might be a mass murderer or something. She was a bit untidy looking.'

'Not all mass murderers are untidy; look at Ted Bundy.' Laura winked, a smile lifting her soft cheeks. 'And you let a woman with pink hair manage the place, so you're obviously not that picky.'

'Yes, well, you can't choose your family, can you?'

Laura laughed and arched one dark eyebrow just as her phone began to trill in her pocket.

'Hello,' she said, her eyes widening in surprise. 'You're ringing about the job?' She looked at Alice and gave a thumbs up. Alice listened, unease tightening the muscles in her back, pinching the nerve until sharp pain shot down her leg. Laura used a voice Alice barely recognised, even pronouncing consonants at the ends of words. 'That's great. Could you email your CV?'

There was quiet before Laura said, 'Could you come in for an interview the day after tomorrow? That will give us time to go through your CV and think up some quasi-intelligent questions.' She laughed at the reply before saying, 'Great. I look forward to meeting you then.'

'That was a bit premature.' Alice bit back the desire to tell Laura exactly how dicey their financial situation was. It wouldn't do any good to burden her daughter. She'd given up so much already. Even a part-time salary would put more strain on an overstretched budget, but she had the money from the loan now, and maybe giving Laura some time to work towards her dream would be a good way to use it. Anyway, in six months the fear that gripped her insides every time she thought about money would be a distant memory. She was sure of it.

Laura skipped from the room. 'No time like the present.'

Alice opened the drawer where they kept spare batteries and keys and took out the property listings she'd stashed there. She flicked through the glossy sheets, stopping at a small, terraced house, then a flat in a modern block. She tried to imagine her little family living there.

No time like the present, eh? she thought as she took a packet of ibuprofen from the cupboard next to the sink, popped two from the foil and swallowed them, feeling them snake their way down her throat. *But what about the future? Who's going to take care of that?*

Chapter Four

Alice

Present Day

Laura tidied the tiny staffroom behind reception, ready for the interview. She whirled around the small, functional room, polishing the sink, wiping down the cupboard, and the front of the fridge. As she ran a cloth over the square table with four plastic chairs, Alice scanned the room, suppressing the bitter thought that Laura rarely channelled her inner clean freak at home. It was her own fault really – it was easier to do the clearing up herself; that way, she knew it had been done properly. Somewhere over the years, the rest of the family had stopped asking if she needed any help, and even though she now did, the pattern of her making everything tick was established and set.

Taking in the uneven walls, covered in the same shiny white paint as the reception, and uncomfortable furniture, she was forced to acknowledge that she'd made little effort to make it a cheery place to work. It had never seemed worth it since they'd bought the place planning to knock it straight down. But three years was a long time for someone in their twenties to be stuck in a job where there was nothing of beauty; especially for someone like Laura.

She watched her daughter polish the aluminium sink until it shone, crossing her fingers behind her back and silently praying that this place would soon be an unpleasant memory, like a turbulent flight, or a hospital stay. She quickly shook the last thought from her head.

'You've dressed to impress.'

Laura wore black linen trousers instead of her usual jeans, her pink waves corralled in a neat bun on top of her head. She looked beautiful.

'I'm going to take that as a compliment. Thank you.' Laura carried on scrubbing. 'You look very nice too.'

Alice's grey cashmere roll neck with the tie at the throat was a little too warm for the stuffy room.

'I don't know why you're making so much effort,' she said, watching Laura wipe the kettle over with a damp cloth. 'She probably won't even turn up. Even if she does, we should interview more than one person before committing to working with someone.'

'Yeah, because it's everyone's dream job. They'll be queueing up for the chance to work here.'

Ignoring her daughter's sarcasm, Alice rushed to the door as a banging noise came from reception.

'Ah, Jim!' she said to the elderly man who was opening and closing the red door that led through to the storage units. His hooded eyes narrowed as he moved the door backwards and forwards on its hinges, head cocked to one side.

'Now then,' he said. 'I think it's stopped squeaking. Can you hear anything?'

Alice stepped out from behind the desk, listening intently, eyes dipping from the cracks appearing in the shiny paint on the high ceiling, to the threadbare carpet tiles. The damned place was falling apart. 'I don't think I can.'

They both stood in silence, staring at the door as Jim moved it to and fro like a fan in front of a fainting maiden's face.

'I think you've fixed it!' Alice broke the silence, clapping her hands as Jim slowly straightened with his hand supporting the small of his back.

'I think I have.' A smile bounded onto his face and his wrinkled cheeks flushed as he stole a glance at Alice then looked away.

'It's been bothering me for so long, and now it's gone. You're a marvel, Jim Morton.'

'Glad to help.' His voice was gruff, as though warming up for the first words of the day. 'Nice to see both of you in this morning. Laura looks very smart.'

'Yes.' Alice opened and closed the door experimentally, her smile fading. 'We're meant to be interviewing a new receptionist this morning, but I'm rather hoping she doesn't turn up.'

'You're not thinking of leaving here, are you?' Jim flushed again. 'I mean, it would be strange not to see you every day.'

She could've kissed his lovely old face. 'It's only a part-time post, so Laura can spend more time painting bloody pictures.' She covered her mouth and put her hand on Jim's arm. 'Don't tell her I said that. I just worry about her future. I don't know how she thinks she'll make a living with a master's in Fine Art. I wish she'd do something with her business degree. That's more likely to give

25

her a stable income. You can't underestimate that, can you?'

Jim put his hand over hers. 'These young 'uns don't value stability like we did at their age, do they? Your secret's safe with me.'

'Now, what do I owe you for fixing this door?'

Jim flapped his arm dismissively. 'Don't be daft, it only took a minute, and I was here anyway.'

Alice pursed her lips. 'You can't—'

'I can do what I like,' Jim interrupted, standing tall. 'It's one of the few perks of getting old.'

'What must your wife think of me? I'm sure she must curse me for taking advantage of you.' She knew how she'd react if Richard regularly did unpaid work for another woman. Jim's wife was either oblivious or a saint.

Jim dropped his eyes to the floor. 'She thinks nothing of the sort. She's glad to have me out from under her feet.' He bent to pick up his toolbox, then looked up at Alice with kind eyes. 'I'm always happy to help, so please don't stop letting me know what needs doing. It's nice to feel useful.'

She squeezed his arm, hating herself for thinking up a list of repairs she would ask Jim to do when the shame of not paying him for this one abated. A loud buzzer sounded behind the desk and they both turned to see Laura bounce in from the staffroom and press the button to release the blue door.

The woman who entered looked very different from the untidy creature who'd taken the leaflet. Her hair was still a bit wild, the strawberry blonde, wispy fringe tucked ineffectually behind her ears, but her silk blouse looked expensive, as did her tailored culottes. It was the kind of outfit Alice admired in magazines – blues clashing with

26

greens in contrasting prints – but knew she'd never be brave enough to try.

'You must be Bonita.' Laura approached the woman, hand outstretched.

When the woman took her hand and shook it, Alice was surprised to see she was trembling. She actually looked like she might cry. Was she really that frightened of interviewing for a part-time job?

'Yes, at least that's the name on my driving licence, so I put it on my CV, but most people call me Bonnie.' The woman gave a short, nervous-sounding laugh.

'Okay, Bonnie.' Laura gestured to Alice and Jim. 'I believe you've met my mother, Alice.'

Alice nodded as the small woman looked up at her.

'And that's Jim. He's a customer, but he very kindly helps out around the place.'

'Hello.' Jim thrust out his hand and Bonnie shook it, seemingly recovered from the trauma of her entrance. Her smile was broad, eyes darting between the three of them like a skittish puppy, deciding who to lick first.

'Nice to meet you all.' She wiped her hands on her trousers. 'I'm surprised how nervous I am, it's a long time since I had an interview.'

Alice stepped forwards, aware of her height as she looked down on Bonnie. 'Yes, I saw that on your CV. I'm a little confused to be honest—'

'Let's go through to the staff room, shall we?' Laura interrupted. 'I'm sure you'll be less nervous with a nice cup of tea.'

* * *

Seated on the plastic chairs, Alice watched Bonnie wipe sweat from her top lip as she and Laura leafed through a copy of her CV. She put the paper on the table and looked directly into Bonnie's green eyes. 'You're an interior designer, I see?'

'That's right.'

'And you had your own business in Glasgow?'

'That's correct.'

Alice sat back in her chair and crossed her arms, then uncrossed them again, aware she might appear unapproachable. 'Could you explain why, as a businesswoman in a creative field, you're applying for a part-time job in a storage facility?' If her husband hadn't bought the units then nearly died a few days later, she wouldn't have chosen to spend a moment of her precious time cloistered in this stultifying place.

She felt Laura tense beside her, but the question needed to be asked.

Bonnie wrapped her fingers around her mug of tea. She bit her bottom lip. 'I know it might seem a little odd, but I've had to rethink my life recently and I believe this job would be perfect for me.'

'Could you expand?' Alice was sure she heard Laura tut, as though she didn't spend her life complaining about having to work there. But she was undeterred. 'Why would it be perfect?'

Bonnie let go of the mug and lay her fingers flat on the table. She took a deep breath. 'I've recently sold my business and moved to a new area. I have my reasons for all of that, which I would rather not disclose now, but it's fair to say that having arrived at this time in my life' – she looked at Alice, who recognised the inference – 'I have taken stock and carefully considered what's important to me and now I aim to do my best to pursue it.'

Alice wondered if an interview was the right time to

tell a prospective employer you had secrets but couldn't think of a question that wouldn't sound inappropriately probing. 'And how does taking on a minimum wage job fit in with your grand, new life plan?' If she thought she'd be able to work her way up, she was wrong. 'There're no options for promotion or pay rises; this isn't that kind of business. It's repetitive and boring and we don't have a TV company coming and auctioning off forgotten bins.'

Laura threw daggers at her.

'I'm only saying that if your grand plan involves world domination of the storage business, there really isn't anything to dominate.' Alice hated sounding so pessimistic, but she couldn't understand why this woman wanted this job. She didn't need the hassle of taking her on and training her only for her to disappear in a few weeks, leaving Alice to pick up the pieces.

'There's nothing grand about my plan,' said Bonnie, her freckles dancing as she scratched her nose.

Laura shot Alice a cold glance. 'I think what my mother is trying to say, is, why does this job appeal to you?'

'Okay, to be perfectly honest, my artwork is what makes me happy. I want time and space to paint and draw and enjoy my life without the demands of a stressful job.'

Alice had to close her eyes to stop the other two women seeing her eyeballs roll to the back of her head. Another bloody artist. Didn't anyone know how hard it was trying to make a living doing the most mundane jobs, never mind following your artistic passions? She focused on containing the muscles in her face and opened her eyes again, avoiding looking at Laura. Bonnie was still talking.

'But I don't know a soul, so I'd like a job where I can meet people, but where I wouldn't have to take work home. I don't need the money, it's true, but I do need some structure in my days, some company, and so I think this job would suit me perfectly.'

Lucky you, thought Alice sourly. 'Wouldn't retail be a better option if you want to meet people?' Her tone sounded abrupt, even to her.

'I'm not a big fan of shops.'

Alice wondered why Bonnie's cheeks coloured but didn't feel she could ask.

'Our customers are lovely,' Laura interjected, 'and everyone has an interesting story to tell about why they need storage, so I'm sure you'd meet new friends here. Jim, who you met outside, retired a few years ago and his wife likes to keep the house perfect so he stores all of his tools and bits and bobs here, which is enormously useful when bits fall off the building.'

Why was Laura prattling like that? Alice gave her a tap on the ankle with her shoe and Laura kicked her back.

'What personal strengths would you bring to the job?' Alice was pleased she'd read a couple of articles on interview techniques with her morning coffee and hoped this overqualified woman wouldn't see through her bravado.

Bonnie chewed her bottom lip again and looked up to the left. 'I'm loyal and hardworking.' She paused. 'I'm friendly and have a creative approach to problems.' She nodded at the bare walls. 'And I think I've got a few pictures I could hang in here to cheer the place up a bit.' She pulled her lips back in a grimace. 'If that's not over-stepping the job description.'

Laura chortled and shook her head. 'It sounds like a perfect collection of skills to me, especially the last one. I might join you!'

'Anyway,' said Alice, forcing a polite smile and keen to bring the meeting to an end. 'I think we've asked everything we need.' She folded the CV into quarters. 'Do you have any questions?'

'Erm.' Bonnie looked from one woman to the other. 'How do the shifts work at the moment? Is there more than one person on site at a time?'

'My husband has a heart condition,' said Alice, 'so it's just Laura and I taking it in turns. That wouldn't be a problem if people didn't need us to be open at peculiar hours of the day.'

'Those pesky customers, they will go and have day jobs themselves.' Laura wobbled her head comedically.

Alice ignored her and continued. 'So, in answer to your question, no, there isn't usually more than one of us on site, so if we do take someone on, we have to trust them not only with our business, but with the belongings of all of our customers.'

'I'm sorry to hear about your husband.'

'Thank you.' Alice noted she hadn't said anything more about being trustworthy, but she hadn't asked directly and didn't feel like she could now. She wished Richard were there, he'd know what to say. Interviewing was like trying to cross a stream with slippery steppingstones. Surely it was the interviewee who should feel out of their depth.

'This isn't a permanent job. You know that, don't you?' Alice scrutinised the woman's face. 'When we get planning permission, we will probably be closing the units.' She crossed her fingers under the table, then felt foolish at trying to harness superstition like a silly child.

'That's fine by me.'

Was there no way of putting this woman off? 'We'd need you to carry out a police check, for security purposes.' Alice watched Bonnie's face carefully. She was sure she

31

detected a tensing of the muscles in her cheeks, as though she'd clenched her teeth.

'That won't be a problem.'

Maybe she'd imagined it. 'We appreciate you coming in, Bonnie.' She stood and held her hand across the table.

Bonnie's chair legs scraped across the lino floor as she stood quickly and took Alice's hand, shaking it firmly. 'Thank you for seeing me. I enjoyed meeting you both.'

Laura was now on her feet and Alice noted when they shook hands, Bonnie covered Laura's hand with both of hers. Something about this woman made her uneasy. Perhaps it was just the thought of spending more money that caused her to feel like taking this woman on would be a huge mistake.

* * *

As they watched her walk across the car park and turn left along the main road Alice felt a heat coming off her daughter that reminded her of when she was younger and she wanted something very badly. An energy would build in her and escape through her pores, filling the air around her with something tangible. As a small child she would jump up and down, torrents of words pouring out of her, putting her case for why she couldn't possibly live without whatever was her passion in that moment.

These days, the vibrations were smaller, the words fewer, but the passions still burned with a fire that terrified Alice because it was out of her control.

* * *

The wind whipped fallen leaves against the windows on three sides of the dining table when they sat down to eat that evening. Alice watched the branches of the trees in the garden sway. She usually loved that their dining table was surrounded by glass, but in unpredictable weather like this, she'd prefer to be cocooned by solid brickwork.

Almost as soon as Alice placed her plate in front of her, Laura took up her knife and fork and said, 'You'll like the new receptionist, Dad. She's nice.'

Alice stopped chewing the chicken in her mouth and considered how best to approach this. She swallowed with some effort. 'We didn't agree to give her a job, Laura. There's still a conversation to be had about this.'

Laura put her cutlery down on the table. 'Oh, come on. She was perfect.'

Alice steeled herself. 'I don't agree. She was strange.'

'Strange how?' said Richard, without finishing his mouthful.

'Secretive.'

Laura rolled her eyes and took a drink. 'She didn't have to tell us anything about her personal life and it's none of our business anyway. Just because she didn't go into whether she's left a shag-about husband or anything doesn't mean she's being dishonest.'

Alice ignored Richard's laughter. 'No need to be crass. She looked at you all the while I was talking and, anyway, she's ridiculously overqualified. She's got a degree for goodness' sake.'

Laura's glass hovered in front of her face as she spoke. 'You're right, Mother, of course. It would be a million times better to employ someone who doesn't have a single GCSE to take care of our family business.' She took a loud slurp, which Alice knew was meant to provoke her.

'It would be better not to employ anyone at all.'

Laura slammed her glass on the table and Alice automatically looked to see if Richard was all right. His eyebrows were raised, but his skin had colour as his eyes flicked between the two women, the amusement gone.

The muscles in Laura's jaw pushed up under her skin. 'Then why did we interview her in the first place?'

'I don't know.' Alice rubbed the bridge of her nose. 'I shouldn't have let it get this far. I'm sorry. It's my fault.' Alice attempted a sorry smile but was met with fire in Laura's eyes.

'I knew you were humouring me.' She looked between her parents, then shook her head. 'You know what? I think it's time for me to look for something else.'

The hair at the nape of Alice's neck lifted. She looked across at Richard, but his eyes didn't shift from Laura's face.

'I'll get a part-time job somewhere, then you can use my salary to employ whoever you choose, and I can get on with my life. It's ridiculous us all living in each other's pockets like this. I need to do something for myself and that's the only way I can think of resolving this.'

She stood, but Alice caught her by the wrist. 'Don't.' She moved her hand down and took Laura's fingers and was transported back twenty years, holding her little girl's hand as they stood in front of Laura's infant school on her first day. Laura's hand had slipped from hers so quickly as she skipped towards the building and Alice had felt the ghost of her tiny fingers in her palm all day. 'Please. Let's talk about it.'

'There's not much point, is there?' She dragged her hand free. 'I've stalled my life for years and it was never meant to be permanent, was it? It's all a bit laughable, really. Twenty-four and living at home with my parents . . .'

'We know you only moved back to help us out. We are grateful,' Alice said. She didn't add that without Laura to support her, she was worried she might crumble under the weight of her life.

'I tried to compromise by going part-time, so, really, it's not much more expensive, is it?'

Alice couldn't argue without telling the two of them that even a small change in their finances could send a dangerous ripple across their already precarious situation.

'Even the most perfect candidate isn't good enough for you,' continued Laura, 'so I need to take myself out of the equation altogether.'

'No, you don't.' Richard's low voice made them both turn. He'd taken off his glasses and was rubbing his eyes. 'We can sort this out. Maybe I can do some shifts?'

'No.' Both women spoke at once.

Alice had made a vow to keep Richard's life stress-free. She was almost there. She leaned on her elbows and sighed, trying not to look in the direction of the drawer with the property details and think about the sacrifices they might all have to make. 'If you're serious about doing your MA in the autumn, then maybe we should give this Bonnie a trial.'

'I'm sure I'm well enough—'

'Please, Richard. I'd much prefer it if you didn't go back to work.'

He nodded and she could see it cost him to allow his wife and daughter to take care of him. 'You looked after us for decades. Now it's our turn.'

Laura's arms were limp at her sides. 'Mum, I still think it might be time I took a step back.'

Alice's heart swelled as she looked at her hard-won girl. 'You've done enough for us over the last few years. You're right, it's time we made some concessions for you. I admit, I worry about you pinning your hopes on a career in the arts, but we don't want to stop you following your dreams. And when things come good, we'll all reap the benefits, and none of us will have to worry too much about the future.'

'It's time to let me worry about my future, Mum. I'm a big girl now.'

'I know, but I'm your mother. Worrying about you is my job. And I like having you around. It's the only good thing to come out of what happened.' She looked down at the table, aware that Laura probably didn't see it that way. Alice knew that having Laura at home was her ideal, not Laura's.

She glanced across at Richard, his eyebrows still knitted in concern, when there was a bang then a crackle at the window. They all turned to see a plastic bag flat against the glass, as though prostrating itself, begging to be let in. Slowly, it peeled away then flew at speed, skidding across the grass as though it had seen what was inside and couldn't escape fast enough.

Alice rubbed her temples; her head ached, and needles of pain were jabbing at her back. 'Give Bonnie a ring in the morning and see when she can start,' she said with more positivity than she felt.

'You sure?'

She looked at Richard again and he nodded. She silently thanked the universe she still had him to guide and support her. 'I'm sure.'

Laura sat back down, picking up her knife and fork, and continuing her meal. The wind licked at the glass as the light fell away, hiding the chaos in the dark as Alice silently calculated how much of the loan would go on salary payments to a woman who she didn't trust.

36

Chapter Five

Bonnie

Present Day

Since Bonnie had learned about the police check, she'd struggled to eat. She dug a Dorito into a pot of hummus and raised it to her mouth, but her stomach said no. She tried an olive but had to chew it to a pulp then spit it out. The salty brine stayed in her mouth as she tried to research whether her DBS check was likely to come back clear.

She needed to know if she had to let all hope of the job go before she'd even started. The internet didn't seem to want to give her a definitive answer. She only knew one person who might be able to tell her with any authority: Ross. She looked up her cousin's number in her phone.

Every word Bonnie had practised in her head evaporated when she heard the dial tone. After the third ring she decided it was a stupid idea to call Ross. Just because he was a solicitor, didn't mean her would know the ins and outs of both Scottish and English legislation.

She pulled the phone away from her ear just as a deep voice said, 'Hello.'

It was too late. She placed it back near her ear. 'Ross. How are you? It's Bonnie. Bonita.'

'Hello, stranger. How are you doing?'

'Yeah. Good, thanks. You? How are Annie and the kids?'

'Alright, yeah, good. Growing up fast, you know. The kids, I mean, not Annie.' He laughed, then his voice sounded serious as he added, 'Haven't heard from you since your mum's funeral. I should have called after that—'

'No, don't worry,' she cut him off. 'I was in a bit of a state. Best left alone when I'm like that.'

'Right.' There was an uncomfortable pause. 'Anyway, what can I do for you?'

The question made her cringe. She vowed silently to keep in regular touch after she'd asked for this favour. 'I wanted to pick your brains about DBS checks.'

'What do you want to know?'

Bonnie filled her lungs, then forced out the words. 'The difference between the basic check and the enhanced one. What will show up, that kind of thing.'

'You mean like the stuff that happened after uni?' The sound of Ross's voice changed, as if he had switched the call off loudspeaker.

Bonnie scrunched her eyes tight. 'Yeah, and . . . there was one more thing when I first moved to Glasgow. That's more than ten years ago now, though.'

'Cuz . . .'

'I know, I know.' She lay back on the sofa, covering her eyes with her hand. 'I'm mortified to be asking you. I've moved back to England, to a to a town called Hamblin, and I've applied for a job I really want—'

'I thought you were self-employed?'

'I was but I sold the business last year and . . . it's a long story, but I really want this job and I need a clear police check for it.'

'Are you alright now?' There was concern in his voice.

Bonnie assessed her mind and body: her muscles were tense, she was regularly close to tears, she found it hard to sleep, and her head permanently chased one negative thought with another. 'I'm fine. Honestly, I'm in a good place. At least, I will be when I can stop worrying about this check.'

'Okay. I don't know off the top of my head. Give me a day to get all the information and I'll call you back. Alright?'

Bonnie let her hand fall from her eyes. 'Thanks, love. I really appreciate it. And let's get together soon, yeah?'

'I'd like that. Look after yourself. I'll be in touch.'

She'd made the call. That was the first step. Now she just had to get through the hours until she heard the results.

* * *

The next morning, bleary-eyed, Bonnie flicked through the clothes in her wardrobe, the hangers clanging on the rail. She wanted to make the right second impression when she started work. She'd felt an immediate affinity with Laura, but Alice was going to be difficult to win over.

She snorted a half laugh, remembering the day she'd been invited to Glamis Castle to quote for redesigning the private suite of the Earl of Strathmore. She hadn't even thought about what to wear then, and here she was now, agonising about an outfit to sit behind a dusty desk and hand over keys to customers at Bocks. Though she'd only been given a couple of shifts so far and she might not be allowed behind reception until her check came back. The thought made her insides churn.

She straightened the peacock feather throw on the bed and walloped the green and gold cushions to the floor. She lay out an array of shirts and trousers, shift dresses and leggings, and moved them around like pieces in a colourful jigsaw. She glanced at the clock on the bedside table and saw that she was running out of time. She grabbed a ruby red shirt and white trousers and put them on, fingers fumbling with the buttons. The trousers were loose. She knew she wouldn't be able to force down any breakfast so promised herself she'd eat lunch.

* * *

Pressing the buzzer beside the blue door of her new workplace, she hoped the sweat she could feel under her armpits hadn't stained the silk. She lifted her fringe and stuck out her bottom lip, trying to blow air upwards to dry her damp face. Was she hot from the exertion of leaping down the communal stairs two at a time, then running along the road to get here on time, or were the night sweats turning into daytime hot flushes? She could do without that now.

When the door clicked open, she tucked the hair quickly behind her ear and pulled back her shoulders, stepping into the reception. She must stop thinking of it as her junior school, but the cavernous room made her feel even smaller than usual.

A loud whistle made her jump. Heart racing, she turned to see Laura standing with her back to the staffroom door. Bonnie tried to look more composed than she felt.

'Whit woo,' Laura said. 'You look fabulous!'

Alice emerged from behind her and looked Bonnie up and down. 'Goodness, you're putting us all to shame.'

There was a bitter tone to her voice and Bonnie's cheeks burned. She'd got it wrong. What was she thinking, dressing up like this for a desk job?

'I wanted to make a good impression.' She opened her arms and looked down, hoping to allow some air to her armpits. 'Too much?'

'Not at all.' Laura bounced forwards. 'I love that top!'

Laura loved her top. Result. She would wear gorgeous clothes every day and get validation from this young and clearly very trendy woman. She could feel her mood lifting already.

Alice stayed behind the desk. She was wearing a cream blouse and dark red lipstick, which Bonnie thought made her look a bit like a walking corpse. *It's not a competition*, she reminded herself, *but if it were, I'd win this round*.

'Come through to the back and we'll fill in all the boring forms.' Laura raised her arm as though she was going to lead Bonnie by the hand but Bonnie resisted the urge to take it. God, imagine Alice's reaction if this well-dressed woman grabbed her daughter's outstretched hand.

She curled her fingers into fists and followed Laura behind the desk and through the door to the staffroom, Alice following behind like a shadow on a warm day.

'First things first.' Laura's voice was upbeat. 'This is where we keep the tea and coffee' – she tapped on the lids of the containers, then opened the fridge – 'and the milk, obviously.'

'And the whisky?' It was out of Bonnie's mouth before she could stop it. The sweat under her arms trickled down her sides. 'I'm joking.' She thought Alice's eyebrows might leap into her hairline. 'I don't drink very much, actually. It doesn't agree with me, and my god, the hangover if I drink white wine. The menopause, eh?' She looked at Alice again and clamped her mouth shut. If she could've torn out her tongue, she would.

'I think whisky would be a very good idea. What do you think, Mother?'

'I think we'd better fill in these forms.' Alice picked up a pen and thrust it in Bonnie's direction.

The scratching of the Biro on the forms was the only sound for an agonising minute. In her head, Bonnie scolded herself for not reading everything before signing it, but she was so busy trying not to cry at her stupid runaway mouth that she just signed where she was told. She needed to get a grip on her emotions; they were as unpredictable as her internal thermostat these days.

'This is a trial period, and after that it will be a rolling, temporary contract with a week's notice on both sides,' Laura explained.

'Understood.' If she only gave one-word answers, perhaps she could stop herself from appearing like a court jester. There was a silence. The fridge hummed. She heard herself swallow. Was it loud enough for the others to hear? She swallowed again and watched for their responses, but they still looked at her with wide eyes.

'And you said you were flexible as to which shifts you work?' Alice asked.

'Yes.'

'Do you have any questions?'

'No.'

Alice squinted at her, obviously finding the monosyllabic version of her equally as confusing as the one with verbal incontinence. She gave her head a quick shake and turned to face Laura, who was leaning against the sink. 'You may as well go home, then.'

'I can stay and help Bonnie settle in.'

Yes, thought Bonnie, *do that*. She didn't want to be left alone with hostile Alice.

'No need. After all, she's here so you can have more time to yourself, so you should take full advantage of that, don't you think?'

Something passed between them that Bonnie couldn't translate, but Laura smiled tightly and took her denim jacket from the hook on the back of the door.

'You're right. Welcome to the team, Bonnie. Have a good day. I'll pop back later to see how you're getting on.'

'No need,' said Alice again and Bonnie watched Laura ignore her mother's tone, wave, and leave the room.

Alice stood and smoothed the creases in her trousers. 'Since we don't have the results of your police disclosure check yet, I can't allow you to have sole responsibility for our client's possessions, so you won't be here alone until that comes through.'

Bonnie nodded as she stood. Unsure of what to do with her hands, she hooked them together. Feeling awkward, she dropped them to her sides, then felt like a Coldstream Guard. How did people stand naturally? She'd completely forgotten.

'So, I'm afraid you're stuck with the filing.'

Alice led Bonnie across the echoing reception, through the red door at the far end, and down the maze of white corridors. They passed various sized doors and roller shutters with numbers on red plaques beside them, to a door with an older padlock than the others. Alice unlocked it with a key dangling from a keyring with a picture of a small girl on it.

Bonnie pointed to the keyring. 'Is that Laura?'

Alice's face softened as she extracted the picture from the jumble of keys and held it in her palm. 'Yes, she must've been about seven in this. I had it made from her school photo.'

Bonnie shifted closer, looking at the picture of the dark-haired, brown-eyed girl in a blue gingham school dress, two front teeth missing from her face-splitting grin. 'She was gorgeous.'

'Hmm.' Alice dropped the picture back into the keys with a clank. 'She was a spirited child, even then.'

'Better than being dull.'

'Oh, it's never dull with my daughter.' She took a breath and gestured to the piles of papers strewn on the floor of the narrow, rectangular space. 'And this is a fine example of her keeping things interesting. All of these old client records are meant to have been put into alphabetised folders and stored in those boxes.'

Bonnie saw a stack of flat cardboard propped against the far wall.

'But Laura shoved them in here for another day, and it seems that day has arrived.'

'Ah, right.' Was she really going to sit in a windowless room and fight with age-old papers for minimum wage?

'Not the most stimulating start, but then, it's not the most stimulating job, is it?'

Bonnie saw a glint in Alice's eye and realised she was being challenged. How much do you want this job, she was asking? Bonnie would just have to show her.

* * *

At the end of her shift, Bonnie's back ached, and her fingers were lacerated with paper cuts. She rubbed her left buttock, which was numb from sitting on the cold concrete floor. She'd tried sitting on the chair Alice had given to her, but the bending made her spine cry out, so she'd slumped back on the ground. She rubbed her eyes, dry and tired from the dust and staring at small print under the harsh fluorescent light, then blinked away the dirt her fingers left there.

She stood and leaned against the wall to try to straighten out her spine. The blood seemed to drop away from her head, making it spin. She breathed slowly, until her vision steadied. Brushing away the grey smudges from her white trousers with filthy hands, she made them worse. So much for the effort she'd put into choosing the perfect outfit. Overalls would have been more appropriate, or maybe she should've stripped off and worked in the nude. Then at least she'd only need a shower instead of bleach and a ninety-degree wash.

The clack of heels snapped on the laminate floor of the corridor, getting louder as they neared. Her heart sank with the knowledge that it was Alice approaching. She wiped her eyes with her wrist, imagining this is what a new army recruit would feel like when the sergeant major came to inspect the barracks. She resisted the urge to stand, feet together, chin up, and salute as the clipped march reached the unit.

Alice stood in the doorway, eyes assessing the neat boxes that now filled the space where the scattered papers had been.

'Have you done them all?'

Bonnie noted the surprise in her voice, and inwardly pumped her fist at her small victory. 'I have.'

Alice took the lid off the nearest box and leafed through the files, all slotted in perfectly, the information written in neat capitals at the top of each one.

'Well done.'

Where's my medal? thought Bonnie, forcing her lips into a smile. 'No problem. I'll get my bag and make a move.' She stepped past Alice out of the unit, her legs wobbly with the movement and hunger.

'Just a second.' Alice looked her up and down. Bonnie felt like an urchin in comparison to her sleek and polished employer. 'Didn't you come in looking for a storage unit that first day?'

Bonnie remembered her feet tripping over themselves to cross the car park when she saw Bocks on her way to the Chinese takeaway. 'That's right, I did.'

'Do you still need storage?'

Bonnie thought about her flat, now unpacked, the rug she thought was too big now the ideal runner for the hallway and the Roman urn filled with bamboo on the balcony. She'd found a place for everything.

'I do, actually. Just a small unit.'

'We'll sort that out tomorrow then.'

'Great,' said Bonnie. What was she going to put inside a unit? Nothing. She crossed her fingers behind her back, squeezing them tightly together, praying she would find the strength to keep it completely empty for as long as she stayed in town.

Chapter Six

Bonnie

Present Day

Two weeks to the day after her interview at Bocks, Bonnie checked her metal mailbox in the lobby at the base of the communal stairs and found the official-looking envelope. Her mouth dry, she rushed up the stairs to her flat, heart pounding in her ears as she closed the door behind her. She leaned her back against it, ripping open the envelope and throwing it onto the rug.

Even though Ross had reassured her she was very unlikely to fail as long as it was only the basic check, *unlikely* wasn't good enough. She wouldn't believe it until she saw it in print. She ignored the pattern of turquoise with lilac waves spreading out from the centre of the paper and squinted at the black type, past the applicant's personal details, date of issue, then to the police record of convictions, cautions, reprimands, and warnings.

None recorded.

She read it again.

None recorded.

There it was for the world to examine, and now she could breathe again. She kissed the paper with a smack of her lips and shoved it in her handbag.

* * *

She sang as she showered and chose smarter clothes, beaming with the knowledge that Alice couldn't restrict her from being at the front desk, dealing with the customers now she had a piece of paper saying she was trustworthy. The April sunshine danced warmly on her face as she left the tarmacked car park and turned left onto the main road.

She pressed the buzzer by Bocks' front door, listening to the flapping of the roped banner, then the buzz of the lock releasing. 'Ta da!' She waved the certificate above her head as she approached the reception desk where Alice sat, hair perfectly blow-dried, dark lipstick on pursed lips, scrutinising the computer screen.

She looked up. 'What's that?'

'My DBS form.'

Alice took it from her and scanned the paper. 'This is a basic check.'

'Yes.' Bonnie's pulse quickened.

'I asked you to get a standard check.'

Bonnie wrinkled her nose and took the paper back. 'Really?' Alice glared at her. Bonnie changed direction, hoping Alice wouldn't detect the wobble in her voice. 'I'm sorry. I thought the basic would be fine because when I read the criteria it said the standard and enhanced checks were for people working with children or social workers and people who wanted to adopt? Things like that.'

Alice eyed her, her lips a tight slit. 'We are working

with potentially high value—' She was interrupted by a muffled thumping on the door. She turned to look at the small monitor on the left-hand side of the desk, muttering, 'What on earth?'

She released the lock and a woman carrying a huge black bin liner tumbled in, large bottom first. 'Sorry about that.' She staggered around to face them. 'This is heavy, and I didn't have any hands free to press the buzzer.'

Alice's face lifted into a warm smile and Bonnie was struck by how attractive she was when she wasn't frowning. She imagined springing out from behind a door and shouting *boo!* to make her laugh. On second thought, that probably wasn't the best way to tease a laugh from Alice. She seemed more like a person who reserved their laughter for reruns of *The Good Life*.

'What have you got in there, Polly?' Alice asked, then looked at Bonnie, her face stern again. 'Give her a hand, would you?' She turned back to the woman and Bonnie rushed forwards, awkwardly putting her arms under the bag and taking some of the weight.

Polly laughed, wrestling the bag from Bonnie and plonking it unceremoniously on the ground. 'Don't worry, it's fine. It's just a load of tat I picked up at a car boot sale on Saturday. I haven't decided where to put it in my flat yet.'

'I love a good car boot sale,' Bonnie said. 'I found three ceramic pieces by Clarice Cliff at one once. The woman selling it wouldn't believe they were collectable. I had to force her to take a fair price.'

'That's not really the idea though, is it? You're supposed to be looking for a bargain.' Polly lifted her thick black hair away from her neck and flapped her other hand like a fan in front of her face.

49

'Yes, but my conscience wouldn't let me pay two pounds for something worth two hundred. Anyway, I gave her fifty quid and sold it to a client for full market value, so, win, win.'

Polly's chin puckered. 'A client?'

'I used to be an interior designer, in another lifetime.' She raised her arms, as though that made the sentence more believable. Going by the crumpled look on Polly's face, it hadn't worked.

'And now you work here?'

Alice stood. 'She does, and I'm about to train her on how the reception desk functions, so . . .' She trailed off and raised an eyebrow.

Polly stuck her hand in the canvas bag hooked over her shoulder. 'Righty-ho. I'll find my keys and let you get on with it.' She carried on rummaging, eventually looking up, pulling an apologetic face. 'I don't suppose you could find my spare key, could you? Looks like I've forgotten mine again.'

'Now's a good time to show you where we keep the customers' spare keys.' Alice gestured for Bonnie to join her behind the desk, which she did, relief washing through her.

* * *

The instructions went on for some time.

'And finally, this is where we store all the clients' details, and then you must remember to press save,' said Alice, in a painfully slow manner more suitable for teaching an eight-year-old than someone who'd won Businesswoman of the Year at the Glasgow Design Guild only three years ago.

'Do you think you've got it?' she asked, swivelling the

chair to look at Bonnie, who was watching the screen over her shoulder. The instructions were so laborious she'd spent more time marvelling at the many honey tones in Alice's hair and breathing in her grapefruit scent than following what seemed so patently obvious.

'It's not rocket science, is it?' Her feet throbbed from standing and watching while Alice sat in the padded office chair.

'That may be the case,' Alice replied curtly. 'But we have a duty of care, which I take very seriously.'

Bonnie thought *duty of care* would be more fitting to describe looking after school children, or geriatrics in a care home, not Jim's jigsaw or Polly's car boot sale treasure, but she didn't say so. 'Absolutely. I think I've got it.'

Polly reappeared just then, shuffling through the red door that led to the units, and Alice jumped up from her chair. 'Polly, do you have a minute? Sit down,' she instructed Bonnie, then turned back to Polly. 'Can you be a customer so Bonnie can practice?'

'I am a customer.'

'Yes, yes, but be a new one, checking in.'

Polly nodded then shuffled up to the desk, her lips pursed and shoulders back.

'How can I help you, madam?' asked Bonnie.

Polly sniggered, then resumed her peculiar stance. 'G'day. I'd like to hire a unit to store all my precious thingies.'

Alice observed the exchange, thumb rubbing along her chin, eyes like an eagle watching the progress of a mouse along a hedgerow.

Bonnie peered up at Alice at the end of the process, daring her to be critical.

'All okay?'

She knew she'd performed in exactly the way she'd been taught. She'd been courteous and warm to Polly, whose grin spread the full way across her plump face.

After a pause Alice conceded, 'Yes. Good.'

'I love a role play!' said Polly. 'I used to like drama at school.' Her smile dropped. 'My brothers say I'm rubbish at accents though.'

'That was a brilliant Welsh accent,' Bonnie said.

'I thought it was Australian?' Alice's brow furrowed.

'I was joking.' Bonnie looked between the two perplexed faces. 'It was obviously Australian. Somewhere between Sydney and Brisbane, am I right?'

Polly's cheeks reddened, and she grinned. 'I couldn't be that specific. It was based on wherever they film *Neighbours*.'

'You have a talent.'

Polly giggled. 'Thanks. I'm going to come in here more often if you carry on being that nice.'

She dipped her hand into her canvas bag and the material puckered as she shifted her hand around inside, looking up intermittently to roll her eyes. Eventually she produced a set of keys with a flourish. 'There we are! I knew they were in there somewhere, otherwise I wouldn't have been able to drive here, would I?'

* * *

An hour later, Alice emerged from the staffroom and announced she was going home. She slung her tan leather bag over her shoulder and clipped towards the door, pausing before pressing the button to unlock it. 'Are you sure you'll be okay?'

Bonnie would be more relaxed knowing Alice wasn't hovering. 'I have your number. I'll ring if I need any help.'

'Alright. Make sure you do. One of us will be back to lock up.'

* * *

Nothing happened for four long hours. Bonnie didn't know what she expected to occur on a Tuesday afternoon in spring, in a storage facility in Hamblin, but the silence jangled her nerves. She hadn't considered how much time she would have to think while the place was quiet. She would need to find something to keep the dark thoughts from jumping out and assailing her.

Scanning the room, she noted how the red fire extinguisher in the far corner stood out like slashed skin against the pockmarked walls, whose cracks and uneven surfaces were amplified by the shiny white paint. It was an exhausted-looking room, everything about it worn and past its best. She knew how it felt.

She turned over one of the signing-in sheets and doodled on it, the scratching of pen on paper soothing her. At four o'clock she watched a tall, thin man walk up the ramp through the black-and-white monitor and stand patiently as he pressed the buzzer and waited to be let in. He barely glanced at her, signing in on the lined sheet on the desk, then disappearing through the red door to what Bonnie thought of as the warren. She carried on doodling.

* * *

Half an hour later, Bonnie was drawing on the back of one of the sign-in sheets when the door clattered open and Laura appeared. She looked bright and full of life, her pink hair waving around her shoulders.

'Hello.' Even her voice bounced. 'How did you get on?'

'Absolutely fine,' Bonnie replied. 'Nothing to report.' She shifted the signing-in sheet around so she could see it. 'Just a' – she tried to read the scrawled signature – 'Mr Booth in at the moment.'

'Wildly interesting as ever, then?' Laura leaned both forearms on the reception desk, resting her chin on her clasped hands. 'How are you passing the hours?'

'I wait with bated breath for someone to need my help,' Bonnie said, primly.

'Yeah, right.' Laura examined the line drawing under Bonnie's hand and gasped. 'That's Polly!'

Bonnie grimaced. 'Sorry, I should probably be doing something more productive.'

Laura reached out and lifted the paper. 'That's bloody brilliant.' She studied the sketch. 'You have got her likeness perfectly. How did you make it so detailed with so few strokes?'

'Practice.' Bonnie shrugged, trying to mask her delight with nonchalance. 'That's not my first ever drawing, you'll be surprised to discover.'

'It's so, so good.' Laura sounded pained. 'I'm so jealous of your talent.'

A lump appeared in Bonnie's throat and she had to blink to stop tears from forming. She lifted the drawing in front of her face, pretending to inspect it so she could compose herself. 'Thank you. That's lovely of you. Didn't you say you were an artist too?'

Laura dropped back onto the desk, laying her cheek on her arm and expelling a long breath. 'I'm a wannabe artist.'

'Wannabe how?'

'I haven't done anything about it since A levels. I was a complete idiot and let my parents talk me into doing a business degree because my mum is obsessed with "generating a reliable income", then Dad got sick and I moved back home to help out with the business and now here I am, twenty-four years old and still a wannabe.'

Bonnie bit back the indignation she felt on Laura's behalf. Surely only someone soulless would deny their daughter the joy of following their dreams. She remembered her own mother's reluctance to her taking an art course and how hard she'd had to fight to get to Glasgow. She'd proved herself right, but not until it was too late for her and her mother to mend their splintered relationship.

'You said it, you're only twenty-four. You've got loads of time to change whatever you want.' Perhaps she could be the one to help Laura, to push her in the right direction. That could give her the project she needed to keep the dread under control. The busier she was, the better she would cope.

'You don't think I've left it too late?'

Bonnie dug her nails into her thighs under the desk as she said, 'It's never too late.' And she hoped with every fibre of her being that it wasn't too late: for Laura to make her dreams come true, and for herself to bring her nightmares to a close.

Chapter Seven

Bonnie

Present Day

That evening, Bonnie pulled the balcony doors closed and dragged the pink throw from the back of the sofa, draping it over herself. The soft wool felt like the touch of a warm hand against her neck.

She lifted her laptop from the coffee table. When she turned it on, the screen came to life with a picture of a sandy-coloured house, vivid bougainvillea flowering against the wall where a man leaned, pictured in profile, looking out over a glistening lake. Bonnie felt time slow as the background photograph faded and brightened with another of her leaning against an ornate railing, sunhat on and freckles across her nose, the same sparkling, still expanse of water behind her as she held up a champagne glass as though raising a toast to the camera.

Onto the screen slid another picture of a lake-view room in an exquisite hotel on Lake Como. With a monumental effort she forced herself to shift the arrow across the shimmering water and onto the search engine icon. She clicked the mouse pad and let out her breath as the lake disappeared and the screen turned white, waiting for her to tell it what to do.

Art classes Hamblin she typed into the search bar and sent her request into the world.

Unfortunately, it seemed everything she clicked on was aimed at children. Growling at the screen, she flicked from site to site, each showing primary-aged kids holding up paint-covered fingers, or teenagers leaning over intricate pencil sketches.

She went back to the search bar and typed *Life Drawing Hamblin*. Scrolling past all the national events and sponsored posts, one entry caught her eye. It said, '*Life Drawing with Angie*', and when she clicked on the link a rudimentary page about a life drawing session, which took place every Tuesday evening at a church hall in the next town, flashed onto her screen. It was exactly what she was looking for. She found the same link on her phone and added a bookmark, shutting the laptop down before it could show her any more photos of the life she'd left behind.

* * *

Two days later, Laura was with Jim in the staffroom when Bonnie finished her shift. It was a squeeze at the best of times, and she had to step over Jim's legs as he knelt with his head inside the fridge.

'Don't do it!' she said in mock horror.

'Ha!' Jim laughed.

Laura looked from one to the other, face screwed up. 'Do what?'

'Kill myself,' Jim said.

'What?'

'She's too young to get it. They changed the gas in the seventies,' said Jim, head emerging from inside the fridge.

'Get what? Who kills themselves with a fridge?'

'Sorry, it was a crap joke. It looked like he had his head in an oven.'

'Ah, like Sylvia Plath?' Laura nodded. 'Gotcha.'

'Like who?' said Jim.

'Oh, never mind.' Bonnie gestured to Jim. 'What's going on here?'

'The thermostat's on the blink and it keeps freezing the milk, so Jim's trying to sort it out.'

'Is there nothing you can't do, Jim?' Bonnie watched the old man put his hand on the sink and hoist himself to standing.

'Fix that thermostat, for one.' He smoothed down his white moustache. 'I think I'll have to order a new one.' He turned to Laura. 'All right if I use the computer on reception to check the prices?'

'Knock yourself out.'

'Not literally. We've only just saved you from your last suicide attempt,' Bonnie said, then wished she hadn't as they both gave her a quizzical look. Why was she such an idiot?

As Jim left the room, she lifted herself onto her toes then dropped onto her heels, drumming her fingers against her thighs, trying to find the right words to start the conversation. 'I've got something to show you.'

'Said the actress to the bishop.' Laura laughed. 'Or is that the other way around?'

Bonnie pulled a chair out from under the table and

gestured for Laura to sit. She took the seat next to her and pulled her phone from the pocket of her yellow tunic. 'Have a look at this.' She opened the page about Angie's life drawing class and handed the phone to Laura.

'Life drawing?' Laura touched the screen, scrolling through the information. 'Drawing naked people?'

'Yes.' Bonnie suddenly felt very warm. 'I thought you might be interested, but maybe it's not your thing.' She took the phone out of Laura's hand, her head fuzzy. What had she been thinking? Who wants to stare at nudes with someone twice their age who they've only just met? 'Sorry. It was a stupid idea. Forget I mentioned it.'

'No, it looks good.' Laura laughed. 'Well, interesting, anyway. I've never done life drawing though. Isn't it a bit embarrassing, all those boobs and bums?'

'When the model first takes their robe off, it's a bit weird, but it's surprising how quickly the body becomes shapes, light and textures rather than' – she paused – 'boobs and bums and willies.'

'Willies!' Laura's mouth fell open. 'There are real penises?'

'I think they're real, but I've never given one a tweak, so I can't say for certain.'

'Ah! Tweak!' Laura shouted, then covered her mouth and banged her other hand on the table.

Jim's head appeared around the door. 'Everything all right in here?'

Bonnie snorted through her nose and Jim's brow furrowed.

'Ever done a life drawing class, Jim?' Laura said when she caught her breath.

Jim's chin retracted into his neck. 'I don't think my

missus would be keen on me partaking in that sort of thing.' His head dipped back out of the room and they caught the words '*price*' and '*thermostat*' before the door banged closed again.

'Poor Jim. I think we've shocked him.'

'It's not that shocking, it's art,' Bonnie said.

'I wonder if my mother would see it that way.'

Bonnie tensed. 'Surely she doesn't try to stop you doing things that make you happy?'

The apples of Laura's cheeks flattened, and the room seemed to chill. 'Mum has never stopped me from doing what I want.'

'That wasn't what I was saying.' Bonnie wanted to suck the words back in. 'Sorry, that came out completely wrong. I just thought this might be useful experience, for your course?'

Laura took a hairband from her wrist and scooped her hair up into a ponytail, tying the band tightly around it. 'Nobody's making me do anything I don't want to. I chose to help because it was the right thing to do after Dad got sick.' The usual brightness had left her eyes, and with her hair scraped back she suddenly resembled Alice. 'I've been here longer than I thought I would be and I know that's not ideal, but it won't be forever. At least, not if Mum has her way, and she usually does.'

'Absolutely, I wasn't trying to suggest anything else.' Bonnie wanted to slap her own cheeks. How could she have been so stupid?

'No biggie.' Suddenly Laura's tone was lighter, and Bonnie heard the chair legs clack back on the lino.

Bonnie pretended to be engrossed in her phone as Laura thrust her arms into her denim jacket. She was surprised by Laura's voice, back to its cheerful norm, as she said,

'I'll have a think about that life drawing thing. It might be fun. I'm not going on my own though; you'd have to come with me.'

'I could do that,' she said lightly. She waited until Laura left the room to lay her hot cheeks against the cold of the table and let out a long sigh of relief.

Chapter Eight

Alice

Present Day

Alice's phone flashed its white light alarm. She kept it on silent so the shock of a sudden awakening didn't tip Richard's heart into overdrive. It was very unlikely – the doctors had reassured her of that – but she couldn't be too careful. She reached over to the bedside table and tapped the screen, shutting off the alarm, then lay as she did every morning, staring into the half-light, listening, muscles rigid, until she heard Richard breathe.

He snorted unceremoniously through his nose and shifted in the bed, so Alice could release her clenched jaw, tip herself carefully off the mattress, and start another tedious day.

* * *

She was chopping strawberries on the island in the middle of the kitchen when Laura shuffled in, wearing rumpled pyjamas, hair fluffy around her face.

'I swear we used to eat toast and Marmite like normal people before I went to university. When did we turn into a family from one of those nauseating adverts who eat fresh berries in the morning?' She picked a strawberry from the bowl and shoved it in her mouth.

'When your father nearly dropped dead from heart disease.' Alice swiped the rest of the fruit into the bowl from the chopping board. 'If anything is going to make you look at your lifestyle, that will.'

Laura filled the kettle from the tap, water splashing all over the pristine sink. 'But didn't the doctors say his cardiac arrest was more to do with genetics plus the stress when everything went tits up with the business?'

'Nicely put.' Alice dried the spilled water with a tea towel. 'The worst of it was probably caused by stress, but those arteries didn't clog themselves.'

'Grandpa was skinny, and he still died of heart disease.'

Alice gripped the sink. 'So, I should give up, should I? Your dad has congenital heart disease, made worse by years of stress, so I should accept he's going to drop dead any minute and give him a fry-up for breakfast? God knows, it'd be cheaper.'

'Whoa! Where did that come from?' Laura put her hand on Alice's shoulder and Alice realised how tense she was. She allowed her muscles to relax under her daughter's warm hand.

'Sorry. I didn't sleep well.'

'Sit down, I'll make some coffee.' Laura paused. 'Decaf. Promise.' She winked at Alice and more tension slid away.

'You are very annoying.'

'I know, but you wouldn't have me any other way.'

She was right. Living with Laura was like having a

bright diffuser in the house, zapping the tension molecules with her positive energy.

Richard walked into the kitchen, yawning. 'Morning.' His voice was gruff. 'Sleep well?'

'Yes.' She didn't look at Laura, but she could feel her eyes on her back. Richard didn't need to know she'd lain awake half the night worrying. What good would that do? 'You?'

'Like a corpse.'

'I wish you wouldn't say that.'

Richard pulled her towards him and kissed her cheek, his breath minty, his stubble grazing her chin. 'You're a big softy underneath that veneer, aren't you?'

'Get off and go eat your fruit. I'm going to be late if I don't head out now.'

'I'm in early today, remember? You're doing the later shift.' Laura slurped her coffee and put it down clumsily on the island, a ring of dark liquid sploshing out and spreading.

Alice batted Richard away and ripped off a piece of kitchen roll, lifting Laura's mug and wiping the mess. 'But it's Tuesday.'

'I know. That's why you're doing the later shift – so Bonnie and I can go to that art thing.'

Alice stopped wiping. She had a vague memory of Laura mentioning an art class, but certainly didn't remember her saying she planned to go with the new receptionist. 'What *art thing*?'

'Life drawing. I'm going to stare at bums, boobs, and willies while holding a pencil.'

Richard bellowed out a laugh. 'Can I come?'

Alice glared at him, then at Laura. 'You want to go and look at naked people with our new employee? Isn't that a bit unprofessional?' She didn't add that she would have liked an invitation. If Laura was now hanging around with people a generation older, why wasn't she included?

'It's not like I'm a teacher taking one of the sixth formers. She's an artist. It was her who found the class and asked me along.'

Unease crept along Alice's shoulders. 'It's still a bit weird. Why doesn't she find some friends her own age?'

Laura puffed out her cheeks. 'Give her a break. She's just moved into the area and we have a common interest. Stop being so ageist.' She wandered towards the door. 'She might have asked you if you hadn't been so frosty.'

'I'm not frosty, I'm professional,' she said as Laura left the room, sticking out her tongue at her parents as she went.

'Mature!' shouted Alice after her.

'It's what you get if you're going to treat me like a child!' Laura yelled back.

Alice wondered what Laura would've said if she'd suggested they went to an evening course together. She thought she knew the answer. She waited until she was sure Laura was out of earshot then turned to Richard. 'There's something odd about that woman. I don't like Laura getting close to her.'

'I don't think you're going to have much say in the matter. She's old enough to choose her own friends.' Richard sat at the table and Alice pulled a face at his back. She knew exactly how old Laura was, but it was still her job to protect her child.

'I trust my instinct on this. She's hiding something and I think Laura needs to be careful.' She sipped her coffee, drumming her fingers on the side of the cup.

* * *

When Alice heard Laura bluster through the front door, she looked at her watch and her stomach balled. She'd been sitting at the kitchen table analysing the business's profit-and-loss sheets and wasn't expecting Laura back for hours. She glanced towards Richard who was outside on the patio, snoozing on a garden chair. His face was turned up towards the sun, despite Alice having insisted he sit in the shade. She jumped from the chair and rushed into the hall.

'What are you doing back? I told you I couldn't take over this evening, I sent you a message.'

'I know.' Laura struggled out of her jacket. 'But I didn't think two hours on a Tuesday would make that much difference, and I wanted to see how Dad was.'

Alice put her hands on her hips, legs splayed, trying to create a barrier between Laura and the kitchen. 'You can't leave the facility unattended. We have set opening hours.'

Laura frowned. 'I know, but I think Dad's health is more important.'

'So do I, which is why I asked you to stay at work this evening so I could keep an eye on him.' Laura stepped forwards but Alice didn't move.

'Why are you acting so weird. Where's Dad? Is he okay? What are you hiding?'

'He's resting, so I think you should go back and finish your shift.'

'It's not my bloody shift. I told you, I'm going to life drawing tonight, so I want to check on Dad and grab a sandwich before I set off.'

Alice dropped her arms as she heard the click of the patio doors being opened. Laura marched past her into the bright kitchen. She followed, heart pattering in her chest. She came to stop at the granite island and put her hand on the cool stone, wanting to hold on to something solid when the inevitable explosion happened.

'Dad, are you okay?'

'Hello, love. Yes, why wouldn't I be?' He looked between the two of them, taking off his glasses and putting the stem between his teeth. 'What's going on? Your mum said you wouldn't be back until eight.' He looked at his watch. 'Is the new girl covering at Bocks?'

'She's not a girl; she's old enough to be her mother,' Alice snapped.

Laura tutted. 'Is that why you don't like her? Because I want to hang out with her but not with you?'

Alice felt that like a slap. 'Don't be ridiculous.'

'Am I missing something?' Richard said.

'Have you been in pain today, Dad?' Laura scrutinised Richard and Alice closed her eyes.

'Not especially, why?'

Laura turned to Alice. 'Do you want to tell him or shall I?' she snarled.

Alice climbed onto one of the high stools at the island and sat with her back straight. She wasn't going to apologise for doing the right thing. 'I sent Laura a message asking her to stay at the facility until eight, so I didn't have to go in.'

'Why? Aren't you feeling well?' Richard stepped towards her and lay a hand on her back, stroking her gently.

Laura made a snorting sound. 'She said you'd had a bad day, and she didn't want to leave you.'

Richard's hand stilled. 'I've been fine.' He paused. 'Alice?' She didn't look up. 'Why would you say that?'

'Yes.' Laura's tone cut. 'Why would you say that?'

Alice shifted on the small circular seat. 'Okay, I shouldn't have lied, but I couldn't face that place today.'

'Bollocks.'

They both turned to face Laura.

She pointed her finger. 'It's because you wanted me to miss the art class. You need to control everything I do. You couldn't bear to let me have something for myself, could you?'

'Alice?' Richard's blue eyes searched her face.

She'd been caught in her own net and now she had to wriggle out. 'I'm just worried for you, darling. The more involved you get in that world, the worse it will be if things don't work out the way you want them to.' If she admitted she was trying to slow Laura and Bonnie's burgeoning friendship, it wouldn't go down well. She saw now how selfish and irrational she'd been. But she wasn't ready to apologise.

'Bullshit. You're bitter because your life is miserable, and you want the rest of us to rot with you. Well, I'm not.' Her dark eyes glowed. 'That was low, what you did today. How am I meant to believe you if Dad really is sick when you pull a stunt like that?'

Alice hadn't considered that. She'd wanted Laura to come home at eight, to gloss over what she'd implied in the message by saying Richard was fine now, and for everything to get back to normal.

'I'm getting sick of being manipulated into doing what you want, Mum. I'm getting changed, then I'm going to pick Bonnie up, and we're going to the life drawing class.' She stepped towards the door, then spun back. 'And I won't be coming back here tonight, so don't wait up.'

* * *

Richard went to bed early to read and Alice's heart, weighted like a heavy pendulum, came to a slow, low drop at 11 p.m. when she accepted Laura wasn't coming home. She pushed the latch across the top and bottom of the front door and stepped up the thickly carpeted stairs one by one. On the landing she switched off the chandelier, now a mocking reminder of her extravagant spending in the past when business was good, when Richard was in robust health and they had so much to look forward to.

Alice pushed open the door to their dark bedroom, then hovered by the side of the bed, holding her breath until she was sure she'd heard one of his.

Chapter Nine

Alice

Three Years Ago

The bell above the door tinkled when Alice pushed it open. Laura came rushing from the back of the gallery, her fresh, youthful face brightening at the sight of her mother. Alice had missed her so much when she was away at university, and the day she said she was coming back to Hamblin to look for a job had been one of her happiest.

'Hello!' Laura lifted a plastic carrier bag. 'I've bought us lunch.'

'From the garage, by the looks of it. Aren't we going out?'

Laura gestured to the desk where she'd positioned two chairs. Shoving the papers piled on the surface to one side, she said, 'I thought this would be nice. Just the two of us and a meal deal.'

Alice unpacked the plastic bag, peering at the sell-by date of the sandwiches as Laura shook her head.

'I saw a management position advertised at that new

development off the dual carriageway,' Alice said, halfway through a prawn sandwich, stopping to dab the corners of her mouth with a paper napkin. She looked around the gallery, white walls spattered with bright paintings that looked to her like the daubings of primary school children. 'If you were thinking of applying for something with more prospects.'

'Oh, bore off, Mother,' said Laura, flicking her thick dark waves over her shoulder. 'Managing a gallery is a proper job. Anyway, it's only temporary.'

'You'll be paying for lunch next time we go to Chez Pierre then?'

'Ha bloody ha. Money isn't everything, you know.' Laura bit off a chunk of her sandwich and chewed. 'I'm surprised you're even thinking about going to that place. I thought it would be out of your price range these days?'

'Your dad has worked very hard to get things back on track since the recession. He seems hopeful this property deal he's working on will be the one to secure things going forwards.' She unscrewed the top on her bottle of water. 'Can I have a glass?'

Laura didn't move. 'What is this *big deal*?'

'I'm not quite sure, to be honest. Something to do with some land in town. It's got a storage facility or something like that on it, so Dad's going to buy it as a going concern, but he's been assured that the planning application to change its designation from commercial to residential is a formality.'

'Assured by who?'

'Whom.'

Laura sighed and raised her eyebrows.

'By the vendor.'

'And people who want to sell things never lie, do they?'

Alice shrugged. 'I trust your father to do all the due diligence. He's never let us down before, has he? He couldn't help what happened in the crash. Millions of people went bankrupt. We were lucky to keep hold of the house.' She sighed. 'I just hope this deal is as good as he thinks. If it is, it could put us back in a very good position financially.'

She wrinkled her nose at her water bottle. 'Couldn't you have stretched to one of those little bottles of Malbec?'

'You've made me want one now.'

'I don't think that would be a good idea after last week, do you?' Alice allowed the sound of Laura crying down the phone about a date not showing up and the bottle of vodka she'd had to soften the blow to infect her mind momentarily, then shooed it away.

'Fair point.' Laura shuddered, crossing her arms over her chest. She slumped back and her plastic chair squeaked.

'And don't you have to work this afternoon?' Alice regarded the glass front door. Nobody had come into the space in the last half an hour. She wondered what Laura did all day in this silent shop, surrounded by these bizarre paintings.

Laura lifted one of the pieces of paper and shook it at her mother. 'Yes, we're not all ladies who lunch. Some of us have to work for a living.'

'It's not all lunching, you know. The charity work takes up a lot of my time these days.'

'You're so Home Counties! I'm surprised you don't wear a tweed suit and have a beagle drinking water from a monogrammed bowl under the table.'

Alice laughed. 'I was thinking about getting a dog. It would be nice to have a reason to go for a walk. Your dad needs to get fit too. I heard him wheezing yesterday, and he's always tired. He's getting ridiculously forgetful too. He left a whole ream of paperwork in a restaurant on Tuesday. It had completely disappeared when we rang up to see if anyone had found it.'

'He was looking a bit pale when I last saw him,' said Laura. 'Maybe you should get a dog and get him out in the fresh air. Wouldn't that interfere with your cruise habit though?'

'I do not have a cruise habit!' Alice shifted in her chair, trying to get comfortable on the moulded plastic seat. 'Anyway, if we did get one, you could look after it if we went away.'

Laura took her sandwich in her fingers and picked off the crust. 'That might not be possible, actually.' She paused, biting her bottom lip.

Alice narrowed her eyes. 'Why not?'

'Working in the gallery is okay, but it's not what I want to do long term.'

Alice threw her arms up. 'At last. I knew you'd see sense. You need to use that business degree for something a bit grander than managing a backstreet art gallery no one has heard of.'

'You are such a snob!'

'Well, for goodness' sake, this place is a graveyard. It pays buttons, you live in a bedsit, and it's not as if you're going to get a big promotion or even meet a nice boy somewhere like this.' She brushed crumbs from her pencil skirt into her hand and dropped them onto a napkin. 'And if you want to move home so you have fewer costs while you get settled, you know your room is ready and waiting.'

'I'd feel like a right loser moving home now. Anyway, I might go travelling.'

The bread Alice was chewing solidified in her mouth.

'Travelling?' Surely Laura wasn't going to go away again? It was bad enough when she'd gone to university and they'd only seen her for the odd weekend and in the holidays. What if she went to Australia and met someone? She might never come back.

Before Alice could reply her phone rang on the table in front of her and she swallowed the balled-up bread, snatched it up, and took the call. As she listened to the voice on the other end of the line, the blood drained from her face.

* * *

Alice gulped in a lungful of air before approaching Richard's bed in the hospital's critical ward. It felt like she was watching things play out on TV, going through the motions since she'd got the call to say Richard had been taken to hospital in an ambulance with a suspected cardiac arrest; like she was experiencing everything second-hand.

'He is unlikely to respond for now,' said the ward sister in a rich Nigerian accent, 'but talk to him. He can hear you.' She gave Alice's arm a squeeze and smiled before going back to her desk.

Alice had tried to take in all the information when the earnest-looking doctor explained why Richard had been put into an induced coma, but all of her words slipped through Alice's brain before she could capture them.

The kindness in the doctor's eyes and the sympathy in her voice did lodge itself in Alice's head though.

She wished the doctor had talked in clipped, officious tones. That would have told her Richard's condition wasn't life-threatening, he was just a malingerer the doctor had to see to before sneaking off for a well-earned cup of tea.

75

But one look at her husband told Alice that Richard was no malingerer. And the oxygen mask covering his face and the machines on both sides of the bed with jumping lines chasing each other across dark screens confirmed it.

A man with a shaved head, wearing blue scrubs, was reading the screen on the right of Richard's bed when Alice approached. He looked up and smiled. More sympathy. Alice bit her bottom lip.

'You're Richard's wife?' he asked.

Alice nodded.

'I'm Pete. I'm looking after Richard.' He turned back to the bed. 'Aren't I, Richard? And you're doing alright, mate, aren't you?' Back to Alice. 'He's responding well. Getting some colour back in those cheeks.'

Alice leaned forwards, hopeful. But to her, Richard's skin looked shiny and pale like raw chicken.

Pete looked at the screen again then nodded as though satisfied. 'Sit yourself down.' He patted the back of a plastic chair. 'I'll leave you alone for a bit. I'm just out there if you need me. Alright?'

Alice nodded again. She sat and tried to look past the wires and tubes to find her husband. His eyelid flickered and the movement made everything real. This was Richard, the man she'd loved and relied on for thirty years, fighting for his life.

His life.

The thought was like a jolt of electricity forcing her back into consciousness. She'd been on autopilot, but now she was back in her body, the smell of antiseptic rushing up her nostrils, the electronic beeping of the machines stinging her eardrums.

She gasped, covering her mouth with her hand. 'Richard,' she whispered. 'Oh god. Please don't die. Please don't die,

Richard.' She couldn't believe she was saying those words out loud. It seemed absurd. Maybe she shouldn't talk like that; he might find it disturbing. He wasn't going to actually die. Surely? He wouldn't leave her. He couldn't.

She reached for his hand, careful not to touch the canula spiked into the back. She wrapped her fingers around his and willed the strength from her body to transfer to his through their skin.

'I love you,' she said, through her tears. 'I love you so much. I might not tell you often, but I do.' She gasped in another breath. 'I can't lose you. I can't. Me and you, we're a team. We only work when we're together.' She reached to the bedside cabinet for a tissue. Wiping her face dry, she realised how true it was that she couldn't imagine existing without Richard. So many of their friends who'd married around the same time as they did were now divorced. Others moaned relentlessly about their partners, but her and Richard, they were two halves of a whole.

'Let's make a deal,' she said, rubbing her thumb back and forth over his knuckles. 'You get better, and I'll stop complaining about how much time you spend playing golf. How's that?' She blew her nose and tried to stop her voice trembling as she continued to bargain. 'When you're better, we'll go on a long weekend up to St Andrews, shall we? We could ask Laura to come. The two of us could go to a spa or something while you play golf, and we'll meet you at the nineteenth hole. That would be lovely, wouldn't it?'

Sobs blocked her throat, forcing her to pause, swallow, and breathe. 'Richard,' she said when she could speak again. 'I can't bear the fact that I've never said thank you to you, not properly. Thank you for being the kindest, most forgiving man I've ever met. I know it wasn't easy . . . I wasn't easy to live with after I lost the . . . after the miscarriages. I know it must have been hard on you, too, but you always made sure I was alright, put me first. You never made me feel like I was to blame, even when I railed against everything, against you especially. I couldn't understand how you could just carry on, you see, how the loss didn't suffocate you like it did me. I couldn't breathe because of it.

'I know I punished you back then. I'm sorry. It was never about you. I just felt cheated. Everyone else had what I wanted so badly. It wasn't fair. Sometimes I thought the longing and the grief would send me mad.'

The words continued to rush out. 'Then, when Laura came along, you were the most perfect father. You still are. I'm ashamed to admit I'm sometimes jealous of the bond you two have. She worships you, you know. I'm sorry I said you worked too hard when she was little, that you were missing all the important bits. I understand why you had to. Honestly, I do. You've given us such a wonderful life. And I'm grateful. I'm grateful to you for so much.'

She leaned her forehead against his motionless fingers. 'I love you. Laura loves you. When you come home things are going to be different, I promise. I won't ever take you for granted again. I'll take better care of you. Whatever it takes to keep you healthy and well, I'll do it. Because I can't bear this. I can't imagine my life without you. Please come back to me, Richard. Please. I'll do anything.'

Quiet footsteps approached and she lifted her head to see Pete holding out a tissue. She took it and dabbed at her eyes. She gazed at Richard's face, desperate to see whether he'd heard what she'd said. But his head was still tilted to the side, eyes closed, face slack.

Whether he'd heard or not wasn't the point, she realised. What she'd said was true and saying the words out loud gave her a new energy. Richard would get better, and she would spend the rest of her life caring for him in the way he had always cared for her and their child.

* * *

Alice and Laura sat at the kitchen table; the paperwork spread out in front of them.

'The solicitor is certain there's nothing we can do?' Laura's voice was gentle.

Alice shook her head, lifting her reading glasses and resting them in her greasy hair, which sat flatly against her scalp. She tried to remember when she'd last washed it, but the days since Richard's collapse had all blurred together. She rubbed at the bridge of her nose where her glasses had made a ridge as she'd sifted through the paperwork, trying to find a clause the solicitors might have missed that meant Richard hadn't spent all of their savings and taken out a huge mortgage secured against their home to buy an overpriced storage facility with no planning permission.

'But he wasn't well,' Laura said. 'Surely that has to be relevant?'

'The papers were signed, and the money transferred. It's all legal.'

'But—'

'There are no buts. It was your dad's responsibility to make sure everything was in order. The solicitor says he was adamant he wanted to go ahead, despite his concerns, so we just have to live with it.'

'But the doctor said Dad might not have been thinking clearly and he won't be able to work for months.'

Alice pulled air in through her nose. 'At least he's alive. God, what if—' She covered her mouth, pushing her teeth into the soft flesh at the base of her thumb to stop herself wailing. 'It could be years until he's back to full strength, maybe never . . .' She broke off, taking a faltering breath. 'If his condition was made worse by stress, then it's down to me to make sure he doesn't have any.'

'How do you plan to do that?'

'I'll just have to find a way.'

Laura reached across the table and Alice felt the warmth of her hands on her cold fingers. 'We both will.'

'No.' Alice shook her head, releasing her hands. 'None of this is your fault. You shouldn't have to help dig us out of this hole.'

'After everything you've done for me? God only knows where I'd have ended up without you two. I want to help, Mum. Please let me.'

Alice looked into her daughter's soft brown eyes and relief washed through her. This is what families did, looked after each other.

'What about your plans?'

'I can go travelling any time. Dad needs me to be around.'

'It won't be forever, I promise,' she said. And she hoped, for all their sakes, that was true.

Chapter Ten

Bonnie

Present Day

The buzz of the intercom in her flat came twenty minutes earlier than Bonnie expected. She'd been surprised when Laura offered to drive them both to the art class, but accepted, grateful she wouldn't have to navigate her way around Hamblin's unfamiliar roads.

She pressed the speaker and heard Laura's voice. 'Sorry I'm early. That's really annoying, isn't it? If you're not ready, I can wait in the car.'

'Nope, it's fine. Come on up.'

She pressed the button to let her in. Nerves twitched her fingers. She was still surprised Laura was willing to hang out with her. She glanced down at her skinny jeans and lilac cashmere jumper. Did she look too frumpy? New friendships were a kind of date, she mused. It felt like there was a lot at stake. Then she felt stupid at even thinking Laura might want to befriend her. Was she making a fool of herself even trying?

The rap of knuckles against the door of her flat stopped her thoughts vaulting over each other. Almost tripping on the edge of the rug, she rushed along the hallway, then forced herself to slow down. She stretched up to the spyhole and saw Laura's face, round like a chipmunk's, and suppressed a giggle.

'Welcome to my humble abode.' She stepped back and threw her arm wide, inviting Laura in.

'I love that rug.'

'Thanks. I got in in Patara in Turkey, years ago. I tried to barter, but I think I probably still paid four times more than a local would have.' The word Turkey caught in her throat, and she was glad when Laura bent to touch the rug.

Laura stroked the intricately woven threads. 'It's gorgeous.'

'It's all downhill from here.' Bonnie squeezed past her towards the sitting-room. 'I like to peak early.'

Laura followed her and stopped, jaw gaping as she stood at the entrance to the room. 'You're a bloody liar,' she said.

Bonnie allowed herself to feel some satisfaction, surveying the room and accepting she'd done a pretty good job with the boxy space. She'd chosen the lightest curtain fabric in a shimmering, almost opaque pewter, and it fluttered against the open balcony doors like silver butterfly wings. The evening sun slanted in, filtering the room in soft focus.

Laura ran her hand along the hot pink throw on the back of the sofa, then touched the silver cushions with the tips of her fingers. She walked towards the largest painting.

'Don't tell me you painted that.'

Bonnie's breath caught in her throat. 'Okay, I won't.'

Laura peeped over her shoulder at her, then again at the painting. Bonnie clenched her fingers, nails biting into her palms, as she let the swirls of blues pull them both into its luminescent centre. Stepping slowly around the room, Laura's eyes were wide. She stood silently in front of each piece until she reached the orange painting. Bonnie's breath quickened as she waited for her to speak.

'I love this one. It's got so much emotion in it. I hope you don't think I'm being too personal, but this looks like a mother and child.' She pointed at the rust figures. 'And there's an intensity, like a protectiveness between the figures. You don't have children, do you? Is it meant to be you and your mother?'

Bonnie was glad Laura didn't turn around to see her face, it would have been difficult to hide the depth of sadness this question mined. 'That's an interesting question. I had a complicated relationship with my mum.'

'Had? I'm sorry.'

Bonnie walked towards the window, willing the breeze to blow away the memories. 'Ah, thanks. It was a while ago now.'

She pushed the curtain to the side and stepped onto the wooden slats of the balcony. Laura followed, her fingers brushing the curtains then the enormous pot and green-knuckled bamboo.

'I've had a row with my mum.'

Bonnie kept her gaze on a horse and rider trotting along the towpath, trying to align her breathing with the steady clack of the hooves. 'Mums can be tricky.'

'Don't get me started.'

Bonnie didn't intend to. It hadn't gone well last time she criticised Alice, and she wasn't going to make the same mistake twice.

Laura must have taken her silence as an invitation to carry on. 'It's like she's forgotten I had a life of my own before Dad got sick. I'm twenty-four, for god's sake, and I live at home with my parents and work in the family business. What else can she possibly want from me?'

Bonnie pinned her lips together, resentment towards Alice curdling inside. What else could she ask of Laura? She watched a barge painted in vibrant colours like a gypsy caravan sidle along the canal, its elderly captain, in a greying vest and peaked cap, smoking a cigarette on the stubby deck. He blew smoke rings into the air like he was the king of all he surveyed.

'That would make a good painting.' Bonnie pointed at the barge just as the old man looked up. He gave them a gummy smile and saluted. They both waved back. The man doffed his cap then blew them a kiss.

'Shouldn't we get going?' Bonnie pushed back from the railings. She stepped inside, waiting for Laura to follow, then locked the doors.

'This is a gorgeous place.' Laura assessed the room from the new angle. 'All these colours shouldn't go, but they do. Our house is so . . . tasteful.'

'That could be taken two ways.' Bonnie put her hands on her hips.

'You know what I mean.' Laura laughed, glancing back through the doors to outside. 'And the view is fabulous. I can imagine you sitting on that balcony on a summer evening, sipping a Pinot Grigio, watching the world go by.'

'Ha, I can't go near white wine anymore.'

'Why not?'

'Menopause. I was always a lightweight, but since my hormones buggered off, so did my capacity to tolerate

Sauvignon Blanc. Two glasses and I'm dancing on the bar waving my bra around my head. Then the hangover's so bad I can't get off the sofa for the next two days. They don't tell you that in the leaflets the doctors give you.'

Laura wiggled her eyebrows. 'I'd like to see that.'

'You wouldn't.' Bonnie cringed. 'I don't know why I'm telling you all this. You must think I'm a nightmare.'

'Not at all. I'm a rubbish drinker myself. My uni friends used to think it was hilarious I would be properly pissed after a couple of pints.' She followed Bonnie through to the hall as she pulled on her leather jacket. 'That's another thing; Mum gets angry when I get drunk, but she can have all the red wine she wants. It's as though I'm some kind of irresponsible child.'

'Everyone's tolerance is different.' A shiver brought the hairs on her arms to attention. 'So she's probably just being protective.'

'I thought you were on my side!'

'I don't want to be on anybody's side. You're both my bosses, remember?'

She picked up the bags she'd put near the door, filled with two drawing boards, a sketch pad, graphite pencils, and charcoals. She lifted one to hand to Laura, but she was poking her head into the second doorway along the corridor. 'Is this a two-bed flat?'

'It is.' Bonnie shook the bag, so the pencils rattled. 'This is for you. It's what you'll need for starters.'

'Wow, thanks. I didn't expect you to get the stuff for me.'

'Did you bring anything yourself?'

Laura scrunched her face. 'No. I kind of stormed out without thinking anything through. I think I revert to childhood when I'm with my mum. That's not ideal at my age, is it? Still, she was out of order today.'

Bonnie didn't comment, feeling a hint of sympathy for Alice, dealing with a self-confessed overgrown child. Still, you reap what you sow. 'Good job I got these then, isn't it?'

When Laura said a meek, 'What would I do without you?' Bonnie flushed and bent, pretending to pick a piece of fluff from the rug.

* * *

Laura parked outside the church hall's entrance on the steep hill, dragging the handbrake up and unclipping her seat belt. It was an old building with a thick stone trim around the double doors. They collected the bags from the boot and approached the entrance just as a woman with long, twisted blonde and grey tresses, like a middle-aged heroine in a renaissance painting, filled the space.

'Hello!' Her face was made up of three circles, two red apples for cheeks and a smaller ring for a chin. Her eyes twinkled behind rimless glasses, and Bonnie immediately liked her.

'I'm Angie and you must be our new girls.' She looked them up and down. 'When I saw you get out of the car, I thought you were mother and daughter, but looking at you now, I'm not so sure.'

Laura chuckled. 'Is it because she doesn't have pink hair?'

'I love your hair.' Angie stroked Laura's waves and Laura's eyes widened, but she didn't move. 'So, friends? Work colleagues?'

'She's my boss.' Bonnie pointed a thumb towards Laura who shrugged and grinned.

'Okay . . .' Angie looked between them, lines crinkling around her eyes, as though waiting for this to make sense, then abruptly giving up. 'Well, welcome both of you. Can I help you with those bags?'

'No, thank you, we can manage.'

'Through here.'

They trailed behind Angie past a square kitchen, where a gaggle of people interrupted their conversations to grin and nod in their direction, to a cavernous hall with curtains drawn in front of a stage to their right and enormous windows straight ahead and on the far wall. In the centre of the scarred, dull parquet floor was a seat covered in a red velvet fabric, which fell in waves to the ground.

Facing the stage, gold framed chairs with red cushioned seats were set in a semi-circle, interrupted here and there by skinny easels.

'Find a chair that hasn't already been snaffled,' said Angie. 'And feel free to shift into whatever space you want as long as you don't block anyone's view. I'm here.' She pointed at a large easel with a canvas propped on it. Paint tubes, pencils, and brushes were scattered in a mess at its base.

'This all looks very professional.' Laura's voice was tremulous. 'I think I might be out of my depth.'

Angie let out a throaty laugh. 'Don't be silly. I'm a professional artist, so I've got all this shit, but Trudy, who's sitting over there' – she pointed at a chair with a plastic bag leaning against its leg – 'has retired from being an accounts clerk and this is only her second week. I told her I didn't care if she draws stick men, as long as she enjoys it.' She peered into Bonnie's bag. 'What medium are you using?'

Bonnie lifted the charcoal sticks out. 'I'm going to start with charcoal and might do some colour later.'

'Nice, bit of mess. Love it.' Angie grinned. 'Find a spot, I'll get everyone through, and we'll start in five minutes.'

They tiptoed through the maze of art materials and Laura turned to her and grinned when they found two seats next to each other. Bonnie showed her how to clip the sheets of paper onto the board and gave her a clear pencil case filled with soft pencils, charcoal sticks, an eraser, a Stanley knife, and a small packet of wet wipes.

'Wow, that's very organised and really kind.' Laura opened the case and examined the contents.

'Just experiment with everything. You'll soon find out what works for you.'

Laura leaned towards her and whispered, 'I'm nervous. I think I'm going to show myself up.'

'Impossible,' Bonnie whispered. 'Trying new things is brave. I'm already impressed with you.' She was delighted to see a sparkle in Laura's dark eyes as she straightened and balanced the board on her knee.

Quiet classical music played from a portable radio plugged in at the base of the stage, and two fan heaters, directed at the central chair, emitted a soft hum as people of all ages wandered into the room. A man with grey hair and a cravat, which clashed with his brilliant white trainers, gave them the thumbs up as he sat opposite. The woman she presumed must be Trudy sat stiffly, sharpened pencil poised.

'Everyone settled?' yelled Angie, taking a paintbrush out of her mouth and waving it to get their attention. 'Today we've got a lovely lady modelling for us, so if we're all ready, let's get on with it.'

A woman with long dark hair stepped from behind the stage curtains and down the stairs to the wooden floor. She wore a white towelling bathrobe which, as she approached the velvet-covered chair, she dropped from her shoulders and handed to Angie. Eyes lowered, she flicked her straight hair over her shoulders, revealing large breasts a shade lighter than her smooth, tanned arms, and sat, one leg crossed over the other, on the seat. She draped her left arm across her full, soft stomach, resting her hand above her neat black triangle of pubic hair. Then she opened her eyes and looked at them.

Bonnie felt the colour rise in her cheeks at the same time as the model's cheeks flared red. She flicked a glance at Laura to see her eyes as round as saucers as she mouthed, 'Polly?'

Chapter Eleven

Bonnie

Present Day

Bonnie had been to many life drawing classes over the years, but none where she'd recently met the model in an entirely different arena. She'd always found it easy to stop seeing naked breasts and instead see where light hit curves and the difference in shade between the nipple and flesh. But now the nipples were Polly's, and the pubic hair was Polly's, and her cheeks were flaming, and it all felt very awkward indeed.

'We'll do three two-minute poses, then two five-minute ones to get into the groove, as it were, then we'll go on to the longer, more detailed stuff, okay?' said Angie.

Laura intermittently glanced over at Bonnie as Polly stretched her arm over her head, enormous bosom lifting and hanging, leg extended behind her. Bonnie tried not to catch either Laura or Polly's eye as she scratched at her paper with her charcoal. She rubbed the shading with her finger, erasing the curves of Polly's bottom and redrafting, worried she might upset her if she made it as broad as it looked in the early evening light.

When Angie announced it was time for a break, Polly grabbed her bathrobe, giving Angie a quick smile and disappearing behind the stage curtain without a backwards glance.

'Polly!' Laura whispered loudly to Bonnie. 'I've seen Polly's tits.' She turned her board and showed it to Bonnie. 'I couldn't bring myself to draw her pubes, it felt so wrong.'

The paper was covered in beautiful, curved lines; small, fine drawings of the different poses, each one stopping at the round stomach.

'You are such a child.' Bonnie tried not to laugh. 'It's about the shapes and the light, not the body parts.'

'But' – Laura clenched her teeth and drew her lips back – 'Polly's tits.'

'Stop it.' Bonnie took Laura's board and examined the drawings, suddenly serious. 'These are good.' She flicked onto another sheet filled with even smaller studies. 'Really, really good.'

'Shut up.' Laura pointed at Bonnie's paper. 'Look at yours. They look so much like Polly she could walk off the paper.'

Bonnie wasn't interested in hers. She examined Laura's drawings more closely. 'Do you mind if I give you some advice?'

'Knock yourself out.'

'Hold the pencil further up, it will give you more freedom of movement, or better still, try some charcoal because it's impossible to be tidy with this stuff.' She took a long black stick from the pencil case and passed it to Laura. 'I'd like to see what you do when you're not trying to get it right.'

92

'Good work, you two.' They looked up to see Angie's apple cheeks glowing. 'You're both doing brilliantly. You've got Polly's likeness in that.' She pointed at Bonnie's largest drawing. 'Cuppa?' She grinned and walked towards the kitchen.

'Do we let on we know her?' Laura asked.

'I think we should let Polly take the lead. Let's get a drink and if she comes in, we'll take it from there.' As she wiped the black mess from her fingers with a wet wipe, Bonnie felt like a sage. It was clear Laura thought she knew the answers, so she was going to pretend she did until Laura found out how clueless she really was.

Polly didn't come into the kitchen to join them, which was clearly unusual. Angie blustered around looking for her, left the kitchen, and came back saying, 'Polly's got some emails to do, so I'm taking her a cup of tea through. We'll start again in ten minutes, okay? Don't forget to wash your cups or I'll have the caretaker on the blower again.'

Bonnie and Laura finished their drinks and washed the chipped mugs in the ancient porcelain sink, drying them with a musty tea towel.

As they returned to their seats, they saw the chair in the centre of the room was gone and cushions were scattered over the red fabric on the floor. Angie called out, 'Polly, we're ready!' She turned back to the group. 'This time, Polly's going to pose for a full hour so you can do a more detailed study.'

Polly descended the steps, holding her bathrobe across her chest. She seemed more hesitant when she unwrapped herself and handed over the robe, and she didn't raise her eyes from the material as she lay on her right-hand side on the cushions, facing away from Bonnie and Laura.

'You comfy, love?' asked Angie, and Polly gave a small nod. The room filled with the sound of scratching brushes and the classical music seemed to rise in volume. Soon Bonnie forgot she knew the voluptuous woman, concentrating on capturing the way the rich tan of her thigh caught the light, rising to a golden shine on her hip, then dipping to a dark shadow at the roll of her stomach. Her skin was youthful and flawless. Bonnie imagined it felt much like the velvet she was now colouring, trying to catch the folds and highlights on the paper with her soft pastels.

She looked at Laura who was squinting, her lips pinched, and was pleased to see she'd followed her advice and held the black charcoal stick near its end, making much larger, bolder marks. She turned and caught Bonnie's eye and tipped her board towards her. Bonnie gave a quick thumbs up and Laura smiled, smudging a line, giving it depth.

Bonnie's brain released itself from the tensions of life and let all of her focus seep in through her eyes, down through her body, and flow out through the tips of her fingers. Her breathing slowed, the music lulled her. She felt peaceful for the first time since she'd come to Hamblin to start her new life.

A beeping sound made her jump, her yellow pastel skidding across the paper, leaving a trail along Polly's leg.

'Time's up.' Angie pressed her phone screen and the noise stopped. She handed the gown to Polly. 'Can we give our lovely model a round of applause? She's been brilliant today, hasn't she?'

Everyone clapped and Polly dipped her head in a little bow and pulled the towelling cord around her middle.

'Do you want to have a look at the work?' Angie asked her. 'You all right, love? You're quieter than usual.'

Bonnie couldn't hear what Polly said in reply, but saw

Angie put her hand on her forearm before Polly scuttled up the steps and behind the curtain.

After a quick scoot around the room to look at the drawings and paintings the others had done, they gathered their materials.

'Yours are the best in the room,' Laura whispered to Bonnie. 'The way you use colour is inspired. I would never have thought to use purple to shade.'

'Practice, that's all. I've been doing this for twenty years longer than you.'

'Why didn't you become a professional artist?'

'No money in it.' Bonnie zipped her pencil case and dropped it in the bag. 'I did an art foundation course, but when it came to university, I did interior design because I could persuade my mum I'd be able to make a living doing that.'

Laura flicked through the paper on her board. 'That's why my mum persuaded me to do a business course. I hate it when she's right.'

Again, Bonnie buttoned her lips. She didn't think Alice was right, but she couldn't say that. She remembered the fierce rows with her mum about what she was going to do with her future, how she'd told a young, troubled Bonnie she'd ruined everything and pushed her to make different decisions. Her mum had been wrong, too, and their relationship had never recovered after she moved back to Scotland. By the time Bonnie had realised everything her mother had done was out of a misguided notion of what was right for her, it was too late.

'It doesn't mean you can't do something creative, though. There's a lot that could fill the gap between business and art. I managed to run an arty business, didn't I?'

'But now you've decided to be a receptionist in a storage

95

facility?' Laura tipped her head to one side and Bonnie looked away. Suddenly, she spied Polly's face pop out from behind the curtain. She looked like a child at the start of a school show, searching for their mum in the audience. She saw Bonnie spot her and disappeared.

'Just a minute,' she said to Laura before heading towards the stage. At the top of the steps she stopped and said, 'Polly?' There was no reply at first, so she said a little louder, 'Polly.' There was a slight shift of the material and a sliver of Polly's face appeared.

'Hi.'

'Hi.' Bonnie paused. 'You want to see what we drew?'

'I know what you drew. My fat arse.'

Bonnie couldn't help but snort with laughter. 'You looked gorgeous, come and see.'

The curtain shifted wider and Polly scanned the hall. Bonnie followed her gaze and saw Laura waving. Polly's hand appeared and gave a flutter.

'Come on, Mrs. It's a bit late to be bashful now.'

Polly rolled her eyes and stepped out from her hiding place. She was dressed in a T-shirt and jeans, and it seemed hard to believe that fifteen minutes ago she was laid on the floor with nothing on. 'I'm mortified.'

'Why?'

'You've just seen my muff.'

They both laughed as they stepped into the hall. 'I made it purple.' Bonnie sniggered, and she lifted the board for Polly to see. 'Look, purple pubes.'

'Oh my god, that's brilliant!' Polly seemed to have forgotten her coyness and stared, eyes wide, at Bonnie's picture. 'You've made me look pretty in this.'

'You are pretty,' said Laura. 'I wish I had your flawless skin.'

'You're only saying that to make me feel better. I can't believe you've both seen me naked. I could die.'

Bonnie frowned. 'If you feel like that, why do you model for life drawing?'

'It's a long story—'

'Hold that thought,' Laura interrupted. 'How do you two fancy going for a drink and you can fill us in over a glass of wine?'

'Genius idea.' Polly visibly brightened. 'I could mainline vodka after the shock of seeing you two staring at my undercarriage.'

'I didn't stare.' Laura grinned. 'It was all about the light and shade for me.'

'You've learned something.' Bonnie punched Laura playfully on the arm. 'Let's pack up and get that drink.'

* * *

Standing at the bar in the empty snug of The Horse and Groom, Bonnie tried to remember the last time she'd been to the pub with girlfriends. Most of her friendships had fallen away over the years as the women she was close to got married and had babies. It wasn't that they weren't friends anymore, just that they didn't have the same opportunities to go for a spontaneous night out or girly weekend away.

She looked at the two young women sitting at the round table, chatting over the top of the cardboard menu shoved wonkily in a holder. They looked like natural friends. They were a similar age and would have things in common. A cloud passed across Bonnie's bright mood. What was she doing out with these two twenty-somethings? They probably wanted her to go home to a hot chocolate and warm bath and leave them alone.

The barman startled her as he clonked a pint of lime and soda on the sticky bar next to two gin and tonics. When she looked up, he gave her a plastic smile, and she saw how young he was, hair in a top knot, black circles in both his ears, stretching the skin into gaping holes. He probably wondered what she was doing here too.

Back at the table, Laura raised her glass in a toast. 'To new friends,' she said, as they clinked their glasses together. Bonnie searched her face to see if she meant it, and there didn't seem to be anything other than open delight. Laura leaned in. 'You were going to tell us the story of how you became a glamour model, Polly.'

She sat back and lifted an eyebrow as Polly's jaw dropped.

'I'm not a glamour model!' She glanced at the bar, then lowered her voice as she saw the young man was looking in her direction. 'You make it sound like I pose for the bloody tabloids.'

'Do you?'

'No!'

'I wouldn't judge you if you did. If I had your boobs, I'd be getting them out all over the place. I'd have them sitting on the table in front of us, right here.' Laura mimed popping her chest onto the table and they laughed as Polly shook her head.

'I've only ever done life drawing classes, and' – she paused – 'you'll think I'm mad.'

'Go on,' said Bonnie.

Polly sat back and took a sip of her drink, looking at the two of them over the top of the glass as if assessing whether she could trust them. 'It's kind of like, to try to get some body confidence.'

'Boobs-out therapy?' said Laura, nodding gravely. 'I've heard of that. Very popular in Scandinavia.'

'I'm trying to stop thinking of myself as a fat, ugly, useless lump.' Polly's voice was quiet.

Bonnie blinked. She looked across at Laura who seemed equally lost for words.

'Sorry.' Polly flushed. 'Got a bit heavy there, didn't I?'

'No, no. Not at all.' Bonnie put her hand over Polly's. 'It's just I can't imagine you feeling that way about yourself. You are so, so gorgeous and when I met you before, you seemed so confident and comfortable in your own skin.'

'I'm trying, but after years of being told negative stuff, it sinks in.'

'Who said that to you?' Laura's voice had dropped an octave.

'My whole family, really, but Mum mainly. I'm the family's running joke.'

'Oh. Seems a bit harsh.' Bonnie wanted to say more, but she'd only just met these women.

'Yeah.' Polly sipped her drink. 'I don't think they notice they're doing it anymore to be honest. You know what families are like, you get pigeonholed, and that's it for the rest of your life. I'm just the fat, messy one and if I complain they say I can't take a joke.' She shrugged.

'Want me to kill them all for you?' Bonnie and Polly turned to Laura, who was making karate moves with her arms, looking down her straight nose, lips tight. Bonnie watched in confusion, wondering if Laura was actually some kind of martial artist. 'High ya!' Laura pretended to chop through the air.

'Can you do karate?' Bonnie asked.

'No, but you were convinced, weren't you?'

'That's very kind, you nutter,' Polly said. 'But I don't

99

think slaughtering my entire family is necessary. I'm trying to ignore their comments and work on myself.'

'That's impressive,' Bonnie said. 'Well done, you. Is it working?'

'Clearly not as well as I thought since I could have happily smashed my head against the floor like a watermelon if it had meant escaping when I saw you two there today.'

'Sorry about that.' Bonnie grimaced.

'You should give her your picture to make up for seeing her knockers.' Laura nudged Bonnie, spilling her drink onto the table. Bonnie wondered if any thoughts happened inside Laura's head that didn't escape straight out of her mouth.

'She might not want it.'

'I do!' said Polly. 'I'll pay you for it if you like? It's beautiful. I've never seen myself like that.'

'With purple pubes?'

Bonnie tutted at Laura, who dipped her head and took a drink, sniggering childishly. 'You are welcome to have it. If I can be a positive part of your boobs-out therapy, it would be my pleasure.'

* * *

When they drew up in the car park outside Bonnie's flat, Bonnie unplugged her seat belt and looked over at Laura. 'Thank you for tonight. That was the most fun I've had in ages.'

'Good, because there's something I wanted to ask you.' Laura was grimacing.

'What's that?'

'You know how I flounced out earlier? Of home, I mean?'

Bonnie tensed. 'Yes.'

'Say no if you want to. I know I'm being presumptuous but . . . I said I wouldn't be back tonight, so Mum's probably put the latch and the alarm on. Don't suppose I could stay at yours?'

It was too soon. She'd only known Laura for a couple of weeks, and she was painfully aware Alice wasn't her greatest fan.

'Of course, no problem.'

What else could she say?

Chapter Twelve

Bonnie

Present Day

It felt strange to hear someone else moving around the flat in the morning. Bonnie had got used to the noise of the neighbours in the communal spaces, but the sound of the shower running and the spare room door opening and closing seemed intimate and unnerving. There was a knock at her bedroom door.

'Come in.' She pulled the duvet up to her neck, then realised she probably looked like Little Red Riding Hood's grandma, which was foolish, because Laura was more like a Labrador puppy than a big bad wolf.

The door shifted, brushing across the unworn carpet. Bonnie clicked on her bedside light as Laura walked in carrying a steaming mug. 'I've made coffee. Hope you don't mind? I'm overstepping all kinds of marks, aren't I? I bet you wish you'd never seen Bocks.'

Bonnie shuffled to sitting and took the coffee from her.

'Don't be daft. I'd only be sitting here on my own, listening to *Radio 4*, and knitting tea cosies.'

'Yeah, you definitely seem like the tea cosy type.' Laura's head turned to take in the room. 'Bloody hell.'

'What?'

'This room!' She lay her hand on the peacock throw. Bonnie liked how she touched everything. It was like a small child, needing to use more than one sense at a time to experience the world.

'Is that an original?' Laura pointed at the Bakelite clock.

'It is.'

'Wow.'

Bonnie sipped the coffee. It was strong and sweet. She lifted her mug. 'This is nice.'

'It's not hard to make good coffee when you've got a fancy machine like that.' She sat on the end of the bed and Bonnie shifted her feet out of the way. 'I've been wondering . . .' Laura continued. 'You're clearly not short of funds, so why the hell are you working at our place?'

Bonnie took another drink, buying time to think. 'When you get as old as me' – she made her voice waver like a very old woman – 'you realise what's important and what's not.'

'And storage facilities are crucial for the continuation of the species?' Laura nodded. 'I hear ya.'

'Purpose is important.' Bonnie put the coffee on a glass coaster on her bedside table and swung her legs out of bed, pulling the old T-shirt she wore to bed down over her thighs. 'Purpose, choice, and hope are the things that make people happy, in my experience.' She took her dressing gown from the back of the door and put it on. 'We all need a reason to get up in the morning, and, while I'm choosing to spend much more time painting and drawing than I had a chance to when I ran my own business, I need somewhere to go and be useful and meet people. That's where you lot come in.' She opened her arms. 'And look how well it's turned out so far.'

'Very well indeed.' Laura grinned.

'I'm not sure your mother would say the same.'

Laura dropped backwards onto the mattress, her pink hair splayed across the blues and greens. 'My mother doesn't agree with anything I say or do. I don't see why you should be any different.'

'You know what you sound like?'

'What?'

'A sulky teenager.'

Laura sat back up. 'Are you surprised? It's like she's stored me in formaldehyde.' She put her finger in the air. 'No, it's like she's put me in a tower and she's keeping me there.' She shook her hair forwards towards the floor. 'Laura, Laura, let down your hair!' She flicked it back up, the waves rippling around her face. 'And you're my Prince Charming, saving me with paintbrushes and charcoal.'

Bonnie laughed. 'I'm not your Prince Charming. I haven't ridden into town to save you.' She picked up her coffee and headed for the kitchen. 'This is the twenty-first century, pal. You can save yourself.'

Chapter Thirteen

Alice

Present Day

The following morning, Alice put her newspaper on her lap when she heard Laura's key in the lock. She and Richard had talked about what she needed to say to smooth things over, but she simmered with resentment that she had to apologise. She might have gone about it in the wrong way, but she still thought that putting some distance between Laura and Bonnie was the right course of action.

She sensed Richard looking at her over the top of his newspaper from his chair, but she wouldn't give him the satisfaction of reminding her what she needed to do. The sound of Laura's boots clonking onto the hall floor was almost enough to make her pick the paper up and finish the article she was reading about property prices, but with Richard's eyes following her, she folded it and got to her feet.

In the kitchen, Laura was drinking orange juice from the carton.

'How many times . . .' She stopped. 'How was the class?'

'Good.'

She was clearly not yet ready for small talk.

'I'm sorry I wasn't completely truthful about Dad yesterday.'

Laura snorted. 'Not completely truthful? You purposefully lied.'

'Yes, well . . .' Alice didn't know how to end the sentence. 'Was it a man or a woman?'

Laura's nose wrinkled. 'What?'

'At the class. The model?'

Laura's face lit up. She screwed the top back on the carton and wiped her mouth with her hand. 'Oh my god! You're not going to believe this.'

Alice's mind raced. Surely Laura wasn't going to disclose that the receptionist was actually the nude model? 'Believe what?'

'Who it was. The model.'

'Dear lord, it wasn't—'

'Polly. It was Polly.' Laura's eyes were wide. 'From Bocks.'

Alice frowned. 'I know who Polly is. I just can't believe—'

'I know, right? She's got a cracking pair of boobs on her.'

Alice took the juice carton from the island and put it in the fridge. 'I'd really rather not know the details.' Turning back to Laura she felt brave enough to ask what she really wanted to know. 'So, you stayed at Bonnie's?'

'Yeah.'

'And?'

'And what?'

She could be infuriating sometimes. 'I'm just interested in your new friend. That's allowed, isn't it? What's her house like? Have you learned any more about her?'

Laura turned away, opening the fridge and looking inside. 'Her flat's really nice. Colourful.' She plucked out a packet of ham, extracted a slice, rolled it into a tube and shoved it in her mouth. 'Stylish.'

Alice sniffed.

'What?'

'Nothing.' She opened a drawer and passed a roll of cellophane to Laura. She watched her daughter cut off a ridiculously large portion of film and wrap it around the packet. She knew she should have done it herself. 'I was wondering whether you'd like to come and see some properties with me next week.'

'What for?'

'Just for fun. On the off-chance the planning application doesn't get approved, we could think about downsizing.' She kept all emotion out of her voice. She didn't want Laura to suspect that the clock was ticking. She certainly didn't want her to know that the last three years might have been for nothing; that they might lose the house, the business, everything they'd worked so hard for.

'Ha, can't imagine you and Dad in a two up two down.'

'It would just be nice to scope out the market. I thought it might be something fun for us to do together.'

Laura nodded. 'When were you thinking?'

Alice rubbed her temple. She plucked a date out of the air. 'Next Tuesday evening?'

'Tuesday? Are you kidding me?'

Alice blinked. 'Or . . .'

'Is that your plan, to make me choose?'

'What?'

Laura dropped the packet onto the shelf and slammed the fridge door. 'First you lie to stop me going to Life Drawing, then you ask me to do something with you instead when you know it's on every Tuesday. Manipulating much?'

Colour rushed to Alice's cheeks. 'No, you've misunderstood.'

'Really?' Laura dropped her head to one side. 'As if you'd honestly consider downsizing from this place. It's your pride and joy. Be honest, it was just another plan to stop me having a life of my own. The sooner I get out of here the better.'

'Laura—'

But Laura had already stormed out of the room and Alice heard her footsteps stomping up the stairs. She thought about following her and shouting that she, Laura, was her pride and joy, not the bloody house, but as she paused to find the words, her phone dinged on the counter, demanding her attention. She picked it up to see an alert from the loan company. Her mouth went dry when she saw the first words of the message: 'Your loan repayment is due.'

Chapter Fourteen

Alice

Twenty-Two Years Ago

Alice breathed in the smell of damp plaster and then emptied her lungs in a satisfied sigh. Everything was coming together. After all those years of trying for a baby, the waking in the middle of the night with searing stomach pain and watching the blood of another miscarriage drip into the toilet bowl, here she was with her perfect daughter, about to move into their perfect forever home.

Laura sat heavily on her hip as she closed the front door, the echo of the slam reverberating around the empty hall. She popped her three-year-old down on the floorboards, pulling a grey stuffed elephant out of her bag and handing it to her.

'What do you think, poppet?' she asked the dark-haired child. 'Do you and Ellie the Elephant like our new house?'

'No,' said Laura, curling the elephant's velvet ear around her finger. 'Ellie says it smells funny.'

Alice laughed. 'That's just because it's new. It will smell

better when it's decorated, and all our things are here. It will smell exactly like home.'

'Where's Daddy?'

Alice dropped the plastic bag with all the tiny cans of paint she'd bought at the DIY superstore by the door. 'He's at work.' She didn't add that he was always at work these days. It was a necessary evil, she supposed, so they could buy this gorgeous house on this desirable road and be able to save towards a more secure future. It was a shame he had to miss out on so much though.

She took Laura's little hands. 'Imagine what this is going to be like when it's finished.' She twirled them both around and Laura giggled as their shoes clattered on the floorboards. Alice stopped and pointed to the left of the door. 'I'm going to put a table there and we can have lots of family photos on it and pictures from all the lovely holidays we'll go on.' Sweeping her eyes up the curved staircase to the high ceiling of the second floor, she pointed. 'And, when we have enough pennies, I'm going to buy a chandelier that drops from up there.'

The little girl followed her gaze. 'What's a chamblier?'

'A chandelier. It's a sparkly light made of glass baubles and every time we switch it on it will be like Christmas.' Her heart swelled. It felt like her dreams were truly becoming reality. She crouched by the plastic bag, lifting out the pots of paint and lining them up against the naked skirting board. 'We're both going to do some painting.' She unrolled a strip of wallpaper lining and dropped a pot of paint on each corner to hold it flat. 'You can paint on this. Here's your brush.'

Laura took the brush in her pudgy fingers. 'I like painting.'

'I know you do. Make sure you stay on the paper

though. I'm going to try out some colours on the walls while you make a picture. You'll need to stay here, though. Don't go exploring when I'm in another room, okay?'

Laura nodded, her cherub-like lips in a serious line.

'What are you going to paint?'

Laura rubbed her fingers across the bristles, and Alice smiled at the familiar way her plump hands with indented knuckles always had to touch things.

'I'm going to paint you and Daddy and me in our new house.'

Alice didn't think she'd ever felt happier as she set out brightly coloured paints in the middle of the hallway for Laura and started to daub neutral colours with names like 'Sandstorm' and 'Oat Biscuit' on the wall nearest the door.

She moved through to the kitchen and was considering whether a light grey might be better than cream for the woodwork of the huge windows in the dining area, when she noticed how quiet the hallway was. Laura's chattering to the elephant and quiet singing had been the background music to her splodging of colours on the dry plaster. She balanced her brush across the top of the open paint tin and cocked her head.

Unease crept into the pit of her stomach as the silence hummed. She strode past the granite island and into the hall, but Laura wasn't leaning over the bright colours on the paper. Instead, her brush lay next to a big pink circle with crude blue eyes and a red gash for a mouth.

Alice scanned the empty room. 'Laura?'

Bouncing footsteps clattered on the floorboards upstairs.

'Laura, what are you doing up there?' Her voice was sharp, and Laura's chin puckered as she appeared at the top of the stairs.

'Sorry, Mummy.' She held out the elephant. 'Ellie wanted to see what was up here.'

The elephant fell from her fingers and before Alice could stop her, Laura leaped forwards after the toy and her feet missed the step and then she was falling, her tiny body tumbling head over little Velcro shoes, her precious bones crashing against the wooden steps. Alice sprinted towards her, but there was nothing she could do to stop her fall. That inability to save her daughter imprinted itself on her heart, and the screaming that started seconds after Laura stilled would be the soundtrack to Alice's nightmares for decades to come.

* * *

In the children's ward, when Laura came around from the operation to set the broken bone in her wrist, Alice stroked the hair back from her bruised forehead and kissed her pale cheek. 'I'm so sorry, poppet,' she said. 'I'm so, so sorry.'

'It wasn't your fault,' said Laura. 'It was Ellie's. Naughty Ellie.'

But Alice knew that she'd put her new home above caring for her child, and in that moment, she vowed to always put her family first.

Chapter Fifteen

Bonnie

Present Day

'Long time no see.' Ross jumped up from the bench and opened his arms. Bonnie allowed herself to be wrapped up and the feeling of being held by her cousin weakened her knees. For a moment, she regretted not keeping in regular touch with this lovely man. But even now, in this much-needed hug, he was a reminder of the most painful time in her life.

He let go and looked her up and down. 'You look well.'

She detected surprise in his voice. 'You too. Baldy, but well.'

Ross ran his fingers through his thinning hair. 'The cheek. This is how all the cool dudes wear their hair these days. Can't blame me if you're behind the times.'

Bonnie laughed. 'Yeah, all the cool dudes say, "*cool dudes*", too.'

They both grinned. 'Sorry I couldn't invite you to the flat, by the way,' Bonnie said. 'The smell of paint is awful.

It's given me a banging headache. Nice to be out in the fresh air.' When Ross rang to say he was in town and wanted to pop by, Bonnie had hurriedly invented a story about the communal spaces being decorated and suggested they instead meet in the grounds of the folly for a walk. She wasn't exactly sure why she couldn't have him in the flat, beyond the fact that she couldn't bear for her past and present to collide. Not right now.

'Shall we walk?' She nodded towards the winding concrete path leading up to the folly. Bonnie had to take two steps for every one of Ross's long strides. 'You do realise I take after our mothers' side of the family?' she said.

'Ha, forgot you were a short-arse for a minute. Sorry. I'll slow down.' He started to walk in exaggerated slow motion and Bonnie slapped him on the arm. How soon they'd fallen back into acting like their childish selves.

'So, you had a meeting in Hamblin?' Bonnie said.

'Yeah. A client who owns some commercial units on the outskirts of town wanted to meet. He's having staffing issues, wanted to know his legal position, you know.' He shrugged.

They walked on towards the stone tower at the top of the grassy hill. 'You've been to Hamblin before then?'

He kept his eyes raised to the folly. 'No. He's a new client.'

'That's a coincidence.' She scrutinised his face. He looked uncomfortable.

'Yeah.'

They walked on, their breathing quickening with the incline and a sense of unease tightened Bonnie's chest. She stopped. 'Why are you really here?'

'I told you—'

116

'No bullshit, Ross. Why have you suddenly turned up here when I haven't seen you for years?'

'You rang me first, remember?'

Bonnie groaned. 'You called Stuart, didn't you?' She stomped away up the path.

It only took seconds for Ross to catch her up. 'What did you expect me to do? He's still your husband. He cares about you. And that time you rang me was weird. It wasn't exactly a normal request, was it? I was worried you were in trouble again.'

'You better not have told Stuart about—'

Ross took her wrist, forcing her to stop and face him. 'Of course I didn't. I promised you and your mum I'd never tell a soul.'

Bonnie searched his face to work out if he was telling the truth.

He peered into her eyes. 'Stuart is worried you might be struggling again though. We both are.'

Bonnie hung her head. 'I'm not.' She looked up. 'There. Happy now?' She shook his hand from her wrist and stomped to the foot of the looming tower.

He followed her. 'Not really.' He walked towards a bench in the shadow of the building. 'Come on. Sit down. Talk to me.'

Reluctantly, Bonnie plonked herself next to Ross. She didn't want to talk. She didn't want Ross to be here at all. 'I can't believe you're spying on me.'

'I'm not spying. I'm checking on you. That's all.'

'Same difference.'

Ross looped his arm around her shoulder and pulled her in.

She was stiff at first, but the warmth of his body eventually made her soften.

117

She felt his ribs expand before he spoke. 'Just because I don't see you often, doesn't mean I don't care. You've had it rough, Shorty.' His hand squeezed her shoulder. 'I mean, it's not always been ideal, being a solicitor and having a criminal for a cousin, but . . .'

Bonnie butted him gently, digging her head into his shoulder. 'Knob.'

'Still classy, then.'

They sat, watching an elderly woman in a rain mac hook her arm through an old man's. After just a few steps he looked like he was crumbling under the weight of pulling them both up the hill.

'I'm not doing anything . . . you know. I promise,' Bonnie said quietly. 'Haven't since I left Glasgow.'

'That's good.'

The old man stumbled and righted himself. He stopped to look at the woman next to him and they both shook their heads and started to laugh. She hooked her arm through his again and they turned to make their descent.

Ross nodded towards the couple. 'Thought you and Stuart would end up like those two.'

'Too knackered to climb a hill?'

'Growing old together.' A minute passed before he spoke again. 'Stuart doesn't know why you won't let him help you.'

Bonnie squeezed her eyes tight, trying to block the image of her husband pleading with her to try therapy from her mind. 'I don't deserve his help. I need to work things out on my own.'

'That's not true.'

Bonnie lifted her head from the comfort of Ross's shoulder. 'I should never have married him. If he hadn't

118

married me, he could have had a better life, children, a proper family. I ruined his life.'

'He doesn't see it like that. Maybe if you'd told him why—'

Bonnie stood. 'Please, Ross, don't. Thank you for coming. Thanks for checking up on me, but as you can see, I'm fine. Don't worry, I'm not about to hurt myself.'

'There's more than one way of harming yourself, Bonnie. I can see you're struggling; you're not thinking rationally.'

She needed to get away. 'You're a solicitor, Ross, not a fucking psychiatrist.' She stood and started down the path. 'Please tell Stuart I'm fine. He doesn't need to worry about me.' She waved her hand behind her. 'And I'm sorry. I know you meant well, but I can't do this.'

Chapter Sixteen

Bonnie

Seven Years Ago

'Happy fortieth birthday!' Stuart handed Bonnie a champagne flute filled with orange liquid. 'Breakfast is almost ready but thought we'd start the day with a cheeky buck's fizz.'

Bonnie took the glass and chinked it against the one in Stuart's hand. 'Forty. Blimey. Sounds old.'

'None of that.' Stuart held his palm up. 'Only positive vibes today. We are going to celebrate your magnificent forty years on this planet. Your wonderful life, your successful career and, of course, your stupendous luck in finding and marrying the perfect man.'

He chinked his glass against hers again, grinning, oblivious to the effect his words had on his wife. *Has my life been wonderful?* she asked herself. The last four years had been, since she'd met Stuart and the business had taken off. But before that . . .

When Stuart led her through to the dining room, the

sun shone through the multicoloured beads hanging across the window frame. The rainbow light dappled on the table set with a feast of pasties. The smell of freshly brewed coffee rose from the silver coffee pot. Bonnie looked at the love Stuart had poured into making this breakfast and put the past out of her mind. Now was all that mattered, and now was perfect.

After devouring two croissants with jam, Stuart wiped pastry flakes from his chin then put his elbows on the table. He eyed Bonnie thoughtfully. 'Forty.'

'Yep.' She widened her eyes. 'Officially middle-aged.'

'Makes you think.'

The way he went quiet and rested his chin on his knitted fingers sent a ripple of nerves through Bonnie. 'Let's get this lot cleared up.' She stood and lifted a plate. 'Then we can—'

'Just a minute.' Stuart's voice was serious.

'Come on. Lots to do before we go out.' She shifted the remaining pasties onto one plate.

'Please, just wait. I want to talk to you about something.'

She had no choice but to put the plate back on the table and sit.

'I've been thinking.'

Bonnie's stomach tipped. She knew what was coming. He'd been making clumsy hints, which she'd been able to brush away so far, but now it was going to be a *conversation*.

'Now you're forty . . .'

Bonnie could see he was nervous by the way he circled his thumbs around each other in front of his mouth.

'I was thinking . . . I mean I know you always said . . .'

Bonnie closed her eyes. Here it came.

'I know you were sure you never wanted to have children,

but . . . well, I wondered if now that time is . . . not running out exactly.'

'Oh, Stuart.' Her heart felt heavy in her chest.

'This might not be the best time to talk about it . . . I mean, I don't want to spoil your birthday, but I just wanted to say, if you were having second thoughts . . .'

'I'm not.'

He dropped his hands onto the table. 'Okay. Okay, I hear you, but what if . . .'

'What if you've realised you do want children after all?'

He rubbed his hand over his face. 'I thought it was worth having a conversation.'

She stood and walked to the window, looking out into the garden so he couldn't see the anguish on her face. 'I knew this would happen. That's why I made it as clear as I could before we got married. I told you I wasn't going to change my mind. I'm not cut out to be a mother.'

She heard the chair legs scrape back and felt his presence behind her. 'I know that's what you said, and I know I'm the one saying something different to what we agreed. But can't we even talk about it? I don't know why you think you're not cut out for it. You'd be a brilliant mum.'

'I'm telling you, I wouldn't. I know myself. You promised you accepted my decision. I gave you a choice. You should have walked away. I should have made you. It isn't fair on you. I'm sorry.'

He wrapped his arms around her shoulders. 'I think you'd be—'

'Please don't.' Bonnie turned, twisting herself out of his arms. She didn't deserve his faith in her. 'I'm sorry. I can't give you what you want. Maybe I should go now. Give you the opportunity to meet someone who—'

'No.' He pulled her into his chest. 'No.'

123

He pushed his fingers into her back and she felt his desperation. The acid-guilt burned holes in her stomach. 'I'm so sorry,' she whispered.

'It doesn't matter.' She could hear he was trying not to cry. 'I want you. Just you. If it's a choice between spending the rest of my life without you or having children, you win every time.'

'I don't want to win. I can't bear that you've had to make that sacrifice.'

He turned her towards him and took her face between his hands, then kissed her hard. She could still feel the pressure of his mouth when he released her. 'Forget I said anything. Forget it. Please, Bonnie. *You* are enough. I love you and all I want in the world is you.'

But she wasn't enough. She knew that. And knowing now that Stuart wanted more than she could give him opened up a wound she thought had almost healed.

Chapter Seventeen

Bonnie

Six Months Ago

Bonnie jumped when she heard the front door bang shut downstairs. She opened the desk drawer and scooped the mascaras inside. She turned over the envelope, so the address was face down and went to the door of her attic studio. 'Stuart?'

A muffled voice shouted, 'Hiya. Forgot my office keys.'

She let out the breath she was holding and went back to the desk. He'd be gone in a minute so she could carry on bagging up the things she'd taken from Boots and send them to the women's refuge in town.

She didn't know why she'd started to shoplift again. For years after marrying Stuart she'd never experienced the heart-quickening sensation, the tingling in her fingers urging her to lift something from a shelf and slide it into her bag or pocket. But recently, the urges had come back so powerfully she wasn't always able to resist. It was the only time she experienced any relief from the feeling of dread that had crept up on her over the last few years, and now had permanent residence in the pit of her stomach.

She listened for the sound of Stuart moving around, but the house was quiet, so she opened the drawer again. Lifting the three mascaras, she slipped them into the padded envelope and stuck down the lip. Anonymously sending the things she'd stolen to charities allayed a tiny portion of the guilt.

Quick footsteps on the stairs made her jump and she quickly shoved the envelope back in the drawer and took a book of fabric swatches from the desk, pretending to leaf through. Looking up when Stuart reached the doorway, her blood chilled at the grave look on his face.

'Do you have something to ask me?'

Bonnie blinked. 'What?'

'Have I ever given you cause to doubt me?'

She put the fabric book down. 'What are you talking about?'

'Do you think I'm having an affair?'

A surge of laughter burst from her mouth. 'What on earth makes you ask that?'

'This.' Stuart thrust her phone at her.

She took the phone and looked at the blank screen. She shook her head. 'What on earth are you talking about?'

Stuart pointed at the phone. 'Open it. My phone's in the car so I picked up yours to ring work to tell them I was going to be late.'

Bonnie's stomach flipped when she remembered what she'd been researching before leaving her phone to charge in the kitchen. She put the phone on the desk. 'Don't be silly. Of course I don't think you're having an affair.'

'What's going on then?'

She picked up the swatch book again and pretended to be engrossed in it. 'Nothing.'

Stuart came towards her. 'Nothing? Really? You expect me to believe that? I hardly recognise you these days. You don't seem to sleep anymore. You toss and turn all night.'

'I think it's the menopause. My mum started having symptoms at forty-five, so that's probably why I'm not myself.'

'That doesn't explain why you're researching private investigators.'

'I was just curious. I read something in a novel and I thought—'

'Bollocks. You're permanently on edge. I don't think I've heard you laugh for weeks.' He stepped forwards until he was so close she could feel his breath ruffle her hair. 'What's going on, Bonnie? You need to talk to me.'

She looked down at her feet, trying to think of something that might satisfy him. 'Okay. Alright. But don't go off on one.' She gestured for him to sit next to her on the sofa under the eaves. 'I wanted to see if I could find Cahil's family.'

Stuart's face screwed up. 'Why?'

She dropped her head back to rest on the cushion, unable to look at him when she told him this half-truth. 'The reason I'm not sleeping – one of them, at least – is because that night keeps replaying in my mind. It's like . . . you know when you get that feeling you're falling and you wake up suddenly and you're safe in your own bed?'

She felt Stuart shift. 'Go on.'

'Well, I kind of feel like I'm at that point before I wake up all the time. I have that dread, like I'm falling.' Tears clogged her throat. 'But I can't wake up because it's real. What happened was real. And it was my fault.'

She realised it was true. This was exactly how she felt. All of the time. 'I feel like, if I can find Cahil's family and tell them how sorry I am, the feelings might get easier to bear.'

Stuart took her hand. 'So you wanted an investigator to look for Cahil's family?'

She nodded. Tears streamed down her cheeks.

He sighed. 'I'm not sure that's a good idea. They might not react well. You know that?'

She nodded again, tears dripping off her chin onto their entwined fingers.

'Can I tell you what I think?' He waited for her to respond but she was crying too hard to speak. 'I suspect Cahil's parents have done much of their grieving. They'll never forget him and there'll always be a space where he should have been.' He paused and squeezed her hand. 'But you turning up and telling them how guilty you feel . . . well, that's not going to help them, is it? I'm sorry, this sounds like I'm being cruel, but telling them would be more about assuaging your guilt than helping them. And you have nothing to feel guilty about. Accepting that is the biggest hurdle for you.'

Bonnie knew he was right; in part, at least. She couldn't burden them with what she'd done. Any of it.

Stuart turned his body towards her. 'I think the best thing you could do, for everyone, is to see someone – a therapist. You need to truly believe you have nothing to feel guilty about.'

He had no idea. Bonnie shook her head. Her hair stuck to her wet face.

'Hear me out. You need to get past this feeling that it was all your fault. It's eaten away at you for decades now. You're not yourself anymore, Bonnie. You haven't been for a long time. It's like you've been, I don't know, corroded from the inside. I'm worried about you. I'm worried you'll start all that business again.'

'I won't,' she said. 'I promise.'

She looked over at the desk drawer, the guilt of lying about that too twisting her guts. It didn't matter how much Stuart begged, she wasn't going to see a therapist. How could she put into words what she'd done? The magnitude of it. She didn't even want to feel better. She deserved to feel every sting of shame. She deserved the guilt that poisoned every thought she had.

'Thank you,' she said, wiping the hair from her cheeks. 'Just getting it out of my head has helped.' She picked up his hand and kissed his knuckles. 'What would I do without you?'

'I love you,' he said, holding her tightly.

'I love you, too.' And she did.

It was herself she loathed.

Chapter Eighteen

Bonnie

Two Months Ago

Bonnie heard the rattling of the plastic tubes hitting the mattress next to her pillow. She opened her eyes a slit, then scrunched them tight.

'I found these,' said Stuart, his voice constricted.

She turned over, her damp T-shirt snagging and pulling at her neck. She didn't wrench it away. It was better to be strangled by her nightie than face Stuart's disappointment. Again.

'I know you're awake.' His bare feet thudded on the polished floorboards past the bed and she heard the curtain rings scrape against the rail. The light from the late winter morning washed the inside of her eyelids pink and she emptied her lungs through her nose, admitting defeat.

She blinked at the tall figure of Stuart standing over her, hands on hips, watching his lips move in his shadowy face. Poor sod. He deserved somebody who could feel their heart race outside the cosmetics aisle in Boots. Someone better than her.

'I was looking for the invoices for the Strathmore account this morning and those' – he pointed to the other side of the bed – 'were in the filing cabinet in your studio.'

She didn't turn her head. She knew what was there. Her fingers tingled with the memory of plucking them from the plastic dispenser, palming them as her heart pounded against her ribs, slipping them into her pocket, then walking to the sliding doors and waiting for the relief of sharp, fresh air and the sting of shame.

'I'm tired.'

'I know. You're always tired.'

She turned onto her back, dragging the T-shirt away from her neck with her finger, and flopping her hand back on the bed.

A shadow fell across her as he moved forwards and the mattress sagged as he sat. 'You know what I said last time.'

She turned her head away from his glare, but the tubes of lip gloss stared back at her and tears stung her eyes. She shifted and focused on the high ceiling, watching the lightshade send triangular shadows across the paintwork.

'I'm imagining the headlines when you eventually get prosecuted . . . because you will get caught. You know that, don't you?'

Bonnie put her hand across her eyes and felt her chin pucker.

'Wealthy Woman in Shoplifting Shame.' The air moved as he flapped his hands, as though unfurling a banner. 'Local Interior Designer Caught Stealing Shit She Doesn't Need or Want.' He tried to lift her fingers from her face, but she resisted.

His voice lowered. 'Is that what it's going to take?'

She was too hot. The under sheet was moist against her back, and she could smell the sickly-sweet scent that haunted her as she lay in a half-sleep night after night. She threw the duvet off and heard the tubes scatter across the floorboards. Stuart let out a deep sigh.

'Where are you going now?'

'You wanted me to get up. I'm up.' She flung her arms wide.

'There's a lot of things I want you to do.'

She sighed, her arms dropping limply to her sides. 'I know.'

Stuart stood and walked towards her. He took her hands and the scent of her T-shirt hovered around her nostrils. Why didn't he ever mention it?

He tucked his head down to catch her eyes under her fringe, but she looked away. 'I've found a woman,' he said. 'She sounds like she could help.'

Bonnie snatched her hands from his. 'You went behind my back?'

His fingers grabbed at the hair at his temples. 'What was I meant to do? You won't help yourself. It's gone too far now.'

She tried to imagine sitting opposite someone and telling them what really went on in her head. She tugged at the neck of her T-shirt again, trying to catch her breath. Looking into Stuart's blue eyes she said, 'I'll sort myself out.'

The deep lines between his eyebrows relaxed. 'You'll talk to her?'

She shook her head, her fringe falling into her eyes. 'No, that's not what I meant.'

A primeval roar came from Stuart and she jumped. He

clutched the end of the bed, his knuckles white. 'That's it. I'm done.' His Glaswegian accent was stronger when he was angry, and the words were solid and round.

The damp T-shirt felt like a cold, wet flannel sticking to her back. She shivered. 'What do you mean?'

'Enough.' He let go of the bed and spread his hands wide. 'You have to put a stop to whatever this is.' He gestured to the tubes, scattered on the dark wood floor like bright children's toys. 'I've done what I can to help you, but I'm done fighting. I can't win with you.'

'If you want me to go . . .' At first, she couldn't believe she'd said it, then an idea sprang into her mind, and the solution was obvious. She crossed the thick carpet of the landing onto the cold floorboards of the spare room. Stuart's heavy footsteps followed her. She knelt and dragged the suitcase from under the bed.

'Oh, for god's sake, Bonnie.'

She paused, but when he didn't continue, she swept open the case's zip.

'I can't talk to you when you're like this. I'm going to post those invoices.'

She listened to his footsteps pound down the stairs and then heard him slam the door. She took the case through to their bedroom and filled it with handfuls of underwear from her drawers. Lifting clothes from the wardrobe, she lay them on top and tucked the spilling fabric into the corners, then zipped it closed. She pulled the peacock patterned throw from the spare bed, ran her fingers over the silky material, tracing the blue and gold feathers, then shoved it in a bag.

She glanced down at her thin legs, bare under the enormous T-shirt, the soft, blonde hairs long and lifted with goosebumps, her toenails a chipped dusty pink at the ends.

She curled and uncurled her toes, tapped the tips of her fingers together, then mustered the courage to carry on with the job of leaving her beautiful home and the second man she'd ever loved.

She was in the hallway when she heard Stuart's footsteps crunch on the gravel outside, then his key in the lock. As his shadow appeared behind the stained-glass panel of the door, she lifted their wedding photo from the narrow hall table.

He entered and his eyes flicked between her face and the photograph in her hand, then paused at the case. He blinked and took in a sharp breath. 'You're not really doing this?'

'I think I've got to. I don't want to but . . .' She wished she could find the right words.

'You sure you want to take that? Do people usually take their wedding photos with them when they leave their husband?' Stuart's voice had a bitterness she'd never heard before,

'Don't do this,' he said, softly. She walked past him, so he couldn't see her face crumple, and dropped the case near the door.

They didn't speak as he helped her load the car. As she drove away, she watched him through the rear-view mirror, standing completely still at the end of the driveway, until her tears blurred him from view.

Chapter Nineteen

Bonnie

Present Day

Bonnie was on edge. Whenever she caught sight of movement on the CCTV monitor in reception, her buttocks clenched at the thought of facing Alice for the first time since Laura had stayed over. When she hadn't come into work by the end of Bonnie's shift at lunchtime, she felt like she'd escaped a caning by the headmistress.

She was surprised to see Polly and Laura standing at the desk when she came out of the staffroom.

'I was just saying, I didn't recognise her with her clothes on,' Laura said, 'but she didn't laugh as hard as me.'

'You surprise me.' Bonnie grinned at Polly. 'You alright?'

'I am, thanks. In fact, I'm so all right that I wanted to thank you two for the other night. I think it did me a lot of good.' She held the bottom of her floaty top and curtsied.

'In what way?' Bonnie plonked her suede bag on the desk.

'I've been looking at that picture you did, and I can see it looks like me.'

'It does look like you,' Laura said. 'Everyone commented on the likeness.'

'But the thing is, I can see that it's nice.'

'Nice?'

'Okay, I can see I look beautiful in it.' Polly blushed. 'It sounds awful when I say it, like I'm being arrogant, but it's the first time I've ever seen anything I recognise myself in and not wanted to look away. It's a big step.'

'It doesn't sound arrogant at all. It's bloody brilliant.' Laura hugged a surprised-looking Polly. Releasing her, Laura pointed to the bin liner on the floor next to Polly's feet. 'What's in there?'

'Are you meant to ask that?' Polly said, nervously pulling her top further down over her stomach. 'What if I was an international jewel thief and wanted to store my ill-gotten gains until the heat was off?'

'Are you?' Laura asked, sounding excited.

'Might be.'

Laura stamped her feet and pouted. 'Now I'm interested! And you're right, I'm not supposed to ask.'

'Have you remembered your key?' Bonnie said, and they both watched Polly pretend to be affronted by the question before rummaging in her bag and looking up, nose wrinkled. Then she did a sigh deeper than any Bonnie had ever heard.

'I'm going to regret this.' She looked from Bonnie to Laura. 'But I can trust you two, can't I?'

Laura put her hand on Polly's shoulder, and Bonnie was glad to see she could be serious when necessary. 'Of course.'

'Yes,' said Bonnie. 'What's up?'

Polly's expression shifted, and she gave an unusually

artificial smile. 'Nothing.' She licked her lips and twiddled the knot in the top of the black sack. 'I was going to suggest another outing.'

Bonnie glanced at Laura, who looked equally confused. For a moment it had seemed like Polly was going to make a confession. 'What kind of outing?'

'A car boot sale?' Polly sounded hesitant. 'You said you liked them, Bonnie, so I thought it might be something we could all do?'

Laura's brow dipped in the middle. 'I've never been to one. Do you think I'd like it?'

'They can be treasure troves,' said Bonnie, then hesitated. 'But are you sure you want an old crone like me cramping your style?'

Polly curled her top lip. 'Erm, have you been to a car boot sale recently? They have St John Ambulance there for a reason. And you're not an old crone.'

'Yeah, you've got better fashion sense than us, and you're part of the gang whether you like it or not.' Laura looked at Polly and bit her lip. 'No offence.'

'None taken.'

Bonnie felt light-headed at the praise. She grinned, glad she'd worn her pleated maxi dress and biker jacket combo today. 'Okay then, I'm in.'

'Well, I'm not being left out,' said Laura. 'When and where?'

Polly clapped her hands together. 'Sunday morning. I'll message you the details.' She held her hand out for the spare key and Bonnie dropped it into her palm and they watched her pick up the bag, walk quickly across reception, then disappear through the red door leading to the warren.

'I wonder what's in that bag?' said Laura.

'I guess we'll never know,' said Bonnie, thinking of her own little storage unit, which now had one item inside; the hairbrush that Laura had left in her spare bedroom. She had meant to give it back, but somehow couldn't quite let it go.

* * *

They met in the queue for the car boot sale at 8 a.m. on Sunday. Dew sparkled on the grass, and the atmosphere had the kind of chill that promised to politely step aside when the sun gave it a firm stare. Bonnie assessed the others in the line and noticed her spine was straighter and her skin plumper than most of the queue. Laura and Polly were practically infants in the sea of grey hair and bald pates. She spotted the St John Ambulance van and nudged the others, who nodded and sniggered in recognition. She felt like part of a group for the first time in so long, and some of the load she carried lifted and evaporated.

There was the musty smell in the air that she recognised as dust and clothes from the back of ancient cupboards. She suddenly missed her mother, with her charity shop hauls and wardrobes full of bargains she bought but never wore. They had been the dressing-up box of Bonnie's youth, and where she'd learned to experiment with colours and fabrics. With the benefit of years gone by, she could acknowledge how sad someone must feel if they were compelled to buy gold lamé and feather boas, only to put them away in the dark.

Laura slumped, leaning on one leg, then the other, sighing dramatically.

'What's the matter?'

'It's early.'

140

Bonnie and Polly rolled their eyes at each other. 'You're the same age, you two, right?'

'I'm twenty-five,' said Polly.

'Then you're only a year older than this woman-child.' Bonnie looked Laura up and down as she slouched and stuck out her tongue.

'What's your point?' Laura said petulantly with a laugh. 'But don't you think this is stupidly early for a Sunday?'

'It is,' agreed Polly. 'But it's the only way to find the bargains.'

Eventually reaching the head of the queue, they handed over their entrance money to a woman in a high-vis jacket. They then huddled on the other side of the fence, Polly bouncing like an excited child, as she presented them both with a black plastic sack pulled from her canvas bag. She splayed her fingers and said in a high voice, 'Now, let's talk strategy.'

She spoke with urgency. 'I'm going to go anti-clockwise, which is counter-intuitive. Look' – she pointed at people meandering from what looked like the natural starting point – 'if you don't follow the sheep, you get the baaaar-gins. You get me?'

Laura's top lip curled. 'Wow.' She shook the plastic bag. 'What am I meant to do with this?'

'It's for your stuff.'

Her chin retracted. 'You think I'm going to buy that much second-hand crap?'

Bonnie put her hand on Laura's arm. 'Don't think of it as crap, think of it as treasure.'

Polly's eyes drooped like a puppy whose food bowl had been taken away. 'You can go home and go back to bed if you want. I just thought this might be fun.'

Laura straightened. 'God, sorry, Polly. I was only joking.

141

It will be fun.' She rattled the black plastic. 'Let's have a race to see who can fill theirs first.'

Polly grinned. She nodded and looked at her watch. 'See you in an hour and a half. Happy hunting.' She barged into the thickening crowd and Bonnie watched in amazement as she disappeared from view.

She turned to Laura, whose face had slipped back into confusion as she looked around the huge field peppered with makeshift stalls and cars with their boots gaping. 'I'm not in a hurry to divide and conquer.'

Laura gripped her wrist. 'Don't you dare leave me.' She pulled a comical face and gestured to a nearby man whose hair hung in greasy tendrils from a filthy fishing hat, sitting by a table covered in what looked like broken boxes of jigsaws. 'He looks hungry. I bet he'd eat the likes of us for a snack.'

'Washed down with neat vodka,' Bonnie added, enjoying the feeling of Laura's warm hand on her arm.

They wandered towards the cars on the periphery, Laura walking close to Bonnie so the chill from the morning air only registered on one side. They ambled over the patchy grass, stopping to look when something pretty caught their eye, their companionable silence recharging Bonnie like a battery.

Laura nudged Bonnie with her elbow and she turned to follow her gaze, melting at the sight of a trestle table covered on an antique tablecloth topped with a collection of extraordinary ceramics. Bonnie couldn't believe there weren't hordes of people examining the brightly coloured vases and pots. As they moved towards it, her heart skipped when she saw Laura was as drawn to the colours and shapes as she was, picking them up and turning them in her hands.

'Did you make these?' she asked the woman sitting on a canvas deckchair behind the table. 'They're beautiful.'

'Thanks,' said the woman, putting the flask she was drinking from on the grass beside her chair. 'I had a kiln installed in my back garden when I retired so I could fire them at home.'

Bonnie laughed. 'That's commitment.'

'That's not what my husband said when he saw how much it cost.' The woman raised her thin eyebrows and smiled. 'His words only had four letters.'

Laura held a vase up to the sun, which was emerging from behind wispy clouds. The light caught the blues and greens where they twisted around each other, the colours paling towards the top. 'This reminds me of your painting,' she said, moving it round in her fingers and showing all sides to Bonnie, who swallowed hard, hit by the similarity in tones but also Laura's association of this beautiful vase and the painting that had been dredged up from the very centre of her heart.

'I imagine that with hyacinths in it,' the woman said, and Bonnie visualised the vase filled with white and purple blooms, guarded by tall, green leaves. She could almost smell the heady perfume of the flowers. She reached in her handbag for her purse. 'Sold,' she said. 'How much?'

The vase, wrapped tightly in bubble wrap, banged lightly against her thigh as they explored the rest of the stalls, often exclaiming at the same quirky items at the same time, then laughing at themselves. Laura bought five hand-made cards with rude slogans and a painted floral bookmark in muted tones for her mother. She marvelled at a collection of beaded, fringed shawls, but when she wrapped one around her shoulders, she wrinkled her nose, and quickly disentangled herself, hanging it back up on the rail and pulling Bonnie away.

'What's up?'

'The smell!'

'What kind of smell?'

'Like cabbage and yellowed underpants.'

'You're ridiculous!' Bonnie laughed.

Laura's face dropped. 'That's exactly what my mum says.'

Bonnie felt heat rise up her neck. How could she have been so stupid? She looked at her watch. 'It's almost time to meet Polly.' She searched the field, trying to spot Polly's dark head among the crowds. 'Let's make our way back to the meeting point.'

Polly was already at the gate when they arrived, a heaving bag by her side.

'Is there anything left on the tables?' asked Laura, poking the bag, her face cheerful again.

'Nope,' Polly said, puffing out her chest. 'Or in my purse.'

'Whoops,' said Bonnie, stepping from side to side. 'Hate to ask, but didn't you say you lived close by, Polly? Don't suppose I could pop in for a wee?'

'Erm . . .'

Polly didn't look thrilled by the idea, but over the last year Bonnie's bladder had developed a mind of its own, telling her she needed the toilet just minutes before it decided it was painfully urgent. 'Please. My menopausal bladder is begging you.'

'Okay.' Polly lifted the bag and slung it over her shoulder. They followed her back through the gate and out to the road.

* * *

Polly's flat was a five-minute walk away and as she sat on the toilet, the taut balloon of her bladder released, she looked around the bathroom. Everything was white and the bath, sink, and toilet gleamed so brightly Bonnie half expected to hear the diamond ding of sparkle, like on the adverts for bathroom cleaner.

The towels on the plastic rail next to the sink were white and fluffy and folded so perfectly the corners hung in absolute symmetry. As Bonnie washed her hands, she felt the need to wipe the droplets of water away with a towel to leave it as pristine as she'd found it. She glanced up, expecting to see her face reflected in a mirror, but instead, where a mirror would usually be, was a stark white cabinet front with a gleaming aluminium handle.

Unlocking the bathroom door, she walked into a white hallway that looked like a hospital corridor in a futuristic film and followed Polly and Laura's voices into a dazzling kitchen.

'Better?' asked Polly.

'God, yes.' She nodded. 'Nobody tells you all the weird things the menopause does to a woman.' She reminded herself that twenty-somethings might not want to hear about the effects of her plummeting oestrogen. 'Sorry, too much information.'

'It'll come to us all,' said Laura. 'Forewarned is fore-armed, and all that. I asked my mum about the menopause when she looked like she was having a hot flush, but she said she didn't have time for all that nonsense and left the room.'

Bonnie could imagine Alice finding hot flushes and sleeplessness deeply inconvenient. She wasn't a big fan either but didn't think pretending it wasn't happening was the ideal solution. She didn't tell Laura that though, and

145

instead changed the subject. 'Polly, this place is like a show home!' She took in the polished worktop, wondering how on earth she kept everything so clean.

'Has the cleaner just been?' asked Laura.

Polly laughed. 'I can't afford a cleaner on a PA's salary. I do it myself.' She turned to the cupboard to her left, opening the door and plucking out a white kettle. 'Cuppa?'

'You keep your kettle in a cupboard?' Laura said.

They all turned at the sound of the door opening and closing and a woman's voice shouting, 'Polly, you home?' in a strong Irish accent.

Polly gave a nervous laugh and glanced from Bonnie to Laura. 'In here, Mum.'

'You've visitors?' asked the tiny, thin-lipped woman who now stood in the doorway to the kitchen.

'This is Bonnie, and that's Laura.' Her voice seemed quieter than before as she waved a hand in their direction then folded her arms across her bosom. 'Tea?' She turned on the tap and filled the kettle, wiping away the droplets of water that sprayed into the porcelain sink with a neatly folded tea towel as her mother's quick eyes followed her movements.

'Nice to meet you,' said Bonnie as the woman nodded in her direction

'Likewise,' she said, although her frown suggested otherwise. Bonnie wondered how such a tiny, cross-looking mother could have produced a child as soft and warm as Polly. She turned as Polly nudged her elbow, accepting the white china cup she offered and placing it on the coaster as the mother's beady eyes tracked her.

'I'll not stop, since you have company.'

'It's fine. Have a cup of tea.'

'No, I'm grand. I was just meaning to drop this off.'

She held a bottle of bleach aloft. 'They were two for the price of one and, God knows, you could do with it.'

The colour rose on Polly's cheeks. 'I have bleach, Mum.'

'You can never have enough bleach.' She turned to Bonnie. 'Am I right?'

Bonnie found herself nodding under the woman's gaze, despite having no strong feelings either way.

'I'll be off then.'

She dipped her head and left as abruptly as she arrived.

'Now you've met my mother,' said Polly, widening her eyes.

Bonnie didn't know what to say. When the silence grew uncomfortable, she peered through the doorway into the small sitting-room, with its clear surfaces and said, 'This place isn't how I imagined you living.'

'You thought I'd live like a pig?' Polly's voice wobbled.

'No, absolutely not.' Bonnie chose her words carefully. 'You're a bright and interesting young woman, and so I'm surprised how little' – she paused – 'self-expression there is in your décor.'

'Mum doesn't like clutter.'

'She doesn't live here though, does she?'

Polly's eyes stayed on the liquid in her cup. 'I don't like her thinking I live in a tip.'

'There's a difference between a tip and a home.' Bonnie reached out and took Polly's hand, and they sat for a moment longer. 'I'm sure your mum would agree with that.'

'Would she?'

Bonnie wanted to scoop her up and hug her. 'I let my mum affect my decisions a long time ago, and that didn't end well.' She saw the women's eyes lift with interest and backtracked quickly. 'Ignore me. It's none of my business.'

147

She reminded herself she was lucky these young women wanted to spend time with her. Offering her old-lady wisdom would only remind them how little she belonged in their company and she didn't want to get into a conversation about her past.

Polly lifted her gaze and assessed her kitchen. 'I suppose I keep the flat like this to prove I'm not lazy and messy.'

Bonnie ran her thumb backwards and forwards along the top of Polly's soft hand. 'There's nothing wrong with living like this, as long as you're keeping it this way for you.'

'Is this how you like the flat?' asked Laura.

Polly laughed. 'I don't know if I can tell you this. It's so mad.'

'We're all mad in our own little ways,' Bonnie said, then bit her tongue. Who did she think she was, some kind of worldly sage? She couldn't even control the inside of her own head, so she was in no position to be offering crap platitudes to other people.

'Tell us what?' said Laura.

'Just a minute.' Polly left the room and came back a moment later with the bin bag she'd filled at the car boot sale. She put it on the tiled floor and opened the top. 'Look in there.'

Bonnie reached inside and drew out a mauve velvet square of fabric. 'What's this?'

'A cushion cover. I've got about twenty in my lock-up.'

Bonnie regarded the plain charcoal grey sofa in the sitting-room. 'But you don't have any cushions?'

'Not here, no.' She dug into the bag and pulled out two books. 'I love reading, but Mum says books clutter the place up, so I keep one in the drawer next to my bed, then the rest go in the lock-up.'

Laura shook her head. 'Let me get this straight. You buy all the stuff you'd like to put in your flat and shove it straight in the storage unit, then keep the flat all minimalist because you want your mum to approve of the way you live?'

Polly's cheeks flushed. 'That's about the size of it. You think I'm bonkers, don't you?'

'Have you tried making it a bit more' – Bonnie paused – 'you? Your mum might like it.'

'And does it matter that much if she doesn't?' said Laura, though it was a bit rich coming from someone who still lived at home. Laura's mouth made a tight circle, and she wiggled her fingers. 'If you did want to mix things up, I can think of someone who might have a bit of expertise in this area.' She pointed at Bonnie. 'Ta dah.'

Bonnie cocked her head. 'Do you think you're ready to get some stuff out of the unit and see what it might look like in here? If you don't like it, or you think it would cause too much conflict, we could always put it back again.'

Polly looked from Laura to Bonnie, biting the cuticle on her thumb. She smiled shyly. 'Would you really help me to make this place more homely?'

Bonnie watched Laura nod, her hair shuddering with the vigour. A project, with Laura, doing something she knew she was good at?

'It would be my pleasure,' she said, and she meant every word.

Chapter Twenty

Bonnie

Present Day

Bonnie examined the two keys, turning them over in her hand. She took a deep breath. The responsibility for going through whatever Polly had squirrelled away in her storage unit, then transferring what she thought would make her flat more homely felt suddenly heavier than it had when she and Laura had hatched the plan in Polly's kitchen. It seemed like a good opportunity to spend more time with Laura, and to impart some of her creative know-how, but she had to remember this was about Polly and her issues. She had to get it right.

'We're like exorcists,' she said to Laura, as they stood outside the door of Polly's lock-up. 'Killing demons by interior design.' She waved the first key in the air. 'Wand number one! When I use this, it gives me access to the secret chamber.'

She shoved the key into the padlock as Laura waved her arms like a magician's assistant. The padlock clicked open. Bonnie pulled the latch across and hesitated. 'I'm a bit nervous.'

'Are you scared it'll all be crap and you'll have to try to make the flat look good with old lady's doilies and plastic sunflowers?'

Bonnie slumped. 'No, I hadn't thought of that, but I am now.'

Laura giggled. 'Are you ready?' She put her hand on the handle and widened her eyes. 'Let's do this thing.' She pushed the door open, flicked on the fluorescent light, and stepped inside.

* * *

'Bless her little heart,' said Bonnie, five minutes later, when they'd assessed what was in front of them in the rectangular space. Polly seemed to have divided all of her purchases into categories. There were piles of soft furnishings, ornaments, and books. It looked like a slightly jumbled home furnishing store, where items were grouped on the floor instead of on shelves.

'She does like some order, then,' said Laura, as she lifted a black-and-white circular rug. 'Or she wouldn't have everything piled up so neatly.'

'Yes. I don't get the impression she's a hoarder.' Bonnie picked up a shallow pewter bowl, turning it over in her hands. 'She's got some nice stuff in here.'

'Are you as relieved as I am?' Laura snorted. 'Thank god it's not a load of knackered old rubbish.'

'Ladies.' They started at the sound of Jim's deep voice. He stood in the doorway, eyes on the mounds of Polly's things. 'What are you two up to in here?'

Bonnie felt the flash of an idea. 'Jim. Do you have a minute?' She looked from the books back to Jim and the tool belt he always wore around his waist. 'I want to ask you a favour.'

In the staffroom, the three of them huddled together as Bonnie outlined her plans for Polly's flat. She buzzed like she used to when she was explaining a design idea to Stuart, and a sharp pang of loss froze her voice mid-sentence. She swallowed, then forced herself to carry on. 'I don't want to change it too much, because that might be a shock, but from what I've seen so far, she likes quite monochrome things, with pops of colour.'

'Pop!' said Laura, flicking out her fingers.

'This is like those telly shows my Lou used to watch, where they go in and add a pop of colour and it all looks proper different after.' He made the same gesture as Laura and Bonnie flooded with affection for the two of them.

'Do you think you'd be able to make the bookshelves if I order in the wood?' she asked Jim. 'Then we can add some of the ornaments, like that gorgeous bowl, in between the books.'

'No problem,' said Jim. 'What else?'

Bonnie turned to Laura. 'Why don't we take some photos of the things we think will look good, then we can go to the flat and measure up? We can see if we need anything else after that.'

'Plan,' said Laura and Jim nodded, his smile wide under his bushy moustache.

'It'll be nice to have something meaty to get my teeth into.'

'Doesn't Lou keep you busy enough, Jim?' Laura winked at him and his smile faltered.

'There's always plenty to do at home, but I don't mind helping you lasses out a bit an' all.'

His Yorkshire accent suited his gruff but gentle voice, and Bonnie squeezed his liver-spotted hand. 'Glad to have you on board.' He returned her grip, and she was sure she saw sadness cloud his face before he released her hand, stood abruptly, and left the room.

* * *

Just before closing time, Polly popped into Bocks, her eyes flitting between them. 'How's it going?'

'We have a plan,' said Bonnie.

'An excellent plan!' added Laura, grasping Polly by the hands and twirling her around.

'Are you going to tell me what it is?'

'Nope.' Laura stilled them both. 'You have to wait for the big reveal, like on those TV programmes. I think Jim will have done his bit by the weekend, so, if you're happy to go out for the day on Saturday, we can put it together then. When you come back, we'll do the obligatory blind-fold then reveal thing.'

'Blindfold then reveal?'

'Yep. Standard practice, I believe.' Laura stood tall, her face taut and officious, but she couldn't keep it up. She balled her fists and jumped up and down. 'I'm so excited to see your face when we're done.'

'Gahhh.' Polly knitted and released her fingers. 'I'm a bit scared, to be honest.'

'Don't worry,' said Bonnie. She nodded towards Laura who was still bouncing. 'I'm keeping her in check. I promise to try to make it as pain-free as possible, and you can easily change it back if any of it makes you uncom-fortable. This used to be what I did for a living, you know. I bet the Earl of Strathmore was bricking it when he let

154

me loose on his gaff too.' She winked, then slapped her lips closed.

'The Earl of Strathmore?'

'Secret project, I shouldn't have mentioned it.'

'You're a dark horse, Bonnie,' said Laura.

She didn't know the half of it.

Chapter Twenty-One

Alice

Present Day

It felt good to take a back seat for once. Alice watched Richard and the architect, Phillip, pore over the details of the plan, hopefully for the last time, marvelling at how impressive Richard was in work mode.

'Respectfully,' he said, 'we have to keep the original building as it stands. I like this extension, here.' He pointed at the enormous computer screen. 'But the façade has to stay exactly as it is. That's what most of the objections were about last time. We can't afford to ignore that.'

The words *can't afford* rang in Alice's ears.

Richard took off his glasses and wiped them with his tie. Alice had laughed when he'd dressed in a suit that morning. 'You're the client,' she'd said. 'You could wear a clown suit if you wanted.'

'No harm in keeping things professional,' said Richard. She'd eyed him as he tied a perfect Windsor knot, wondering if she was doing him a disservice, trying to manage everything on her own. He had been the bread-winner for thirty years, and this house was a testament to how successful he'd been.

But then he'd coughed and the colour drained from his face as he sat limply on the bed.

'You alright?' She'd taken his wrist and tried to count his pulse but he had tugged his arm back.

'I'm fine. Just a bit tired. No need to fuss.'

That was all the confirmation she'd needed that handling the stress on her own was the right thing to do.

They shook hands with Phillip after agreeing the last points on the plans. 'Just one more thing,' he said, waving a sealed envelope. 'Here's the invoice. If you could settle it by the end of the week, that would be great.'

He handed it to Richard but Alice plucked the envelope from his hand as soon as they were out of sight. 'I'll take that, thank you.'

'You really don't need—'

'Look at that.' She pointed outside where rain was pelting against the glass doors. 'We're going to get soaked.'

'British weather,' said Richard. 'Who'd have thought this was on its way when we set off this morning? It was glorious.' They stood for a few minutes, peering up at the clouds, hoping for a break in the downpour. Eventually Richard sighed. 'I'll bring the car around from the car park.' That was what he'd done for the first thirty years of their relationship.

'You're not allowed to drive until the doctor says so, remember? It's only a bit of water.' Alice took Richard's arm and they walked into the lashing rain. 'It won't hurt us.'

* * *

158

Sitting in the driver's seat of the car with rainwater dripping down her neck, Alice regretted her decision. She turned the key in the ignition and the engine gave a half-hearted cough, then went quiet. Alice and Richard looked at each other, brows furrowed. She tried again. Nothing.

She lay her head against the steering wheel, flattening her wet hair to her scalp. Richard put a reassuring hand on her back, but that only served to stick her blouse to her skin.

'I'll call the breakdown service,' said Richard, pulling his phone from his inside pocket.

Alice groaned. 'We don't have breakdown cover anymore.'

'What? We've always had cover.'

Alice sat up straight. 'Yes, well, now we don't. We never broke down in all the years we were covered, so I thought it was one of the outgoings we didn't need.'

'Ah.'

'Yes.' She gripped the steering wheel, watching the torrents of rain beat against the windscreen. 'Sorry.'

'Can't be helped,' said Richard, his voice upbeat. 'I'll call the garage and get them to come and look at it.'

'That sounds expensive.'

He shrugged. 'It is what it is.'

'I'm meant to be taking over at Bocks.' She checked her watch. 'The receptionist is supposed to finish in half an hour.'

'Give her a ring,' said Richard, scrolling through listings for local garages. 'She might hold on for a bit.'

Alice didn't want to ask Bonnie for a favour. 'Can you sort the car out if I go into work?'

'Of course I can sort the car out,' he snapped. 'I'm not totally helpless.'

'That's not what I meant.'

'I'll be fine. Call a cab and I'll ring the garage and get this towed.'

A cab? How she'd love to get a cab across town and dry off as they sat in traffic on the ring road, while the metre ticked the pounds and pence away. 'I'll get the bus.'

'The bus?' Richard seemed as surprised as if she'd said she was going to ride to work on an elephant.

'There's a bus stop right there.' She pointed through the rain-spattered window at the glass structure at the side of the road. 'I'll start getting cabs again when we get planning permission.'

'Right,' said Richard. He sounded deflated, like a child who'd been told off by a parent. Alice hated this new dynamic. She hoped they could redress the balance once the plot was sold and she and Richard could get back on an equal footing.

* * *

Alice was already in a foul mood when she arrived at Bocks, so finding Laura there laughing along with Bonnie in reception made her blood boil. 'Why didn't you tell me you were coming in? I could have stayed with your father.'

'What happened to you?' Laura looked her up and down. 'There's actual steam coming off you.'

Alice wasn't surprised. She was so furious she half expected to see fire when she exhaled. 'The car broke down and I had to get the bus.'

'I could have picked you up. You should have rung,' said Laura. 'And why didn't you get a cab?'

Alice tutted. She lifted the hatch to head through to the staffroom for a towel. Bonnie wisely shifted out of her way.

'I thought you said you were busy. You had work to do?' Alice asked Laura.

'I do, but I had some news I wanted to share.'

Alice turned back towards her daughter, who was now dancing around reception, waving her arms above her head. 'What on earth has got into you?'

Laura stilled. 'I got onto my course! I've been accepted.' She resumed her dance.

'Isn't it brilliant?' said Bonnie, her face flushed, as if it was her daughter who had just achieved something amazing.

Alice made her hands into fists, digging them into her sides to stop herself lashing out. 'You can go now, Bonnie.' She turned to Laura. 'Well done. I'm very pleased for you.' She could hear the edge in her own voice but was in no state to recover her mood. She opened the door to the staffroom and dropped into a chair.

She bit back tears as she listened to the murmured voices outside the door. She could imagine Bonnie putting her arm around Laura, telling her she deserved better treatment, that *she* was thrilled for her, at least.

Laura opened the door and joined her at the table.

'So, you told Bonnie first?' Alice couldn't help herself asking.

Laura threw her hands up. 'Oh, for god's sake! That's your problem?'

'It would just have been nice if your father and I heard the news before the receptionist.'

'I knew you were in a meeting. Why are you turning this into a competition?'

'I'm not.' Alice knew she was.

'If I'd thought you'd throw a hissy fit, I'd have waited until you got home. I was just excited, that's all.'

161

Alice knew there was no way Laura would have been able to contain herself long enough to wait for them. She was the kind of person who bubbled over with good news. Sharing her joy and delight with the world was in her DNA. Alice dredged up a smile. 'It's brilliant news. I really am thrilled for you. Your dad will be delighted too.'

The grin had returned to Laura's face. 'I can't believe it. Roll on September!'

'Roll on September, indeed.' Alice meant it, but for different reasons to Laura.

'There is one little problem,' said Laura.

'What's that?' This was all she needed, more problems.

'The payment.'

Alice's mood plummeted even further.

'You remember when we first talked about the MA? You said you'd lend me half the money?' Laura sounded nervous. 'I've saved six thousand, and I could take out another student loan for the rest, but I haven't even started to pay off my last loan yet and . . .' Her voice drifted off. 'Mum?'

Alice realised she'd closed her eyes. The water on her face had dried leaving the skin tight, as though it was a mask. She stood and walked over to the drawer with clean tea towels inside, took one out and rubbed the back of her neck. 'I'm sorry, Laura. Things are tight at the moment. It might be better to take out a loan at first, then, when—'

'That's what I thought.' Laura cut her off.

Alice watched her for signs that she was upset, but her eyes were still bright.

'There might be another solution.'

Alice dropped the towel over her shoulder. 'Go on.'

'I was talking to Bonnie and she said—'

'Bonnie?'

'Yes. She said she could lend me the money and she wouldn't charge any interest. I could pay her back whenever.'

Alice couldn't believe what she was hearing. 'No. Out of the question. We are not taking a penny from that woman.'

Laura leaned away from her, her bottom lip hanging open. 'What?'

'You heard me,' Alice said, her voice hard. 'You can take out a loan and when the—'

Laura stood. 'If I hear "when the planning goes through" one more fucking time I'll scream. It's like we're all frozen until one piece of paper is signed and only then will we get permission to thaw out and come back to life again. I'm twenty-bloody-four. I've been stuck in your self-imposed ice age for three years. I'm not doing what I'm told anymore.' She paced the small room. 'How dare you tell me who I can and can't borrow money from?'

'I will sort—'

'No. No, you won't, because then you'll have even more control over me.' She opened her mouth as if experiencing a revelation. 'That's it, isn't it? You don't want Bonnie to lend me the money because you want me to be in debt to you.'

Alice shook her head. 'No, that's not it.'

Laura shook her head as though she didn't believe a word of what Alice said. 'What is your problem, then? Surely you're not just jealous because someone other than you is willing to help me? Is your saviour complex struggling with the competition?'

'That's cruel, Laura.'

'Then give me a reason I can understand.'

But try as she might, Alice couldn't find a plausible reason for her actions. Maybe she'd invented her suspicions and distrust to give her an excuse to dislike Bonnie. Because, if she was truly honest, she was as jealous as hell of Bonnie Lombard.

Chapter Twenty-Two

Bonnie

Present Day

They started work on Polly's flat early on Saturday. Jim screwed together the white bookcase he'd made, which filled most of one wall, while Bonnie and Laura trailed in and out, carrying bags full of the things they'd chosen from Polly's lock-up. The black-and-white rug looked good in the middle of the sitting-room floor and Bonnie had chosen six brightly coloured cushions of different sizes and arranged them artistically on the grey sofa.

'What do you think?' she asked Laura and Jim.

Jim nodded sagely, then laughed. ''Aven't the foggiest, but it looks all right to me.' He coughed, pulling out a cotton handkerchief and wiping his nose.

'You alright?' Laura asked.

'Just a cold. Nowt to worry about.' He coughed again, then shook his head at the two women. 'Don't start fussing. I'll be alright.'

Turning back to Bonnie, Laura said, 'You're not bad at this, are you?'

She nudged Bonnie's arm and she felt a lightness fly up her throat making her want to giggle.

Bonnie measured and made pencil marks where she wanted Jim to hammer in nails, pushing the memory of her first day in Hamblin, the hammer flying from her hands and smashing the glass, out of her head.

'My Lou loved that film.' Jim pointed a screwdriver at the framed *Casablanca* movie poster they'd found in the unit. They hung it on one plain wall and the print of Audrey Hepburn looking gorgeous in a slinky black dress in a poster for *Breakfast at Tiffany's* on the wall nearest the kitchen.

Laura stood next to the poster, sucking in her stomach and pretending to hold a cat over her shoulder, looking to the side like Audrey. 'Do you think I could get away with that look?'

'You're more *Breakfast Club* than *Breakfast at Tiffany's*.'

'Oh my god, I love that film! You're right. I'm more detention chic.' Laura pushed herself away from the wall. 'I'll take that.' She unpacked a box of books as Bonnie sang, 'Don't You Forget About Me', Laura joining in loudly as Jim looked at them both as though they'd gone mad.

'I bet there's a story behind this,' said Bonnie, as they covered Polly's bed with an exquisite patchwork quilt sewn with reds, yellows, and oranges, and lay a fake bearskin rug on the floor next to the bed.

'A grandma made it from the baby clothes of all of her grown-up grandchildren,' said Laura, 'and now she's looking down from heaven, glad it's gone to a good home.'

'That's lovely. I hope that's true.'

'Yep.' Laura sniggered. 'Until Polly starts shagging some

sexy dude on it and poor old grandma sends bolts of lightning to burn their bare arses!'

'Now you've spoilt it.'

Bonnie slapped her arm playfully.

Laura balanced a large oblong mirror opposite the bed. 'If she's going to have a sexy dude in here, this will add to the ambience.' They both laughed, and Bonnie peeked into the hall to make sure Jim hadn't heard. He was humming as he hung a beautiful circular mirror with sharp fronds spearing out like the rays of the sun in the hall, over another smaller bookcase he'd made for the passage. On the opposite wall they placed ten prints in what looked like a random fashion, but had actually been carefully measured by Bonnie.

Laura took the kettle and toaster out from the cupboards and plugged them in. She also scattered Polly's collection of fridge magnets from the plastic bag she'd kept them in and stuck them on the fridge door, instantly making the room look more lived in.

By five o'clock they were exhausted. Bonnie flopped onto the couch and the others joined her, Laura wriggling close to her to make room for Jim.

'What do you think she'll say?' asked Bonnie, surveying the room.

'It's grand,' said Jim, blowing his nose loudly into his hanky.

'If she doesn't love it, she can move out and I'll have it,' said Laura. 'It's made me crave my own space again. I loved the little flat I rented after uni. When I moved home it was only meant to be for a few months and now it's been three bloody years.'

Bonnie imagined all the reasons Alice would have come up with to make Laura stay at home with her.

'I wouldn't mind living with your mum,' said Jim, and they both swivelled as he went pink and sniggered like a little boy caught leafing through an underwear catalogue. 'Don't look at me like that. She's a fine-looking woman, Alice is.'

'You old dog.' Laura ruffled his thin hair.

He batted her away. 'She's kind an' all. The way she looks out for you and y'dad, it's saintly.' His face was earnest now, and Bonnie suddenly felt like an imposter. Perhaps it should be Alice here with Laura and Jim, making Polly's flat beautiful. These were her family and friends.

'Hmm. Before we canonise my mother, shall I call Polly and tell her she can come home?' Laura said, breaking Bonnie's train of thought. 'I'm dying to see what she thinks of what we've done.'

* * *

When they heard Polly's key in the lock, the three of them stood at the end of the hallway, like soldiers on sentry duty, chins up, lips pursed. Bonnie could see Laura's fists opening and closing, barely able to contain her excitement, and she suppressed an urge to giggle.

As the door closed behind her, Polly stood, looking at the books in the case, their multicoloured spines interrupted by trailing potted ivy and photos in frames. Her head turned to the wall with the prints, then to the sunshine mirror, mouth in a small circle, eyes filling with tears.

'I can't believe it!'

Laura rushed forwards. 'Do you like it?' She grabbed Polly's arm and pulled her over to the bookcase, showing her the black marble bowl on top with white veins spidering through it. 'We've put this here for your keys,

168

so you don't lose them. See, we've been practical as well as designery.'

Polly walked towards the sitting-room, taking Bonnie's hand as she stepped into the space, then letting go as she spun a slow circle, tears now dribbling down her cheeks. She touched the bigger bookcase and looked at Jim. 'Did you make this?'

He nodded shyly, and she clasped his face between her hands and kissed his cheeks before pulling his head onto her shoulder, saying, 'Thank you. Thank you so much.'

Bonnie watched his eyes become watery before he pushed himself upright and patted Polly on the shoulder. 'Now then,' he said. 'It's nowt.'

'It's everything,' said Polly, her voice wavering. 'This is the kindest, most wonderful thing anyone has ever done for me.'

'Do really you like it?' said Laura, then more quietly, 'Do you think your mum will like it?'

'*I* love it.' Polly emphasised the 'I' and Bonnie felt a flash of pride in her. 'That's what matters.' She paused. 'And I told her a professional interior designer was doing the place up for free.' She nudged Bonnie. 'So she was well up for it, tight-arse that she is.'

Laura picked up a cushion and hugged it. 'It's cool, isn't it? I'm moving in.'

'If it wasn't one bedroom, I'd let you.'

Laura clicked her fingers. 'Damn it.' She turned to Bonnie and pouted. 'Will you help me do my place when I move out?'

'Of course,' said Bonnie, and tried not to whoop.

Chapter Twenty-Three

Bonnie

Present Day

Though Jim had made his excuses and gone home, Bonnie drove Laura into town later on to celebrate Polly's flat makeover. When they pulled up on the opposite side of the road to the bar Polly had chosen, Bonnie's shoulders tensed and she wished she'd done the same. A neon sign flashed intermittently, and young men and women leaned against the graffitied wall in cropped T-shirts and low-slung jeans, smoking.

'I'm going to feel ancient in there,' Bonnie said as Laura slammed the passenger door closed.

'You're not. Anyway, age is a state of mind. Plus,' she looked at Bonnie's flared trousers and sheer black shirt, 'you look fabulous.'

Bonnie followed Laura through the narrow room with a bar along the whole of the right-hand wall, squeezing apologetically past people with tattoos and piercings, aware the pounding of the bass would make talking difficult and wondering if there would be anywhere to sit. Laura lifted her arm to wave and Bonnie stood on her tiptoes to see ahead, but everyone was taller than her and whenever she turned her head, her nose was thrust into someone's armpit. When anyone knocked into her, she was sure they were wondering what someone her age was doing in a bar like this.

She felt fingers in her palm and Laura pulled her along by the hand. The bodies cleared and she could see an ornate spiral staircase a metre ahead and Polly on the other side of the rope that barred people from ascending. As they reached the bottom step, Polly unclipped the rope and flung her arms around them.

'Hi,' she shouted. 'Come upstairs, it's much quieter!'

They followed her up the narrow spiral staircase and came out into a dark room with battered leather chair-shaped beanbags slouched around low tables scattered with tea lights. The thud of the bass seemed to bounce the wooden floorboards as they crossed to an empty table, but at least it was quieter than downstairs.

'Welcome to Regret Rien,' said Polly, flopping into a beanbag. 'I know it's poncy, but my brother's friend, Nathan, part owns it, so I get to use this VIP area and always get fabulous service.'

'I like the sound of that.' Laura grinned.

As she sat, Bonnie felt the air escape from the bag and the brown leather swallow her. She wondered how she'd get up again without looking like a fish flapping around on the deck of a boat.

A skinny woman with a sparkly stud in her nose and a matching one in her exposed navel approached. 'Hi, Poll, what would you like?'

'Cocktails?' Polly looked over at them, handing a folded cocktail list across the pocked aluminium table.

'I'm driving, do you do a virgin mojito?' Bonnie asked, and the woman nodded and smiled, then took the younger women's orders. She strode back to the small bar in the corner where a tall, bearded man with glasses was pouring spirits into different sized glasses.

'I've been downstairs a couple of times, but I've never been up here. I like it.' Laura nodded towards the man at the bar. 'Is that Nathan?'

'No, that's Xav. He's the other owner.'

'Cute.'

Bonnie scrutinised the man. A floral-patterned tattoo in red and blue twisted up his forearm and disappeared under the loose sleeve of an old band T-shirt. He looked unkempt, and she didn't see the appeal. 'Really?'

'I like 'em a bit rough,' she said. 'Much to my mother's distaste.'

'You're barking up the wrong tree there then,' said Polly. 'Xavier might look like a roadie for an indie band, but he's a bit square, really.'

The woman came back with their drinks on a tray and Bonnie wiggled her bottom in her seat, trying to push it into a position where she could sit more upright. Her legs were too short to reach the floor, and she felt like a toddler at pre-school, not yet tall enough for the big-girl chairs.

The waitress saw her struggle. 'Would you like a proper chair? Those things can be a nightmare, can't they?'

Bonnie was torn between wanting to fit in with the others and needing to be able to sit in a position where she could lean forwards for her drink without crushing her intestines. 'If you don't mind.'

Minutes later a chair was presented, which thankfully

wasn't too high in comparison to the beanbags. Bonnie hoisted herself out of the beanbag with as much dignity as she could muster, then sat on the four legs with relief. The conversation flowed as Polly told them where she'd found all the pieces they'd used to decorate the flat. Her eyes shone as she talked, and Bonnie felt the glow of having done a good thing.

* * *

The man with the beard and tattoos brought refills over a while later, kissing Polly on both cheeks after putting the tray on the table.

'This is Xavier Smith,' said Polly. 'Remember I told you he owns this place with Nathan?'

Xavier shook their hands, his eyes stopping on Laura. 'Good to meet you.' He turned as a large man with a shock of bright red curls came up behind him and lay a hand on his back.

'Nathan!' Polly squealed and jumped from her seat to embrace him. Bonnie noticed her cheeks were even rosier and wondered if Polly had a crush on this big, open-faced man.

The introductions were made, and Nathan drew up a chair as Xavier went back to the bar and continued to mix drinks. As Polly told Nathan about her flat's makeover, Laura's eyes tracked Xavier as he moved around the bar.

* * *

'Xav!' shouted Nathan, as he passed their table half an hour later. 'Get Cam to take over up here. Come and have a drink with us.' He turned back to the table. 'If that's okay with you?'

Laura shrugged her agreement as Bonnie and Polly

174

insisted, and Bonnie laughed inwardly at Laura's attempt at coyness. It was so transparent that she fancied him. Xavier brought over another tray of drinks and took a seat beside Laura, who seemed unable to find a position she was comfortable in, crossing one leg over the other, leaning forwards then back.

Laura picked up Xavier's bottle of lager. 'Is this non-alcoholic beer?'

'Yep. If you work in a bar long enough, you learn alcohol is not the friend everyone thinks it is.'

'Tasty though.' Laura took a swig of her cocktail.

'Those are stronger than they taste.' Xavier gestured to her drink. 'Some of the sights I've seen in here after people have had one too many would make your hair curl.'

'True,' said Nathan, rubbing at the mop on top of his head. 'I had straight hair before I owned a bar.'

Polly slapped his leg. 'You did not! You've always had mad hair.' She paused. 'Except when you were about fifteen and you went through that *emo* stage.' She turned to the others and leaned in. 'He dyed that lot black, only his roots grew through bright orange, so he shaved it all off.'

Nathan dropped back in his seat. 'I can't believe you're exposing me like that!'

'I'm sure I could come up with worse if I tried.' Polly laughed. Their eyes sparkled as they looked at each other, and Nathan raised a pale eyebrow.

'Bonnie, are you a Bonita?' asked Xavier and Bonnie nodded.

'I like that name,' said Xavier. 'I'm sick of having to spell my name out to everyone. I might change it to Bob.'

'You don't look like a Bob,' said Laura. 'You definitely look like a Xavier.'

'Oh yeah?' Xavier smiled slowly. 'What does a *Xavier* look like?'

Laura bit her bottom lip and smirked, and Bonnie suddenly felt very out of place. There was a frisson around the table, as though pheromones were being openly traded. She was relieved when Xavier and Nathan reluctantly went back to work.

By the time the next round was presented, Bonnie realised she'd laughed more than she had in years. Polly was doing impressions of what her Irish Catholic mother would say if she walked in and found her naked at the life drawing class.

'What would she say if she saw you on your forth Cosmopolitan?' asked Bonnie.

She sipped her drink and imitated her mother. 'How many calories are in that? Do you know how much sugar is in alcohol? You'll end up a drunk and nobody will marry you.'

'Ouch,' said Laura.

'Yep,' said Polly.

'Makes my mum's obsessive controlling seem almost normal.' Laura's voice was loud, and Bonnie noticed people turn to look at them.

'Shh,' she said, but Laura took no notice.

'It's true though.' Laura took another drink, spilling some liquid down her chin and wiping it away with the back of her hand.

Bonnie turned back to Polly. 'Your mum was born in Ireland?'

'Mum and Dad, yep. I think Mum suffers from the Catholic guilt thing. She sees any excess as a lack of self-control, so she hates things like overeating. Everything she buys has to have a function too. There's

176

no excuse for waste or slovenliness, or anything enjoyable really.'

'All sounds a bit puritan for me,' Laura slurred.

'Me too,' said Polly. 'I'm stuck between wanting to stuff my face and buy beautiful trinkets and feeling like I should stick on a hair shirt and say a thousand Hail Marys.'

'To hair shirts and trinkets!' Laura drained her glass and put it precariously down on the table.

'I'll get us some water.' Bonnie moved the glass away from the edge. She approached Xavier and asked for a jug of water and glasses, looking back at the pair on the beanbags. Laura's movements had become loose, and she was gesticulating more than usual. Bonnie shuddered.

'I don't want water,' said Laura when Bonnie poured it into her glass, the ice cubes clinking against each other. 'I want more cocktails.'

'Just have a glass of water first. You'll thank me for it in the morning.'

Laura lifted the glass and took a tiny sip, then waved her hand at the passing waitress. 'More cocktails, please.'

Bonnie shifted in her chair. She could feel the seat hard against her bottom and her spine increasingly rigid against the back. The mocktails now just tasted of sugar and she didn't want any more. She wanted to go home.

'Actually, Laura, I could do with an early night. How about we make a move?'

'No, don't make me go home.' Laura moaned. 'That's boring.' She leaned forward in her beanbag and tweaked Bonnie's chin. 'Just have another one or two, then we'll go. Okay?'

Bonnie sighed. Laura's cheeks were red and her eyelids heavy. 'One more, then we're going home.'

'That's the spirit!' said Laura.

'Just one, though,' said Polly, who wasn't slurring and looked Bonnie directly in the eye conspiratorially. 'Then we'll head home.'

After the final drink, Bonnie and Polly had to hoist Laura out of the beanbag and when she stood it was like watching a newborn foal trying to find its feet. They led her to the top of the steps and glanced at each other.

'You need to be careful on here,' Bonnie said.

'I'm not a toddler,' Laura replied, and took a tentative step.

It was like watching a film in slow motion. Bonnie's hand reached out as Laura's body seemed to buckle and her legs flew out from under her. She fell backwards and Bonnie managed to get her hand under Laura's head before it hit the top wrought-iron step.

One of them must've screamed because the whole of the downstairs bar seemed to have congregated at the bottom of the steps and the waitress was moving upwards towards them.

'Laura!' Bonnie's blood pounded in her ears. 'Laura?'

Laura was horribly still. The world became silent and Bonnie couldn't move or breathe.

'Ooof.' Laura opened her eyes and blew out her cheeks. 'That smarts.'

She started to giggle and fury flared in Bonnie's stomach, rising and gathering momentum until it burst out of her mouth. 'For god's sake, Laura! You bloody idiot. What do you think you're doing? Do you think it's a joke, drinking so much you literally can't stand? Do you know how dangerous that is? Have you any idea what can happen, how badly things can go wrong?'

Laura stared at her, along with everyone else in the bar, because nobody there but her knew how badly a drunken night out could end.

178

Chapter Twenty-Four

Bonnie

Twenty-Six Years Ago

Final exams were over, and the relief was dizzying. Bonnie and Cahil sneaked away from the student union bar where all of their friends were celebrating, giggling like naughty children as they wandered along Scott Street, looking for a quiet pub where they could be alone on their last night together in Glasgow.

'Run me through what you're going to say to your dad again,' she said, as they found a discreet spot in the corner of the old man's pub where they knew none of their art school friends would think to look for them.

'I'll tell my father that I've met the bonniest of all the bonnie lasses in Scotland, and I'm willing to leave the sun, sand, and sea, and all the beautiful five-star hotels he wants me to build, to stay in the cold, wet, grey land of Scotland!'

Bonnie punched his arm. 'Don't say it like that.' She took a slug from her pint and was suddenly painfully

179

aware of the smoke-yellowed walls and stained carpet. 'God, you're on for a first in architecture. If you stay in Turkey, you'll be designing stunning hotels, won't you? How can you bear to give up swimming pools and classy bars for the blackened stone and dingy pubs around here?'

'I don't look at the stone.' He leaned forwards and took her chin in his huge hand, pressing his lips on hers. 'You are all the sunshine I need.'

She laughed. 'You are pure cheese. If I drew a caricature of a smarmy Mediterranean man, you'd be it.'

Cahil sat back. 'That's charming. I say you are my sunshine; you say I am a cartoon!'

'Seriously, though.' Doubt was creeping along her spine. How could this beautiful, clever, funny man be willing to give up the life he was destined to lead, just for her? 'What if you go back and realise all this isn't enough?' She gestured around the grimy room again and grimaced.

'It's not this I'm coming back for. It's you.'

Her voice wobbled. 'And what if I'm not enough?'

'Ah, then I'll go back to Ankara and marry someone my mother chooses.' He tweaked her nose and laughed. 'I've changed since I've been in Scotland, bonnie lass. I arrived a meek and dutiful Muslim boy, but you and your wicked friends have corrupted me.' He swigged his beer.

'That's a big, fat lie!' She hoped he was joking. 'You were drunk the first night I met you.'

'I admit that bit of corruption was not your fault, although I had only drunk one pint.'

'It only takes one pint to get you drunk.'

'True.' He took another slug. 'This is my third. I'll be under the table soon.' He winked. 'And you did corrupt me in another way, you wicked temptress.'

As he ran his hand up her thigh, she remembered their

first night together at the start of their second year, when she led him to her attic bedroom and undressed him. His body shook as he kissed her, and they lay down and made fumbling love as the moon shone through the skylight, illuminating his tanned skin.

'Are you complaining?' She put her hand over his and squeezed his long fingers, her tiny, freckled hand like a child's in comparison.

'Not even slightly.' He lifted her hand and kissed each of her knuckles and she couldn't believe he was hers and they had an entire future together to look forward to.

The squat landlord with mutton chop sideburns opened the side door. The breeze fluttered Bonnie's hair across her face and she closed her eyes, trying to imprint this moment in her memory. She felt the cotton of her miniskirt against her legs, the rough denim of Cahil's jeans under her hand, the warm breeze rising and falling like their breath. She tasted the sweet cider on her tongue and smelt the cigarette smoke from the other side of the bar wafting through, mingling with the citrus smell of Cahil's aftershave.

'I want tonight to last forever.'

'So do I, but—'

'I won't let you go.' She grabbed his wrist and pulled him towards her, kissing his face, 'You have to stay here with me, forever.'

'I will, I promise.' He pulled away gently. 'I just need to make everything right with my family first. Okay?'

She pouted, but knew he was right. 'Just one more drink then? One for the road?'

Cahil sighed, but there was a twinkle in his dark eyes as he unsteadily stood and went to the bar. They giggled as he came back with two pints, a third of each sploshing onto the carpet as he wobbled towards the table. They drank and kissed and made promises to each other, and soon their glasses were empty. Cahil stood. 'I'm going to the bathroom, then we do have to go.'

Bonnie laughed. 'I love the way you call it "the bathroom", as though you're going to find a claw foot bath in there instead of a stinking urinal with a block of blue cake swilled in old man wee.'

'You paint such a beautiful picture.'

As he weaved across the worn carpet and through the door to the toilet, Bonnie took a five-pound note from her purse, approached the bar, and held it aloft. Mutton chops raised his bushy eyebrows. She nodded. He took two pint glasses from under the bar and held one under the pump, pulling it slowly towards him as the frothy liquid filled it.

She was carrying them back to the table when Cahil emerged from the gents, still doing up the buttons on his flies. She raised the glasses in his direction. He shook his head, but she knew he wouldn't be able to resist her.

'Last one,' she said, putting his glass on the soggy beer mat in front of him as he sat back down.

'You said that last time.'

'I mean it this time.' She winked and slurped her drink as he did the same.

All too soon, Bonnie had to accept the perfect evening was over and they had to make their way home. They slipped out of the side door, arm in arm, and walked down the dark alleyway, turning right along the main road. The street lights and car headlights confused Bonnie's senses after the gloom of the pub, and she had to unhook her arm from Cahil's to swerve out of the way as a man walking in the opposite direction almost bumped into them on the narrow pavement.

There was the sound of screeching tyres and the blaring of a car horn, then a thud. When Bonnie spun around to ask Cahil what the hell had happened, he wasn't there.

She closed her eyes, then opened them again, but Cahil still wasn't standing behind her. In her peripheral vision she saw a large white object glowing under the street light, then became aware of a movement, a door opening, and a man with a bald head stepping from it, his face contorted, mouth moving, making ugly sounds.

Her ears rang. The shouting didn't make any sense. The creature dipped out of sight, and she tried to follow it with her eyes, but something was stopping her from moving her head. The yelling got louder. It seemed to be coming from more than one person. The lights in a shop window flickered like the strobe in the Junior Common Room disco.

The shop door opened, and a man sprang from the doorway onto the pavement, then disappeared too, as though sinking into the paving slabs. Perhaps that's what had happened to Cahil. Maybe he'd been sucked down like these poor souls were now. That's why he wasn't behind her, his hand searching for hers.

A heaviness on her shoulder made her turn. She saw a man's hairy hand on the leather, but it wasn't Cahil's.

'Miss?'

He took his hand away and shoved it in the pocket of his jeans. She looked up into his face, trying to distinguish his words from the buzzing in her ears.

'Is this man with you?'

She looked around. She recognised the man who was talking as the one who'd passed them seconds before the bang; the one who was walking along the pavement, causing Cahil to shift out of the way. His head was the only one she could see.

'What?' She felt her nose wrinkle. 'Where is he?'

His face twisted, as though he thought she was joking, then he looked down at the road in front of the white van and her heart bounced from her stomach to her throat.

'No,' she said.

His face snapped back up. 'He's not with you? Poor sod. I wonder who he is.'

'No,' said Bonnie, closing her eyes. 'No, no, no.' She heard her voice get louder, and the man muttered something.

She turned her head and opened her eyes a slit. She looked at the windscreen of the white van, along the bonnet, down towards the bumper, then at the figure that lay, completely still, in the road.

Adrenaline exploded inside her. She screamed, leaping into the road and kneeling next to Cahil, hands hovering over his body, the urge to drag him into her only surpassed by the fear of causing more harm. Through blurred vision she saw his brown eyes staring upwards, the orange street-lamp reflected in his black pupils. Blink, she willed him, blink at the light.

But he didn't blink. As she searched his face, hands held centimetres above his lifeless body, a dark liquid seeped from under his head and spread in a sickly halo around his skull.

* * *

At the hospital, a nurse wrapped her in a blanket that smelt of cheap washing powder. She felt sweat drip from the end of her nose onto the blue wool, but she couldn't stop shivering. The policeman had given her a cup of sweet tea, but her hand shook too much to hold it and the scorching liquid jumped from the cardboard cup and scalded her thigh before the nurse took it from her hand.

The red patch on her leg burned. Her eyes burned. She was freezing cold.

Pulling the blanket into her fists and dragging it until the material stretched against her back, she watched figures walk past the door of the tiny room they'd put her in when they took Cahil away. When they'd taken his body away.

A paramedic had pronounced him dead at the scene. They'd arrived ten minutes after the van hit him and though they'd pummelled and shocked him, from the way his eyes stared into the black sky and the blood from the back of his head dribbled along the road and into the drain by the pavement as she knelt by his motionless body, she knew he was already gone.

Looking down, she saw her knees were pockmarked with tiny stones. She let go of the blanket to pick them out, but when she released the fabric, she felt exposed, like a child who'd lost their parents in a crowd. She dragged it back around her and pulled it tight once more.

A soft voice startled her and she looked up to see Veronica, her course tutor, standing in the doorway, her cheeks flushed. She vaguely remembered telling the policeman that she didn't have anyone she could call, then, when he insisted, giving him Veronica's name. Her thin, dark hair fuzzed around her face and her down-turned mouth had the remnants of red lipstick in the deep smoker's lines around her lips.

'Oh, darling, darling girl.' She walked towards Bonnie and her heavy floral perfume seemed chokingly strong in the airless room. She wrapped her arm around Bonnie's shoulders, pulling her against her warm body. 'Darling girl,' she said again. 'You poor, darling girl.'

A male voice spoke close by and Bonnie burrowed into Veronica's perfumed chest. She ignored the tap on her arm and shifted closer, but the man cleared his voice and spoke more loudly. 'I need to ask you a couple of questions, then you can go home.'

'Do you have to do this now?' Veronica's clipped Queen's English sounded exaggerated after his Scottish burr.

'We need to know exactly what happened,' said the man, and Bonnie wrenched herself upright.

'It was my fault.' She saw Veronica and the man in the police uniform exchange a worried glance. 'It was all my fault.' Bonnie wiped her hand across her eyes to clear her tears. 'I made him have another, and I knew he couldn't take his drink. It was my fault he fell.'

Veronica's fingers rubbed Bonnie's upper arm. 'Don't say that. It wasn't your fault. You couldn't know he was going to topple over. It was a tragic accident, darling.'

She tried to pull Bonnie back towards her, but she resisted, looking from one face to the other. 'It was my fault. I did this to him. I killed him.'

The policeman looked through his notepad, then crouched so his thin face was level with hers. 'I interviewed the other man at the scene, and he said that Mr Osman was walking behind you.' He looked at the pad again. 'That Mr Osman stepped out of the way to allow him to pass, then seemed to trip on the kerb and collapse into the road.'

Bonnie nodded, feeling tears run down her face onto her neck.

'So, you weren't directly next to him when he fell?'

She shook her head.

'So, you couldn't have stopped him from falling, could you?' Veronica said gently.

But Bonnie knew, whatever they tried to tell her, that she was responsible for what happened. Cahil was dead, and it was all her fault.

Chapter Twenty-Five

Alice

Present Day

A banging noise jolted Alice awake. Her heart raced as she tried to make sense of the sound while her eyes adjusted to the dark. Richard stirred beside her, so she jumped out of bed, then put her hand flat against the wall to steady herself as her head spun.

'What's that noise?' Richard asked.

'That's what I'm going to find out.' She opened the door. Moonlight shone onto the landing but she flicked the switch on the wall in the hallway, and the chandelier threw out spangled light. Richard shuffled behind her and she whispered for him to go back to bed, but his feet followed hers down the stairs.

She switched off the alarm and looked through the spyhole. Laura was leaning against the front door and a short woman stood behind her. Alice slipped the bolt open and as she pulled the door ajar Laura tipped forwards into the hall, almost crashing into the table covered in family photographs in polished silver frames. The cold air bit at Alice's naked ankles, making goosebumps prickle her skin.

'What on earth are you doing?' she said, her anxiety replaced by annoyance when she saw Bonnie standing on the doorstep, looking small and meek. Alice looked back at her daughter, who was now propped against the inside wall, and crossed her arms over her chest, feeling very exposed, braless under her thin pyjamas and face washed clean of make-up.

'I've come home,' Laura slurred.

Alice spoke through gritted teeth. 'I can see that. What time is it?'

'Twelve. It's midnight,' said Bonnie.

'Why are you both here at this time? And why didn't you use your key?'

'I'm home now,' said Laura again. 'Couldn't find my key. Lost.' She raised her hands and shrugged.

Alice smelt the alcohol on Laura's breath and felt her stomach ball. 'How much have you had to drink?'

Laura slid down the wall, rubbing at the back of her skull. 'I banged my head.'

Richard knelt next to Laura, touching her head through her hair. 'What happened?' He lifted her eyelids and checked her forehead as though he were a qualified medic. 'That's quite a bump you've got there.'

'What happened?' Alice turned to Bonnie.

'I was trying to get her to come home earlier, but she wanted to drink more.'

'For god's sake,' Alice said to Laura. 'Will you never learn? You're not a bloody teenager anymore. I shouldn't have to worry about what state you're going to come home in.' The wind flapped her pyjamas around her legs.

190

She felt ashamed, telling her daughter off on her doorstep in her nightclothes while Bonnie was fully dressed. 'What happened to her head?'

Bonnie shuffled like a child who'd been caught out. 'She fell on some steps.'

'Christ.'

She turned to where Richard was still checking Laura's head as she lolled. 'Is it bad? Does she need to go to hospital?'

'I don't think it's that bad,' Bonnie said.

Alice snapped her head back around, looking down at Bonnie. 'Forgive me if I don't take the recommendation of the woman who brought my daughter home in this state.' It was the shame speaking, and she immediately felt embarrassed at her outburst.

'I'm just saying, if I thought it needed looking at, I would've taken her to A&E instead of bringing her here.'

'Right.' She shivered and rubbed her upper arms. 'Okay.' She nodded at Bonnie, adding a grudging, 'Thank you. Thank you for bringing her home.' She paused to watch Bonnie step away before closing the door and turning her attention to her family.

'Come on, silly girl.' Richard helped Laura to her feet and led her to the kitchen.

'I don't think silly covers it,' Alice scolded. 'What were you thinking, Laura?'

'Cocktails, mainly,' said Laura.

'I asked what you were thinking, not drinking.'

'The answer's the same either way.'

Richard sniggered. Alice shot him a look. He could always see the funny side. It was something he and Laura had in common, and it made Alice feel like she was outside their circle. It was a feeling she had more and more these days. It wasn't so bad to feel like an outsider when it was Richard on the inside, but Bonnie was a different matter. She watched them now, giggling together as Richard tried to make Laura drink a glass of water, mopping her chin with a tea towel as though she were a toddler in a high-chair again. It was easier when she was. At least then Alice could keep her on her radar, keep her safe.

And, she thought, bitterly, as another snort of laughter erupted from her drunken daughter, it was all very well them finding it amusing now, but when they were both in bed fast asleep, she'd be the one lying awake worrying Laura might choke to death on her own vomit or have a bleed on the brain from banging her head and die in the night.

'Drink all that, then get to bed.'

'Yes, boss.' Laura saluted.

'Come on, Richard.'

'Yes, boss.' He saluted too, and Alice heard her teeth creak as she clenched them. They had no idea how hard it was being the grown-up all the time, how much she'd love to get drunk on cocktails and forget all about Richard's health and their bloody business. But someone had to keep everything together.

She shepherded her small flock up the stairs, hearing the ghost of Laura's three-year-old bones clonking on each step. She turned the alarm back on, the chandelier off, and lay down next to her already snoring husband and tried to quiet her thoughts.

When Alice arrived at work the next morning, Bonnie was sitting at the reception desk. She was dressed in a smart black-and-white shift dress and looked very much like someone who had not been banging on her front door at midnight.

'Good morning.' Her eyes were clear, like she'd had a peaceful night's sleep. Good for her.

'Morning.' She zipped behind the desk and into the staffroom. She'd left the documents she needed for the last part of the planning application in the filing cabinet, otherwise she would have avoided coming into work at all. Her fury at Bonnie might be misplaced, but she felt it all the same. Life had been simpler before this strange woman infiltrated their lives, pulling Laura away into her world of naked models and bars. If Laura had needed a middle-aged woman to spend time with so badly, she might have chosen the one she lived with.

She opened the files and flicked through the papers, trying to find the title deeds she needed. Hearing the door open, she sighed. She could do without Bonnie trying to make amends for last night when all she wanted to do was get on with her work.

'Can I have a word?'

She looked up, pushing her reading glasses on top of her head. 'I'm a bit busy at the moment.'

'I wanted to clarify that I was not encouraging Laura to drink last night. Quite the opposite, in fact.'

'That may be the case, but as I see it, Laura's spending less time at work, less time at home and more time drinking. That's bad enough, but coming home injured—'

'And you think I'm the common denominator in that?' Bonnie stepped into the room, still holding the door as though allowing for a quick exit if necessary.

Alice tipped her head to the side but didn't reply.

'I'm sorry you feel that way.'

Alice's nostrils flared. She tried and failed to swallow her indignation. She noted the '*I'm sorry you feel*' and acknowledged it inferred she was wrong for feeling that way. It was the opposite of an apology, but still masqueraded as one. This woman was infuriating.

'I think we both need to be aware this situation might not be working out.' She felt the colour rise up her neck.

'You mean my working here?'

Alice dropped her glasses back onto her nose and shuffled the papers, avoiding looking at Bonnie. 'The point of taking someone on was so that Laura could do something productive in the time that was freed up. As it stands, she's in bed with a hangover and a bump to the head, so I don't see how we can justify the expense of a member of staff to cover that.'

Bonnie's face had turned pink, and it looked like she was holding back. When she spoke, the words came slowly. 'I'm glad Laura got accepted to her MA course. She's talented.'

Alice narrowed her eyes as she looked at Bonnie. 'I am aware of that, since I'm the one who's paid for every art class she's ever attended. I've been hanging her pictures on my fridge since she could first hold a pencil.' She noticed the papers were creasing in her grip and placed them slowly on the table. 'So, thank you for your input, but I don't need you – who's known her for all of five minutes – to tell me about my own daughter, or to offer her money.' She snarled out the end of the sentence, making it sound grubby.

'Understood.' Bonnie stood in the doorway for a moment, her mouth poised as though words were about to spill from it. But she simply nodded and stepped out of the room, closing the door softly behind her, leaving Alice to imagine what on earth that woman could have left to say.

Chapter Twenty-Six

Alice

Present Day

Laura's birthday was often one of the hottest days of the year so Alice was glad that today was warm, rather than hot. Memories of slathering suntan lotion on her wriggling daughter, desperate to get back to the bouncy castle, karaoke machine, or whatever party entertainment Alice had hired that year, made her smile. The memories of sweat smudging her make-up as she filled party bags and handed out cake to overheated children did not.

Alice had almost broken her back trying to create neat lines in the long lawn last week. Now she rubbed at her aching lower spine, almost wishing she hadn't pretended to Richard that she loved gardening and he should leave her to do it. She hated the mess and the throbbing knees, but the picture in her head of Richard mowing the lawn and dropping to the ground from overexerting himself made her too frightened to take the risk. She couldn't control the images in her head anymore. It was like her brain was constantly tempting fate, showing her what could happen if she didn't watch out.

After checking her watch, she allowed herself time to admire the cotton wool clouds drifting in the pale blue sky through the sash window above the sink as she made a mental note of what else there was to do. Richard opened up the gas BBQ on the patio, stepping back from the heat then twiddling with the knobs. She watched him in his checked chef's apron, knowing full well that he'd genuinely think he'd done all the cooking when he served up the food, which had been bought, marinated overnight, and handed to him by her.

She fast-forwarded to that evening, when he'd sit down with a satisfied groan, righteously leaving all the clearing up because he'd been on his feet all day, working like a slave. She groaned inwardly at her bitter thoughts. Today was about Laura. Lovely, bright, cheerful Laura. Alice must try to keep her spirits up for her daughter. Maybe next year they'd take a trip abroad for her birthday, if . . . God, why was there always that bloody *if*?

She glanced again at her watch; it was twenty minutes until the first guests were expected. She buzzed around the kitchen, checking on the chicken in the sticky sauce in the fridge, then chopping more fruit to go in the punch.

'Are you sure you want this to be a fruit punch?' she asked, as Laura wandered into the kitchen, looking incredibly pretty in an animal print maxi dress. The front of her hair was twisted into two pinned-back braids, leaving the rest to fall in soft curls over her shoulders. It could be taken for the glossy blue-black of her natural colour if Alice only looked at the front. 'I could easily turn it into sangria?'

'No thanks.' Laura unhooked one of the six matching

glass cups that hung on the side of the crystal bowl and ladled in some punch. She sipped it. 'That's good. Not everyone has the same capacity for red wine as you, you know.'

Alice bristled despite Laura's wink. 'I'm not the one who got falling-down drunk a couple of weeks ago, remember? There's a difference between a glass or two of Malbec with dinner and getting so smashed you topple over, thank you very much.'

'You should be pleased I don't want a drunken birthday bash then, shouldn't you?'

Alice stopped slicing strawberries and put the knife down on the chopping board. 'I am. I'm wondering why, that's all.'

Laura pulled out a stool and sat at the island. 'Okay, but don't get weird.'

'Weird about what?'

'I've invited someone I'd like you to meet.'

Alice blinked. It was years since Laura had brought anyone home to meet her and Richard. She tried to remember the last boyfriend they'd met and couldn't conjure up a face. She didn't kid herself that this meant Laura was leading a celibate life, just that either there was no one special, no one she wanted them to know about, or, and this seemed equally likely, her parents were too embarrassing to be presented.

'Someone special?' She tried to keep her enquiry casual, but when she flicked her eyes up to Laura's face, she saw her shaking her head.

'Look at you, trying to act all cool.' Laura laughed. 'You can't fool me. Just try to actually be cool when he's here, okay? We've only been out a couple of times, and I don't want you scaring him off.'

'Him?'

'That's a leading question, Mother. It is a *he*. Did you think I was gay?'

Alice concentrated on chopping a strawberry into symmetrical quarters. 'I didn't like to presume, that's all. It's a long time since you've brought anyone home, I wondered if that was why.'

Laura laughed. 'It's because you say things like "brought anyone home", that's why.' She took a strawberry from the chopping board and popped it in her mouth. 'Nice to know you're fine about it if I do decide to dabble, though.'

'Dabble?' Alice scowled. 'Really, Laura, there's no need to be crass.'

The doorbell rang and Laura jumped off the stool. 'He's called Xavier, and he owns a bar and has lots of tattoos but be nice, anyway.'

Alice sighed. Laura could never make anything easy. It was difficult enough sharing your only child with someone else, without them choosing a man who sounded more like a roadie for a heavy metal band than future husband and father material. She turned with a gracious smile on her face when Laura walked back in, but she was only followed by Bonnie.

'Oh, hello.' She didn't know why Laura insisted on inviting the bloody receptionist. Obviously, they'd invited Jim from work, but he wasn't staff; he was more of a family friend.

'Hello,' said Bonnie. She offered a bottle and when Alice took it, she was surprised at the weight. She glanced at the label. It was champagne, and not a cheap one either.

'Goodness, thank you.' Alice put the bottle on the island, its thick glass bottom clacking on the granite. 'That's very generous.'

Bonnie seemed particularly tiny in the large room. She looked around as though she were in a museum. Alice remembered she used to be an interior designer and tensed.

'Your house is . . . impressive.'

'Thank you.' Despite Bonnie's unnecessary pause, Alice felt a flush of pride in her big, tastefully decorated home, then remembered calling the estate agent when Laura and Richard were both out, and booking a valuation, just in case the application failed. The smug feeling evaporated.

Laura held a beautifully wrapped parcel in her hand. 'She brought me a present too!' Alice was taken back to all the birthday parties before when her lively daughter had exclaimed with the same joyful voice over every last gift, from plasticine to play houses. She knew how to make people feel good. It was one of her gifts.

'It's only small,' said Bonnie, shuffling uncomfortably, her hands in the pockets of her white linen shift dress.

Laura undid the silver bow and tore off the wrapping, opened the box, then froze. She looked at Bonnie and whispered, 'It's beautiful.'

Alice strode forwards and looked in the box. Nestled in folds of cobalt silk was a plain silver bracelet with a bluish green stone in the middle, which seemed to change colour as Laura moved it in the light.

'The stone's alexandrite,' said Bonnie, pointing in the box. 'It's your birthstone.' Her fingers danced nervously. 'I looked it up.'

'Oh my god, that's so thoughtful! My middle name is Alexandra too, so that's even more amazing.' She turned to Alice. 'Isn't it, Mum?'

Alice nodded, biting back the jealousy at how her daughter's eyes glowed when she looked at the gift. She and Richard had given Laura vouchers because that's what she'd asked for. Now she wished she'd insisted on something more personal. She gave her head a shake. She was being ludicrous; she was Laura's mother and had given her hundreds of thoughtful gifts. This woman probably wouldn't even be around this time next year.

'It's absolutely gorgeous.' Laura flung her arms around Bonnie, engulfing the smaller woman. 'I love it, thank you.' She took the bracelet from its nest and circled it around her wrist where it shone against her tanned skin.

'That's very generous,' said Alice, aware she was repeating herself, but it was very generous. Outrageously so, in her opinion. She thought about her question to Laura earlier and it crossed her mind she might ask the same of their new receptionist. She was suddenly very pleased Laura was bringing a man to her party. He, at least, sounded as though he might be her own age and – tattoos withstanding – it was better than if Laura returned the crush of this middle-aged woman. Surely Bonnie could see that Laura wouldn't be interested in her?

The doorbell rang again. Laura released Bonnie and left the room, leaving Alice stuck trying to find something to say to this peculiar woman. She reached for the ladle and stirred the red liquid.

'Drink? Although I wouldn't recommend this. It's like something from an eight-year-old's party, not someone who is turning twenty-five.'

'Why's that?' Bonnie stepped forward and peered into the glass. 'What a gorgeous bowl.'

'Thanks. It belonged to Richard's mother. It's probably the first time it's been filled with a non-alcoholic drink.'

'That's fine for me. I'm driving.'

Alice carefully ladled a portion into one of the glasses and handed it to Bonnie, who took it and sipped. 'Thank you. It's nice.'

She placed the ladle back in the bowl and reached for a bottle of red wine, unscrewing the top, thankful for something to do with her hands. She lifted the bottle. 'Sure I can't tempt you?'

'No, this is fine, thanks.' As Bonnie took another swift drink, the red liquid splashed onto her dress and they both froze for a moment. Alice grabbed a piece of kitchen roll from the worktop and dabbed at the stain while Bonnie stood with her arms to the side. Alice suddenly realised she was poking at the soft flesh of Bonnie's breast and stopped, heat rushing to her face.

'Sorry.'

'It's fine.'

Her mouth was dry. She opened the cupboard with the bin inside, throwing the kitchen roll away and wishing for the tiles to crumble under her feet and swallow her whole, as Laura burst back into the kitchen with a tall, thin man with a beard, looking ill at ease in a pale blue shirt buttoned up to the neck.

He embraced Bonnie, using her name, and Alice bit back the urge to ask how the receptionist was on first-name terms with the new beau already, when she was only just being introduced?

'Mum, meet Xavier.' Laura shoved the man forwards and Alice put out her hand, just as he leaned in to kiss her cheek, and she poked his stomach as his lips grazed her ear. When had she become so socially awkward?

'Sorry,' he said, jumping back.

'Not at all.' She used her most gracious voice, hoping no one had noticed the sweat that had sprung up on her top lip. 'It's lovely to meet you. You have an unusual name. Is there a story behind it?'

'My mother's French,' he replied. 'From Lille.'

Laura took his hand, and Alice noted Bonnie's eyes stayed on their clasped fingers. Laura's voice was bright. 'That's why his bar is called Regret Rien. It was his grandmother's favourite song.'

'How charming.' *If a tad sentimental.* She kept the thought to herself. 'Drink?'

'Something non-alcoholic, please. I don't drink.'

'God, does no one appreciate a good bottle of red wine anymore?' She pretended to be exasperated, but the fact this Xavier didn't drink was music to her ears. Laura and alcohol had never mixed well, so a teetotal boyfriend, even if he was covered in tattoos, could only be a good thing.

Jim was the next to arrive. His face was paler than usual, beads of sweat collected on his forehead.

'You alright, Jim? You look a bit under the weather.'

He nervously handed over a bottle of sweet white wine. 'I'm grand. Just got a bit of a cold I can't shake.' He pointed at the wine. 'I hope that's all right. I'm not a big wine drinker.'

'Thanks, Jim. It's perfect. No Lou?'

Jim looked at his feet. 'She's popped over to her sister's, she said to say 'appy birthday, an' that.'

'I'm beginning to think you've made her up to make me jealous,' said Alice, winking at him. She hooked her arm through his. 'Come outside. I need to keep an eye on Richard, or he'll burn everything.'

Polly and a large, red-haired man called Nathan – who she was told also owned Regret Rien – were the last to arrive. Alice sat at the patio table surveying the groups, trying to force the muscles in her neck to uncoil. Xavier had undone his top button and Alice assessed her daughter's new boyfriend as they stood together on the manicured lawn. An ornate tattoo seeped from under the edge of his shirt sleeve, but it looked floral and quite pretty. She hoped he didn't have any skulls or naked women hidden away up his arm. He smiled often and draped his arm casually around Laura's shoulders, in a way that signified affection rather than ownership. It was going to be difficult sharing Laura with anyone, but she'd have to try to find the best in this man to keep her daughter onside.

Jim stood at the BBQ with Richard, like a couple of Neanderthals poking at the fire with sticks. Polly and Nathan were guffawing at something Xavier had said, while Laura gazed up at him, dark eyes doting. Then there was Bonnie in her expensive-looking, stained dress, standing awkwardly at the periphery of the group, glancing at each of them furtively, her eyes only ever resting for long on Laura. What was she even doing here?

Alice sipped her wine, savouring the soft berry taste, the smell of the meat on the BBQ, and the sound of her daughter's laughter. A phone's ringtone made them all turn and look around for the source of the noise.

'Sorry, I think that's mine.' Bonnie rushed into the kitchen where her bag sat on one of the stools and Alice watched through the open patio door as Bonnie gawked at the screen until the ringing stopped. Then she heard a ding of a message and saw Bonnie blinking at the phone before her eyes closed and a look of pain crossed her face. She glanced through the window and caught Alice's eye, then turned her head away.

When she came back out, there was a sheen of sweat on her face and her smile didn't reach her eyes. 'Sorry,' she said. 'Something's come up. I'm afraid I'll have to love you and leave you.'

'That's a shame,' said Alice, rising from the table and dropping her head to one side. 'Is everything all right?'

'Just a call from my cousin,' said Bonnie, as she quickly distributed kisses then headed back to the kitchen. 'I'll see myself out.'

Alice took her seat again, aware she felt more relaxed now their employee had left. What had changed her mood so abruptly? What secrets was Laura's admirer hiding?

Chapter Twenty-Seven

Bonnie

Present Day

Bonnie waited until she was safely in her flat to listen to the voicemail from Ross. She pressed play, then curled into the crash position, because she knew an impact was coming.

'Bonnie, hi, it's Ross. I don't know if I'm doing the right thing, ringing you today. I know I don't usually acknowledge it, but I thought, because you're not at home and you might be on your own, I thought, well . . . Since your mum, my mum, and me were the only ones who knew, and they're gone, so . . . Anyway, I'm babbling.' He sighed out a long breath that crackled through the phone's speakers. 'I just wanted to say I hope you're okay today. It must be hard, with it being the baby's birthday and everything. I hope you're coping. That's all I wanted to say really. You know where I am if you need me. Lots of love. Bye then. Bye.'

Chapter Twenty-Eight

Alice

Twenty-Five Years Ago

Susie, the social worker in charge of their case, was let into the room by an officious-looking woman who smiled at them, then closed the door, leaving them alone. As she walked across the office towards the small sofa Alice and Richard were perched on, Susie drifted out of focus. Alice could only see the tiny bundle, wrapped in a white blanket, nestled close to her body. She stood, clasping her fingers together to stop herself from holding out her arms before Susie reached her. She sensed Richard by her side and tore her eyes away from the swaddled bundle to give him a quick smile. His eyes were glass, and she loved him for being as excited about this moment as she was.

Susie dipped lower to show her the baby's round face and Alice's abdomen tightened. This was real, and she was oh, so beautiful. She drank in the thick, dark lashes sitting on plump, rosy cheeks. 'Look at all that hair!' she said, bending her arms at the elbow so Susie could place the baby into them. The three babies she'd miscarried never got to cradle there. But this one did, and Alice exhaled as she felt the weight and warmth next to her body. She fit as though that's where she was always meant to be.

Richard's head bowed towards the pink face and the scent of his hair gel mingled with the sweet smell of talcum powder and clean washing. Alice breathed in the aroma of her new family and savoured the moment she'd waited so long for.

'I'm going to be your mummy,' she said to the sleeping child. 'And this is your daddy.'

'She's a lucky little girl,' said Susie, and Alice examined her wide face and wild grey hair escaping from under a bandana, wondering how it felt to watch as people's dreams come true.

'Thank you.' She bit her bottom lip. 'Is the mother . . .' She paused. 'The birth mother. Is she doing okay?'

Susie put a hand on her shoulder and wrinkled her nose. 'Her mum's taking care of her. She's doing all right. She sent this.' She pulled a toy elephant out of her pocket. 'Obviously it's up to you whether you give it to her.' She nudged the baby's cheek with a fat finger. 'You just concentrate on this little pickle. I have a feeling she's going to keep you busy.'

Richard took the soft toy and smiled. 'Please tell her thank you.'

'But what if she changes her mind?' Alice had dreamt of this moment, but she had nightmares too, of her baby being snatched from her by grabbing fingers, disappearing into the darkness, leaving her hollowed with grief.

'Nobody goes into this lightly, and it's a process of law. All the paperwork is ready to be signed and when it is, it's binding.'

Alice lifted the baby, the soft blanket stroking her chin, and she let her lips rest on her downy cheek. Milky breath tickled her nose, and she closed her eyes to allow this feeling to infuse her.

'Do you have a name?' asked Susie. Alice opened her eyes and found Richard gazing at her.

'What is she . . . sorry . . . was she called?'

'Alexandra.'

'We thought Laura,' said Richard.

'What about Alexandra as her middle name?' Alice looked between Susie and Richard, then back at a tiny gasping sound from the baby as her ruby lips widened into a gaping yawn.

'She seems quite relaxed with that.' Susie laughed and Richard nodded, his eyes bright.

'Hello, Laura Alexandra Egerton.' Alice pulled the baby closer into her chest and she knew, in that moment, that she would never want to let her go.

Chapter Twenty-Nine

Bonnie

Present Day

When Bonnie arrived for her shift on Monday, she was buoyed to see Laura behind the desk. She was wearing the alexandrite bracelet, allowing the first shaft of light into Bonnie's dark mood since she'd heard Ross's voicemail after the birthday party. She wished he'd stop checking on her, especially since he was the only one apart from her who knew why she might not be okay. His call had sent her into a downwards spiral and she was struggling to climb out.

'There you are!'

Bonnie checked her watch. 'I'm not late, am I?'

'No, it's just I rang you yesterday, but you didn't pick up.'

Bonnie pushed away the memory of lying in bed, unable to gather the energy to shower or even make herself a meal. When Laura's name lit up the screen of her phone, fresh tears seeped into her pillow as she buried her head.

'Ah, sorry. I was with my cousin,' she lied. 'The one who called on Saturday. He was only in town for the weekend. Sorry I rushed off. He's a pain in the bum, to be honest, always harping back to when we were kids.' She rolled her eyes in mock exasperation. She shrugged off her coat, turning away to mask the shame she felt about her lies. 'Did you enjoy the rest of your birthday?' She lifted the hatch and passed through, heading towards the staffroom.

'I did.' Laura bounced up from the chair and followed her. 'Let's have a cup of tea and I'll fill you in.'

Bonnie made herself smile in all the right places as Laura explained how Alice liked Xavier and how he'd ended up cooking with Richard, after Jim went home early because of his cold.

'Later, Xav and Nath took me and Poll to this exclusive club I hadn't even heard of. It's underground and doesn't have signage or anything. The boys know the owners, so we went straight to the VIP area.'

'Sounds like fun.' Bonnie couldn't find the right word. She thought she sounded old and out of touch, but Laura didn't seem to notice as she took her favourite mug from the cupboard. It was white with 'Sexy Beast' written on the side in pink lettering. She popped a tea bag in and did the same with another plain white mug, then poured boiling water into both.

'It was. I felt ancient in the club, though. All the girls looked about eighteen and wore teeny tiny dresses and eyelashes that reached their eyebrows.'

Bonnie balked. 'If you felt ancient, I can't imagine how I'd have felt.'

'Do you even like clubs?' Laura asked.

An image of her and Cahil dancing until their hair stuck

212

to their faces and sweat ran in rivulets down their necks flashed into Bonnie's mind. She remembered bass lines thumping in her solar plexus, feeling so glad to be alive. She could feel his lips on hers as the music slowed, their hips meeting as they swayed, oblivious to anyone else as they kissed and moved, their sweat mingling, completely absorbed in each other.

'I used to. It's a long time since I last went to a club.' She'd stopped dancing when Cahil died. It was one of the many things she didn't feel she deserved to enjoy any more.

'I bet you were wild when you were my age.' Laura thumped her shoulder and Bonnie wobbled, closing her eyes against the image of a twenty-five-year-old her working in the textile mill in Glasgow until it grew dark, then going home to her studio flat and painting under the harsh artificial lights until she couldn't keep her eyes open any longer.

'You've got me all wrong.' She forced a smile onto her face. 'I was a wallflower.'

'As if!' Laura laughed, handing her the white mug and taking a sip of her own drink. 'Anyway, we're going to have a much more grown-up time next weekend. Nathan knows where there's an old quarry that's filled with clear water, like a lake, apparently. Xavier says there're rocks to jump off and you can sunbathe or swim. If the weather forecast is right, it should be perfect for a day out there.'

'Sounds wonderful.'

'It does, doesn't it?' Laura cradled her mug. Her eyes crinkled as she smiled. 'I really like him.'

'Xavier?'

'No, Jim.' Laura laughed. 'Of course, Xavier.' She finished her drink and stood. 'I'm off then. I said I'd show

213

Xav some of my etchings.' She smirked and took her mug over to the sink.

'I'll wash that. I'm doing this one, anyway.'

'Thanks.' Laura put her mug in the sink and dipped from the room.

Bonnie's skin tingled and acid gurgled in her stomach. It swirled, gathering momentum, until it spread through her blood to the tips of her fingers, making them restless. She took her cup over to the sink and poured out the dregs of her drink, all the time looking at Laura's mug.

With enormous effort, she forced herself to squirt detergent inside, and use the small yellow sponge to rub away the dark ring left by the tea. She turned the porcelain and made her tingling fingers wipe the smudge of pink lipstick clean and rinse it under the running tap. She placed the mug on the draining board, trying not to look at it as she gave her cup a cursory clean and put it next to the other, making the china clink.

Taking a stiff tea towel from the drawer next to the sink, she dried both mugs and placed hers back in the cupboard. She tried to put Laura's in there too, but looking from the shelf to the mug in her hands, her muscles froze. She couldn't make herself do it. She couldn't force her fingers to release the handle.

Her breathing quickened as she pushed the cupboard door closed and moved silently to her grey suede bag, which was hanging on the back of the staffroom door. She opened the zip and, while her heart drummed in her chest, carefully placed the mug inside, then unhooked the bag and dropped it onto her shoulder.

With the same light steps, she tiptoed out of the staffroom. Scanning the reception to make sure she was alone, she opened the hatch to let herself out. The wide space reminded her again of the junior school hall, and she felt like a nervous child, trying not to get caught skipping class as she crossed the carpet tiles and reached the red door to the warren. Once through, she took a left past the rows of red-fronted boxes, then right towards the smaller units. She stopped in front of number 202 and checked again to make sure no one was around.

Her fingers seemed twice their natural size as she fumbled with the key, at last managing to insert it in the padlock and twist it open. She stepped inside the small, bare room, switched on the light, then closed the red door behind her.

Leaning on the cold wall, she tried to catch her breath. She squatted, balancing against the wall, and lay her bag on the polished concrete floor. The zip sounded like a train thundering through a station in the silent room. She listened again for footsteps outside. When she was sure she wasn't going to be interrupted, she reached inside the bag, stood, and placed its contents one by one at the furthest edge of the unit.

Her breath caught when she saw how small and pathetic the hairbrush, crystal glass from the punchbowl in Alice's kitchen, and mug looked on the ground. She stood for two minutes, unable to move, then she opened and closed her fists, pumping blood into her fingers, willing herself to leave. She turned off the light before opening the door, to make sure no one could see inside from the corridor, then clicked the padlock back in place, allowing self-loathing to replace adrenaline. She welcomed the sickening shame like an intimate old friend.

Chapter Thirty

Alice

Present Day

Alice clicked on the *send* button on her laptop with a flourish. 'Done.' She picked up her coffee cup to stop her fingers fidgeting as she looked at the screen, feeling like something should happen. That application would have such a huge impact on their lives, whichever way it went. Surely there should have been a gong sounding or something to mark the occasion? A blank screen wasn't enough.

Suddenly, she was sure she'd sent the wrong documents. She'd sent the old plans by mistake. After spending all that time and money, the application would be rejected out of hand, and it would all be her fault. Her heart pounded. She clicked onto the sent folder, then opened up the application, sweating fingers slipping on the mouse pad. Phew. She'd sent the right plans. Everything was there. She needed to get a grip.

Trying to appear nonchalant, she looked at Richard, who was sitting across from her at the marble-topped table, staring at his newspaper. He exuded a level of calm she couldn't remember experiencing in her life. Certainly not in the last few years. 'Now keep your fingers, toes, and eyes crossed it's approved this time.'

Richard looked up, his blue eyes crossed, and she laughed, some of her tension slipping away. He relaxed his pupils, and his face became serious. 'This is the last time we can apply, you know that, don't you?'

Alice shifted in her seat, the soft leather moving with her. 'Yes, but you heard Phillip say we have a better chance now we've reviewed the spec to keep the original building, and the laws have changed since we put the last one in, so it should be a bit easier this time.'

Richard sighed, folding and unfolding the corner of the paper. 'These things are never easy, and Phillip is only the architect. He doesn't work in the planning office.'

'I know that,' Alice huffed. She knew better than anyone, since she was the one who'd done all the research to find the best local architect. She was also the one who transferred his extortionate fees from their dwindling funds.

'Sorry. Of course, you do.' Richard smoothed the paper with the flat of his hand. 'I'm worried you're going to get your hopes up, be on tenterhooks for the next eight weeks, then have your hopes dashed again.'

Damned right she would. 'Hope is all we have.'

'Now, that's not true, is it?'

Richard had come away from his near-death experience with a new, philosophical outlook on life, which was all very well, but gratitude and mindfulness did not pay the bloody mortgage. She sat back in her chair and looked around her beautiful kitchen, the dining area where they were sitting now, surrounded by glass on all sides, the sunshine bouncing off the rim of Richard's coffee cup, the

218

granite island where she'd prepared their family dinners for years, the expensive cream blinds with the delicate pattern of trees hanging above the huge sash windows overlooking the garden . . .

'I don't want to lose this house. I can't bear the thought of all that hard work being for nothing. We sacrificed so much to get here. When I think of all those family holidays when you even worked on the beach . . .' She sighed. 'We waited for so long for a baby, then I was like a single mother for half the time.'

'That wasn't by choice.'

'I know.' She leaned forwards and let out an exasperated breath. 'But we deserve a secure future, don't we, after everything?'

'People don't always get what they deserve, as you well know. I think we should talk about what happens if this bid doesn't get approved.' He leaned forwards on his elbows, hands clasped under his chin.

'No.'

Richard chortled and looked over the top of his glasses, and Alice's lips twitched in an involuntary smile. He knew her well.

'We'd be all right. A semi on the outskirts of town wouldn't be so bad, would it?'

'Where would I put my chandelier?' She pouted.

'In the hall, like it is here. We'd just have to squeeze around it to get into the house.' He winked. 'I know you've worked so damned hard to make everything right, and I know a lot of it is my fault . . .' His voice caught. 'But we'd be okay, wouldn't we?'

She had worked hard and she and Laura had sacrificed too much for them to give up now, but the wobble in his voice made her put her coffee down and move to his side of the table, wrapping her arms around his neck and resting her chin on his thinning hair. 'We would. Of course we would.' She kissed the top of his head. 'But I've got one last chance to get us back on track, so I'm going to take it.'

'I wouldn't expect anything less.' Richard crossed his arms over hers and squeezed. 'What would I do without you?'

'You'd rot in a ditch.' Alice pulled away, kissing him quickly on the head again. 'And don't you forget it.'

'I won't,' said Richard, letting out a slow, rumbling laugh. 'You keep reminding me.'

'Glad we've got that straight.' She returned to her side of the table and drank what remained of her coffee. 'I'm off to work.'

Richard tipped his head to the side. 'Sorry. I wish I could—'

'I know,' she said, without adding, *so do I.*

* * *

Jim was waiting for her in reception when she pushed open the blue door. The sleeves of his checked shirt were rolled, and a tool belt hung around his waist like a gun sling. His wrinkled face turned to sunshine when he saw her.

'Aye up, Alice. I'm glad you're here. I'm about to give this hinge a seeing to.'

'That means something different where I come from, Jim,' Alice said, popping her handbag on the desk with a thud, then wished she hadn't as his eyes dropped to the floor.

'What about a nice cup of tea before you start?'

He smiled and his moustache lifted, showing his perfect

white teeth. Alice always wondered if he wore dentures but wasn't about to ask. Lifting the hatch for her, the hinges squeaked, and he put his freckled arm out to stop her before she walked through.

'It's this bit that's perished.' He pointed to where the wood was splintered, and the screws had worked their way free. 'If I were you, I'd think about getting a new top for this desk.' He rubbed his square nails along the wood, and she saw how old and tired the surface was. 'It'll cost a bit, mind, but if I put new hinges on, they'll only come away again because the wood's too weak.' He turned away and coughed.

'Have you been to the doctors about that cough yet?' She watched him shake his head and mop his forehead with his handkerchief. 'You should.'

'I don't like to bother 'em. It's only a bit of a cold.'

Alice gave him a stern look. 'That's what they're there for. I bet Lou's told you to go to the surgery.' She took his averted gaze as confirmation. 'Listen to your wife. That's my advice.' She inspected the underside of the hatch and groaned. 'I don't want to spend money on this place.'

'It'll be a saving in the long term. These hinges are pricey.'

'I know, but with any luck, we won't need a desk long term, or anything else in this bloody place.'

Jim's wiry brows knitted. 'What d'you mean? Y'not selling up, are you?'

There was concern in his voice and Alice twinged with guilt. She looked him in the eyes and chose her words carefully. 'It was never our intention to keep this as a storage facility when we bought it, but things have a way of turning out differently than you expect, don't they?'

'Don't they just?' Jim nodded. His eyes concentrated on hers and she wondered what unexpected turns Jim's life had taken and resolved to make the time to find out more about him.

'Ideally, we'd like to sell the land, or develop it, but nothing is certain yet. I promise to let you know what our plans are as soon as we do. We'll still be friends, if we sell Bocks, won't we?'

Jim's eyes stayed on hers as he listened, but he didn't have a chance to reply because Laura's head appeared around the staffroom door.

'I thought I heard you. You haven't seen my mug, have you?'

'What mug?'

'My mug.'

'I didn't know you had a mug.'

Laura blew out her cheeks. 'The one that says "*Sexy Beast*" on it. Who else's could it be?' She lifted her leg and swung it around the edge of the door, moving it up and down as she ran her hand along the paintwork provocatively and made kissing noises.

'You really are ridiculous,' said Alice. 'Stop that, you're embarrassing Jim.' She looked at Jim who was grinning and not looking even slightly embarrassed. 'You're embarrassing yourself, anyway. And I haven't got time to go around reading lewd messages on crockery.'

'It isn't lewd.' Laura stepped from the doorway to join them. 'It's a statement of fact.'

Jim guffawed behind her.

'And now it's missing.'

'You'll have put it down somewhere and forgotten. It's probably growing mould like all those you left in your bedroom when you were a teenager.' She turned to Jim.

'Honestly, Jim, you've never seen anything like it. And I once found—'

'That's enough from you, Mother,' Laura interrupted, her voice sharp. 'Not that you've noticed, but I am an actual grown-up now. Lived on my own and everything until you sucked me back into your web.'

Alice wondered at her tone and arched brows. Laura had used phrases like *web* and *trapped* on more than one occasion. It was like she was choosing her words carefully to hurt Alice. For what? For loving her and protecting her by keeping her close? In Laura's version of events had Alice purposefully given Richard a heart condition in order to stunt Laura's life?

She opened her mouth to challenge her daughter when she remembered the one lonely hook on the edge of Richard's mother's punch bowl, its small crystal glass nowhere to be found. She tipped her head to the side. 'That's weird, actually. Do you remember my glass went missing last Saturday?'

Laura gasped and made jazz hands. 'We have a thief in our midst.' She looked comically from left to right, her pink waves flying across her face. 'A very thirsty thief.'

'You're being ridiculous again,' said Alice, secretly pleased Laura had recovered her sense of humour. She opened the staffroom door and ushered Jim through. 'It is strange though,' she said. 'Very strange indeed.'

Chapter Thirty-One

Bonnie

Present Day

On Tuesday, Polly joined Bonnie and Laura at the life drawing class. This time she was an artist instead of the model.

'Lovely to have you here!' said Angie as the three of them trundled into the hall. Goosebumps rose on Bonnie's arms; the temperature was so much lower than the warm air outside. August had been a scorcher so far and Bonnie's erratic internal thermometer was struggling to cope. Angie hugged Polly into her paint-daubed smock, Polly's face disappearing into her grey and blonde tendrils. 'Look, everybody, it's Polly with her kit on.'

Polly did a small bow, but Bonnie saw her cheeks redden and felt for her.

After saying hello to Trudy, and the others, they pulled their chairs into position and started to unpack their bags.

'I've bought some new materials,' said Laura to Polly. 'So you can borrow anything you like.'

A tall, sinewy man with greasy, dark ringlets to his shoulders stepped from the stage wearing a black silk robe and walked towards the centre of the room where a large swathe of teal material covered the parquet floor. Bonnie looked over to see Polly and Laura's eyes grow wide, then look at each other, lips tight, obviously trying to keep their faces straight. Just before Bonnie turned back, Laura looked at her, and she felt a rush of relief at being included in their silent exchange.

The man disrobed with the ceremony of a courtesan revealing herself in front of a suiter: slowly, but with the air that this was a particularly special treat for the viewer. He slipped the robe to the floor and Bonnie watched in disbelief as Angie leaned forwards to retrieve the robe, almost colliding with the man's drooping testicles.

He clearly took pride in his job. Each pose was held with absolute concentration, his lithe limbs stretched, showing sinuous muscles taut with the effort. Unabashed, he bent and turned. There was no area of his body the three women were unfamiliar with by the time the quick poses were finished and it was time for the first break.

The man draped his robe over his shoulders and followed the other artists out to the kitchen, leaving Bonnie, Laura, and Polly seated. As soon as the last person disappeared, Laura gasped out a giggle, hand covering her mouth. 'I'm far too immature to be here.'

Bonnie shook her head. 'Yes. Yes, you are.'

Polly slapped Laura's leg. 'Stop it. You'll make me paranoid for next time I'm modelling.'

'You're not doing all this, though, are you?' Laura opened her legs, then stretched her arms above her head. 'After that last pose, I think I qualified as that bloke's doctor.'

'He's a professional.' Polly suppressed a snigger. 'And you are a child.' She shifted to face Bonnie. 'Let's have a look at what you've done.'

Bonnie turned her board to show her and grinned as Polly's mouth dropped open.

'You are a genius. I think you should go on that *Portrait Artist of the Year* programme. Shouldn't she?' she asked, turning to Laura who was nodding.

'That is impressive. How do you get the proportions so spot on?'

'It's just practice,' said Bonnie. 'Let's see yours.'

Laura lifted her paper from the floor and leafed through.

'Those are good. I can't believe you've mostly drawn his face though, you big baby.'

Laura dipped her head. 'I was embarrassed. I'm pleased with this one.' She pointed at a profile in browns and oranges.

'It's beautiful. You have a lot of talent.'

Polly held her board to her chest and grimaced. 'Mine's embarrassing.'

'Don't be silly, let's see,' Bonnie encouraged.

Screwing up her face, Polly showed her pencil drawing. It was a good first attempt, but she'd tried to fit too much in. The man's legs were half the length they should be, and his facial features were bunched under his hairline.

'That's not bad at all,' said Bonnie. 'I'm sure lots of people wouldn't even be able to draw a figure the first time they tried.'

'I've enjoyed it,' said Polly, looking down at her board. 'But it's clearly not the hidden talent I'd hoped for.'

'Ah, you were planning to come in and blow us away with your undiscovered brilliance, were you?' said Laura.

'Yep.' Polly sighed. 'But the best-laid plans, and all that.

227

Never mind, we can't all be good at everything. I'll have to stick with getting my boobs out.'

'And what magnificent boobs they are,' said Laura.

'Thank you very much.' Polly patted her chest fondly.

Angie blustered into the hall. 'I'm so sorry.' She screwed tops onto tubes of paint as she spoke. 'Just had a call from my other half. My youngest's having an asthma attack, and they think she needs a go on a nebuliser, so I'm off to meet them at the hospital. Sorry.'

The others followed her from the kitchen and they all helped her collect her things, murmuring offers of assistance.

'I'll refund half the session, or take it off next time,' said Angie, tucking her easel under her arm. 'Can you lock up?' She threw the keys to the model, who caught them with a flick of his wrist.

Followed by a chorus of voices telling her not to worry about the fees and wishing her luck, Angie disappeared.

'Poor Angie,' said Polly. 'I hope her daughter's alright. Must be terrifying to get a call like that.'

'I can't imagine what that's like, having to worry about a child,' said Laura. 'My mum still talks about the time I fell downstairs and broke my wrist. She says she still has nightmares about it.'

'You broke your wrist?' Bonnie said.

Laura held out her arm and pointed at a tiny white scar. 'Yeah. Chasing a stuffed elephant, apparently.' She looked up wistfully. 'I loved that thing. I've still got it somewhere.'

Bonnie stared at Laura's wrist, breathing carefully.

'Bet you're glad you don't have kids, eh?' Laura said to Bonnie. 'All that worry. More trouble than they're worth.'

'That's certainly the impression I get from my mum,'

said Polly, laughing. 'You've got your head screwed on, Bonnie. Child free, carefree. I reckon that's the way forward.'

But Bonnie couldn't go forward. The awful mistakes she'd made held her in her own private purgatory.

She picked up Laura's new pastels from where they'd slid under her seat. She slipped them into her bag, and instantly hated herself a little bit more.

Chapter Thirty-Two

Alice

Present Day

I suppose I'll have to get used to Laura staying out all night, thought Alice, as she dragged herself out of bed after a restless sleep. Richard lay on his back with his mouth open, snoring softly. The duvet fell across his stomach, and the sight of his greying chest hair peeping through the open neck of his pyjama top saddened her. She lifted the cover up to his shoulders, and he grunted quietly and turned onto his side.

He hadn't woken when Alice's phone flashed with a message from Laura at 11 p.m. last night, saying she planned to stay at her boyfriend's house. Oh, to have Richard's peace of mind. Time was running out. More accurately, money was running out, and he had absolutely no idea. Lying awake that night, she'd calculated they had less than three months left before the loan repayments would be more than the money left in the account. She looked at Richard again, now curled in the foetal position, and pulled the bedroom door silently closed.

She heard a car on the driveway as she reached the top of the stairs and gave a quiet growl before rushing down to turn off the alarm.

'Oh, hello,' said Laura, keys in her outstretched hand as Alice opened the door, hiding behind it so the neighbours didn't see her without her make-up on. 'I wasn't expecting you to be up.'

'It's a good job I was,' snapped Alice. 'Because if you'd come in while the alarm was on the night-time setting, it would have started ringing. I don't want your father woken by that! God knows what that would do to his heart.'

'Ah, right.' Laura let her bags drop from her shoulder onto the carpet. 'Sozzles. How is he?'

Alice surveyed Laura's crumpled jeans and T-shirt and even wilder than usual hair and raised an eyebrow before turning and walking to the kitchen. 'Okay, but please can you give me more notice in future if you're going to have a sleepover?'

Laura kicked off her trainers and followed. 'A sleepover? I'm not ten.'

'You could've fooled me.'

Laura plonked herself onto a stool. 'Do you have an issue with me staying at Xavier's? I'm feeling a bit of a chill in the air this morning.'

Alice tutted. 'You're a grown woman, you can come and go as you please, whatever my view is. I just ask that you have some consideration for your father and I.'

'Consideration . . .' She paused as though deciding not to carry on the sentence. 'And what is your view?'

Alice stopped shaking coffee beans from the packet into

the grinder. Why must Laura always make her talk about everything? 'Do you want my honest opinion?'

Laura huffed, rubbing mascara-smudged eyes. 'Go on.'

Alice braced herself. 'It's going too fast. You've only known this boy a matter of weeks and you're spending all your spare time with him.'

'He's not a boy. He's thirty.' Laura sighed. 'And I'm not spending that much time with him. I went to the art class with Bonnie and Polly yesterday.'

'Huh, the less said about that the better.'

Laura jumped off the stool. 'Jesus, do you know what most single women my age are doing? They're on Tinder, having booty calls with randoms. I meet a nice guy and do an evening drawing class and you think I'm going off the rails!'

Alice didn't understand half of what Laura had said, but she was overreacting as always.

'That's not what I said.'

'I knew you wouldn't like Xav.'

'Oh, for heaven's sake. I don't even know him.' She shook the grounds into a filter, spilling brown powder onto the granite.

'You should get to know him because it's getting serious. I really, really like him.'

Alice stiffened. 'You shouldn't rush into things. You hardly know him yourself.'

Laura cocked her head to one side. 'You can't bear it, can you?' She searched Alice's face with her dark eyes, and Alice had to work hard not to look away. 'You can't stand the fact that I'm getting close to someone else.'

'You're being ridiculous.' Alice picked up a cloth, ran it under the tap, and wiped the mess away.

233

'Do you know how often you call me ridiculous?' There were tears in Laura's voice.

Alice tutted, hiding the fact that Laura's words rang true. 'I just want you to be careful, that's all.'

'Why? Because he owns a bar and he's got tattoos? Would it be okay if he wore a suit and worked in insurance?'

Alice scrubbed a non-existent spot of dirt. 'As if you'd ever go for a standard man. I know you better than that.'

'What is it then?' Laura sounded exasperated. 'And don't pretend you're worried for me. Xav hasn't done anything other than look after me since I fell down the stairs in his bar. He doesn't drink, he's solvent, and he's funny and kind. Unless you're expecting Prince Harry to dump Meghan and sweep me off my Converse, I honestly don't know what more you could want.'

What she wanted was for Laura to stay, she realised, allowing her hand to still, the cloth limp under her fingers. She wanted her little girl to remain under her roof, in their business, safe and sound, where she could see her. *And close enough so she could lean on her when it all became too much.* She realised she really wanted Laura to stay as a prop for her, because she no longer felt she could cope. That sent shivers through her. That's not the way it's meant to be. Mothers are supposed to care for their children, not the other way around.

As if Laura could read her mind she said, 'I don't think you'd be happy unless I was sitting here with you and Dad every night, listening to your woes, having a hot chocolate and going to bed at ten.'

'You know full well that's not the case.' She dropped her voice. 'You should be glad I'm concerned about you. I am your mother, after all.'

Laura shook her head. 'You're trapping me, Mum. You're making it hard for me to live the life I want to live. Is that what mothers do?' Tears ran down her face. 'I don't want to hurt you. I know what I owe you—'

'Don't. Please. You don't owe me anything. It's not like that. It never has been.'

Laura folded her arms across her chest. 'If I didn't live here, you'd have no idea where I was or whom I was with. I should move out. It's claustrophobic here.'

'No. Please, Laura.' Alice couldn't look her daughter in the eye. She shook her head. 'I'd worry more then.' She wondered if that was true. She turned away, dropping the cloth into the sink. 'I promise, I'm not trying to make you feel trapped or hold you back. I just don't want you to rush into anything. You're young. There's no race to get to—'

'To what? I'm still where I was at eighteen. At fifteen. Do you honestly think that's healthy?'

'I just want the best for you.' She could hear Laura was crying, but she couldn't force herself to look at her.

'Is that really what you want? Or do you want me to be happy with the caveat that I stay right where you can see me? If you're honest with yourself, you'll admit what you really want isn't what's best for me. It's what's best for you.'

Alice felt the air leave her lungs. Before she could try to defend herself, Laura left the room. It was probably for the best. She was beginning to realise she had no defence at all.

* * *

She wasn't surprised when she heard the door close half an hour later. Or when she got a text saying Laura wouldn't be home that night. She was somehow doing exactly what she wanted to avoid: she was pushing Laura away.

* * *

Alice tensed when Laura returned early the following morning with a bag over her shoulder. 'Morning,' she said. 'Coffee?'

'Thanks.' Laura placed the board she was carrying on the table. She unclipped the papers and laid them out while Alice made coffee for them both, glancing over her shoulder to assess her daughter's mood. She waited to see if Laura had prepared a speech, like she used to when she was little and she felt she'd suffered some injustice at Alice's hands, but the air didn't zing with tension and, despite her bloodshot eyes, Laura's face was relaxed. She had obviously said all she needed to say yesterday and was ready to move on. 'What do you think of these?' she asked. 'They're from the other night. I feel like I'm getting the hang of it.'

Alice's shoulders, which had ached with tension since the argument, dropped a little as she took the steaming cups over to the display. She halted when she saw the beautiful drawings laid out neatly in front of her daughter.

'Wow. They're excellent.'

'It was a fella. Sorry about the penises.' Laura smiled and Alice shook her head, relieved Laura was speaking to her, even if it was about penises.

'I have to say, I prefer the ones of his head.' She picked up a drawing of the model's face in profile, his features made soft by the orange and brown pastels. 'This one is extraordinary.'

Laura narrowed her eyes, as if assessing her work. She smiled. 'I'm quite pleased with that one.'

An idea popped into Alice's head. She glanced towards the hallway to make sure Richard hadn't woken and come downstairs, then whispered, 'You know it's your dad's birthday next month?'

'Yes.'

'What do you think about doing a portrait of him as a present? I think he'd love that.'

'You think he's bored of socks?' Laura gave a knowing nod.

'Seriously.' She seemed to say that all the time to Laura. 'It would be such a thoughtful gift.' She was warming to the idea, not least because if Laura was working on a portrait of Richard, it would make sense for her to be at home to do it. Whatever Laura thought, it wouldn't do any harm to slow things down with that boy and put some distance between her and that strange Bonnie. Alice knew she was being selfish too, but the stress of logging on to see whether any complaints about the plans had been posted was making her into a walking nerve-ending. Having Laura around for a change would be the perfect distraction.

'Okay. If you think he'd like it.'

'I think he'd love it.'

Laura gathered the papers and clipped them back on the board. 'I bought some new materials. I think I'd like to work with different colours for Dad's piece.' She looked up and saw Alice's face. 'Nothing too out there, I won't give him a blue forehead or anything, but I would like to experiment a bit.' She lifted the top of the bag and looked inside, shifting things around. 'I've got some nice soft pastels with greys and blues, but I can't find them.'

She tipped the contents of the bag onto the table. Alice grimaced as pencils, paintbrushes, and a heavy Stanley knife clattered onto the marble.

'They're not here.' Laura rifled through the packets, turning them over to see the labels. She dipped her head and scanned the floor under the table. 'Nope, not here. What can I have done with them?'

'You're losing everything at the moment. You didn't use to be so ditzy.'

'It's weird though.' Laura frowned and repacked the bag, checking the labels again as she popped them inside. 'I clearly remember showing them to Bonnie in the hall as we cleared up. They were unusual colours. She hadn't seen any like them before.'

Alice squinted, about to speak, but then thought better of it.

'Go on,' said Laura. 'I can tell you're holding something back.'

'No,' said Alice. 'You'll only say I'm making things up to serve myself.'

Laura sat on a dining chair, resting her forearms on the table, looking up at Alice with her beautiful dark eyes. 'Come on. Get it off your chest.'

Alice bit her bottom lip, then sat next to Laura. 'Three things have gone missing, right?'

'Three?'

'My crystal glass, your lewd mug, and these art supplies.'

'Okay, Miss Marple. What's your theory?'

It was a risk, but Laura had asked. 'There's one thing they all have in common.'

'What do you mean?'

'The only person who was there on all three occasions when something went missing was . . .'

Laura lifted her hands and flung them in the air. 'Oh, for goodness' sake.'

Alice crossed her arms. 'I knew you wouldn't listen.'

'Because you're jumping to unfair conclusions! You can't just accuse someone of stealing.'

'I'm only going on the evidence.'

'Circumstantial evidence, at best.' Laura stood and collected her things. 'I'm going for a shower.' She gave Alice a harsh glare, pointing her index finger. 'You, stop acting like a madwoman.'

'I don't care what you say,' shouted Alice at Laura's back as she strode from the room. 'I'm going to be keeping an eye on that woman. I think she's hiding something.'

She ignored the tutting sound she heard from her retreating daughter's mouth. She was sure she was right. Now she just had to find out for sure.

Chapter Thirty-Three

Bonnie

Present Day

Bocks was busier than usual, and Bonnie's cheeks ached from smiling at customers and answering their queries. A good night's sleep was a distant memory these days. She was permanently tired, but the minute she fell into bed, her mind and body clicked on like a central heating system on a timer. *Heat up* ordered her body. *Overthink* screamed her brain.

Right now, she wanted to crawl under the desk and go to sleep, but the surprise of Alice and Laura arriving together forced her eyes fully open. She stiffened as Alice nodded a curt greeting. Her disdain for Bonnie radiated from every pore. Someone with less investment would have left this job by now. Bonnie was only just clinging on.

'You haven't seen my *Sexy Beast* mug, have you?' said Laura when she and Alice came out of the staffroom.

The three of them were squeezed behind the desk, and

241

Bonnie had the urge to vault over it and run away. She pushed her forehead up, making it crinkle and said, 'Your what?' Bonnie felt Alice's eyes like lasers of ice trying to freeze their way into her brain. She took a breath and set her face as a shield.

'The white mug I have my coffee in. It's gone.'

'Has it?' She was aware of every muscle in her face, trying to choreograph them to move innocently. Her capillaries opened and the heat of fresh blood flooded her cheeks. She looked from one woman to the other. 'Oh no!' – she put her hand over her mouth – 'I did actually break a mug the other day. I'm so sorry, I forgot to tell you. I can't believe it was your favourite. I'll get you another. Do you know where you got it from?'

Alice eyed her. 'If you put it in the bin, maybe we could find it and glue it together?'

'Ah,' said Bonnie. 'I emptied the bin. Sorry.'

'You emptied the bin?' Alice spoke slowly.

'It was full.' Bonnie's face burned, but she looked directly into Alice's eyes without flinching.

'Oh, well.' Laura's voice split the tension, and Bonnie dared to shift her gaze to her bright face. 'I'll have to find a new mug with a new saucy message.'

'I'm sorry, Laura.'

Alice lifted the hatch, and it tipped out of her hand, smashing back down with an ear-splitting crack.

'You okay?' said Laura, her hand on Alice's shoulder.

'Just about. That thing could've broken my fingers.' She turned to Bonnie. 'Where's Jim? I thought he was fixing this?'

'He hasn't been in for a while.'

Alice lifted the wood more carefully and stepped through the gap to the reception area, dropping it gently back down. 'I can't remember exactly when I last saw him.'

'Me either,' said Laura. 'And he's usually buzzing around, tinkering with something here, isn't he?'

'Give him a call, will you?' Alice said to Bonnie. 'Jim Morton. His mobile number's in the system.'

Bonnie scrolled through the client list on the database until she found his details, then picked up the phone and dialled. She waited, aware of Alice and Laura's eyes watching her. She gave a tight smile as the dialling tone repeated, but Jim didn't pick up.

'Try his home number. Maybe he's one of those people who never answers their mobile,' said Alice. 'And his wife should know where he is.'

Bonnie resisted the urge to say, 'please?' She pressed the digits and waited until a woman's voice answered, repeating the phone number back in a wavery tone, then asking her to leave a message.

'It's an answer machine.'

Alice leaned over the desk and snatched the phone from Bonnie's hand, saying in a higher tone than usual, 'Hello, this is a message for Jim. Could you please call Alice from Bocks when you receive this? Thank you.' She handed the receiver back to Bonnie who took it and held it aloft for a moment, hoping that someone would acknowledge how she was being treated. They didn't. 'You're welcome,' she muttered.

'It's very strange he hasn't done the work he said he would.' Alice tapped her nails on the desk.

Laura scoffed. 'It's not like you pay the poor old sod.'

Alice exhaled loudly. 'I always offer. He'll only ever take money for materials, however hard I push.'

Bonnie tried to remember when she'd last seen Jim.

When she started at Bocks, he was there most days, fixing something, or working in his unit. It was nice having him around, especially when it was quiet, and the place felt like an abandoned school. She made him cups of tea and they chatted about the news or whatever project he was working on. He'd had a dreadful cold and it seemed worse when she saw him at the end of last week. She remembered because she'd taken the mickey out of him for using a cotton handkerchief.

'He wasn't on great form when I saw him last time. I think it was last Friday. He's had that cold for ages, hasn't he?'

'It's not like him to stay away without letting me know what he's up to,' said Alice. 'I hope he's all right.'

Bonnie picked up her Biro and scribbled down the address from the screen. 'I'm finishing my shift soon. I'll pop home and get my car, then I'll go and give him a knock. Make sure he's okay.'

'I'll come with you,' said Laura and Bonnie had to stop her hands from clapping together. 'I've got my car in the car park and you can cover here, can't you, Mum?'

Alice looked like someone had wafted a strong, unpleasant smell under her nose. Her thin eyebrows arched. 'I suppose I'll have to, won't I?'

* * *

They pulled up outside Jim's nineteen thirties semi-detached house, which was indistinguishable from the other houses in the quiet crescent apart from the neatly edged garden and newly painted gate. His grey Yaris was parked on the drive.

'We're like Cagney and Lacey,' said Bonnie.

'Eh?'

Bonnie laughed. 'Philistine. Scott and Bailey? Investigating duo?'

'Oh, yeah.' Laura pointed her fingers and cupped one hand in the other, waving her pretend gun around until a woman passing the car on the pavement stared in through the windscreen, face screwed up. Laura dropped her hands to her lap.

They opened the gate and walked down the driveway, squeezing past the car.

'All indications are good so far,' said Laura. 'The gate doesn't squeak, the car is clean, and there are no weeds in the cracks in the driveway. I deduce that Jim has recently been in the vicinity.'

'Great detective work, but we could have deduced that from the fact we saw him last Friday.'

Laura turned, finger in the air. 'Do not question my skills, officer, or I'll have your badge.'

Bonnie laughed. 'You're the senior detective in this scenario, are you?'

'Naturally.'

Laura pulled back her shoulders theatrically, and they climbed the two concrete steps to the white door with a small, square, frosted window. Bonnie knocked on the moulded plastic and they waited, Bonnie on the top step, Laura on the one below. As they stood there, Bonnie turned and saw she was now the same height as Laura, and they were face to face. Her soft eyes looked almost black. She quickly turned away and lifted her gaze to the grey sky; the clouds were thickening, the new layers darker, and hanging heavy with the threat of rain.

After a minute, Laura stepped down and walked further up the drive to a window at the side of the house. She peered inside. 'What's Jim's wife called?'

'Lou. Why?'

'Come and look in here.'

Bonnie joined Laura and craned her neck to look through the window. 'You know we're going to be arrested for casing the joint, don't you?'

'We'll show them our badges, it'll be fine.' She tapped the nail of her index finger against the glass. 'Look at that.'

Bonnie focused past the reflection of her face into Jim's kitchen and was astonished to see the mess. A bin stood in the far corner, its swing-lid askew, contents overflowing onto the lino. The sink under the window they were looking through was filled with dirty crockery and two crusted pans sat on the draining board.

'I didn't expect Jim to be untidy. He's so capable and, you know, upstanding,' said Laura.

'And, from what he's said about his wife, I thought she'd be a stickler for a clean house.'

Bonnie walked back up the steps and knocked again, more firmly this time, waiting a minute then pressing the bell, hearing it chime inside. She turned when she heard a door opening on the other side of the small brick wall separating the two houses. An old woman appeared, back bent into a question mark, gnarled hand holding onto the handle of the door as though she couldn't stay upright without its support.

She spoke, but Bonnie couldn't hear her. She crossed the drive and stood next to the wall as the woman watched through pinprick eyes.

'I'm sorry, what was that?'

The woman's voice sounded like a clarinet being tuned; reedy, with more air than volume. Bonnie strained to hear.

'Are you looking for Jim?'

'Yes.' Bonnie spoke loudly as the woman turned her ear towards her, the lobe enormous in comparison to her tiny, lined face.

'I don't know where he is,' she said. The effort of speaking looked like it might finish her off.

'You haven't seen him recently?'

'No. I don't know where he is,' she repeated, and Bonnie wondered why she'd made the monumental effort to come to the door if she had no information.

'Have you seen Lou?'

The woman's eyes seemed to disappear as she narrowed them. 'Lou's gone,' she said. 'And now I don't know where Jim is.'

Bonnie felt a wave of sadness for this wizened old lady. 'We'll try to find him, okay?'

The woman nodded, and that seemed to take the last of her energy. She shuffled to turn, slowly closing the door.

'The mystery deepens,' said Laura. 'Where has Lou gone, and what's happened to Jim?'

They stood, looking at the door, then at each other.

'What now?' asked Bonnie, following Laura as she walked around to the back of the house, putting her head close to the glass of each window and squinting inside. They stood in a tidy square of garden, the grass vivid green, with pink and purple blooming hydrangeas along the back wall, and borders of marigolds and heavy-headed peonies.

'That window's open a crack.' Laura pointed up the red brickwork to the second floor where the top pane of a window protruded. Laura pulled her phone from the back pocket of her jeans. 'I'll call Xav.'

Bonnie said, 'Why?' and stopped herself from saying,

'Please don't.' It was a rare treat to spend time alone with Laura. She didn't want it to end.

'I think we need to try to get in through that window, so we need a ladder.'

'You want us to break in?' It hadn't occurred to Bonnie that they would break into Jim's home. She might occasionally shoplift but this was on a different level. The thought of being caught, and what might happen if her previous convictions came to light, made her mouth dry.

Laura glanced up from her screen. 'Jim's disappeared and Methuselah over there' – she nodded towards next door – 'hasn't seen him or his wife, so I think something weird is going on.'

'That doesn't give us the right to go breaking and entering.' The memory of holding her police check form in her trembling fingers was still raw. Thank goodness Alice had been too distracted over the past few weeks to follow up on making Bonnie get the standard check.

Laura pressed the screen then held the phone to her ear. 'You don't have to, but I'm worried . . . Oh, hi, Xav, it's me.'

* * *

Twenty minutes later, Bonnie was holding on to the cold metal of a ladder with Xavier on the opposite side, as Laura's Converse clanked on each step and her backside ascended towards the open window. Xavier leaned against the ladder, wrapping his leg around the bottom as he wiped spots of water off his glasses with the bottom of his T-shirt.

'Come down,' he said, putting his glasses back on and raising his head. 'Let me go up.'

Laura peered down from the fifth rung. 'Why?'

Xavier shuffled his feet, his mouth twitching. 'I just think it should be me.'

Laura tutted. 'I rang you because you've got a ladder and a van, not a white charger.'

'Is she always like this?' asked Xavier, his knuckles whitening as he gripped the ladder.

Bonnie was flattered he presumed she knew Laura so well. She felt like she did, as though every one of Laura's actions was typically her, but in truth, she didn't know. This was the first time in ages she'd had the opportunity to spend some time with her on her own, and Xavier was spoiling it.

'Impetuous?'

'Mad.'

Bonnie bristled. 'She's trying to help an old man.'

Xavier frowned. 'Sorry, yeah, I know that. But this is bonkers, isn't it?'

'If you don't feel okay about what we're doing, you can leave us to it.' She wished he would.

'I'm here now,' he said, and they both stood quietly watching Laura fiddle with the window at the top of the ladder.

'I wish she'd let me go up.'

'She's hardly the damsel in distress type, is she?' Bonnie was torn between wishing Xavier was the one dangling from a great height, then climbing through glass, and being glad Laura didn't rely on a man to do the potentially risky and illegal stuff.

'That's not what I'm saying. I would rather put myself in danger, rather than her. That's not sexist, it's—' He stopped.

'Chivalrous? Gentlemanly?'

Xavier's forehead puckered. 'It's bloody hard to be a

249

decent bloke these days without sounding like a twat. I don't want to take over. I just . . .' He looked up the ladder again and a softness spread across his face. 'I just want her to be okay.'

Bonnie knew that look and he was suddenly the loveliest young man in the world.

'I'm in,' Laura shouted down. 'I'm going to climb into the bathroom then see if I can find Jim.'

'Be careful,' they both said at once, keeping their eyes on Laura as she lifted one leg from the ladder, then the other, and disappeared inside.

There was no noise from inside the house and Bonnie itched to climb up the ladder to make sure Laura hadn't come to any harm. She stared up the rungs, willing Laura's head to appear from the window and let them know Jim was having an afternoon nap and everything was fine. She drummed her fingers against the metal frame and avoided looking at Xavier, who, judging by the vibrations on the ladder, was doing the same on the other side.

'Do you think I should go up after her?' said Xavier after what seemed like an age. 'We don't know what's in there.'

'I'm not sure I'm strong enough to spot the ladder for you. Why don't I go?' He'd grown on her, but she wasn't about to let him be that knight after all. She'd rather gallop up the rungs herself and be the one to take care of Laura. It was about time.

'I'm sure it'll be fine if you hold it on both sides,' Xavier began, then stopped as they both turned sharply at the sound of a door opening at the side of the house. The ladder wobbled as they both let go at once and Bonnie left Xavier to stabilise it. Ignoring his quiet swearing, she rushed around the corner, bumping into Laura as she reached the drive.

Laura's cheeks were wet, and Bonnie pulled her in for a hug. 'What is it? What's wrong.'

'Jim's not well. He's in a bit of a state.'

With difficulty, Bonnie stepped away as Xavier appeared and took her place, tucking Laura into his broad chest as she looked up at him with watery eyes.

'I think we need to get him to hospital.'

She led them through the open door, through the disarray of Jim's kitchen, and into a small hallway with a patterned carpet. They followed her up a flight of stairs. The house smelt of rotting food and mildew and Bonnie's heart broke for Jim, who always had an air of military efficiency when he was at Bocks. He wouldn't have left the house like this unless . . . She didn't want to finish that thought.

They turned left into a room lit by a small lamp on a bedside table and in the bed, under a floral duvet, lay Jim, unrecognisable as the man who was always neat and straight-backed. His thin white hair stuck out from his head like a fluffy dandelion, and his blue eyes seemed to be covered in cling film. He looked skeletal, like his cheeks had been sucked into his mouth, then Bonnie noticed his false teeth in a glass of liquid next to the lamp on the bedside table.

He coughed and tried to raise himself on his elbow, but the effort seemed too much, and he slumped back on his pillow.

'I think you need to see a doctor, sweetheart,' said Bonnie, moving closer to the bed, hearing Jim's breath come out in short, wheezy bursts. He turned his head slightly and opened his mouth, starting to speak, but a

251

hacking cough wracked his body and she heard Laura take in a sharp breath.

'I think it's best we call an ambulance,' said Bonnie.

Xavier made the call and bustled around, closing the open window and dismantling the ladder, attaching it onto the van with Regret Rien emblazoned on its side. He was a good man, Bonnie decided, then remembered with a dipping heart that it wasn't any of her business.

'Drink this.' Bonnie offered Jim a glass of water. 'Small sips.'

'Is it okay if I pack some of your things for the hospital, Jim?' asked Laura in a soft voice Bonnie hadn't heard her use before.

Jim nodded his assent and Bonnie held his clammy hand while Laura opened and closed drawers in the ancient wooden dresser that stood opposite the bed, putting clothes on top of the duvet ready to pack.

'Jim,' Bonnie said, putting her other hand over his to give him some of her warmth, 'Where's Lou?'

She felt the sobs convulse his body and wished she could take back the question as the old man cried like a heartbroken child.

Chapter Thirty-Four

Alice

Present Day

After marching through the entrance of the hospital's Accident and Emergency Department, Alice found Laura and Xavier sitting close together on the fixed seats of the waiting room, holding hands. Bonnie sat opposite, looking like a spare part. Alice averted her gaze from the other seated figures, trying not to rest her eyes on a man holding a bloodied tissue to a gash on his forehead, or the scrawny woman rocking backwards and forwards, her hands circling each other like a heroin-addicted Lady Macbeth.

'What on earth is going on?' she asked the three of them. 'Where's Jim's wife? How did he get so sick without anyone noticing?'

'He's through there. They wouldn't let us go with him.' Laura gestured to the double doors through which staff buzzed like bees in and out of a hive. 'I went to see the old lady next door and Bonnie came in the ambulance with Jim,' said Laura.

Alice contemplated Bonnie, suppressing the feeling that she had no right to be in an emergency with her friends and family. She was taking up too much space in Alice's life, pushing her to the edges of everything.

'The neighbour said Lou died two years ago.'

'What?' She dipped into her memory bank, trying to pluck out any indication Jim had given of having lost his wife, or was even grieving. All she found were images of the taciturn, gentle man, carrying on as she expected.

'I know. It's awful. How didn't we know that?' Tears brimmed in Laura's eyes. Alice knew how she felt.

'How long has Jim been working for you?' asked Bonnie, and Alice resented the censure she was sure she heard in her voice.

'He doesn't work for us, not officially.'

Bonnie sighed, making Alice's hackles rise further. 'Okay. How long has he been helping out at Bocks?'

'Only about eighteen months,' said Laura. 'He had a unit before that, but he just drifted in and out back then. He told me his wife didn't like him keeping his tools and little projects at home, that's why he had a unit. Then he started to spend more time there, and he was the one who found little jobs to do, and we sort of started to rely on him.'

'Why do you think he didn't tell you his wife had died?' Xavier lifted his arm and put it around Laura's shoulders, and she shifted closer, resting her head on his chest.

'Who knows?' said Alice. 'I've given up trying to work out why anyone does anything.'

'Amen to that,' said Bonnie, and they all looked at her. She dropped her eyes to the shiny waiting room floor.

They were quiet, watching nurses in blue scrubs scurry

254

through swinging doors, to a soundtrack of coughs, groans, and whispered conversations.

'Have the doctors told you what's wrong with him?'

'The problem is, we're not family, so they can't say much,' said Bonnie. 'They're trying to find his next of kin. Do you know who that would be?'

Alice sighed, not wanting to admit how little she really knew about him. 'Afraid not.' She turned to Bonnie. 'Thanks for your help today, but you can go home now if you like. We can take it from here.' She saw confusion in Bonnie's eyes, but stared her down, aware how cold her grey eyes could be if she put her mind to it. Jim was *her* friend, he helped with *her* business, and had been found by *her* daughter. She would be the one to put this right, and she didn't need Bonnie's input.

'It's okay. I'm happy to wait.' Bonnie glanced at Laura and Alice felt the muscles in her cheeks twitch as she gritted her teeth.

'There's no point us all staying here. I'll call you if we hear anything.' She turned to Xavier. 'I'm sure you have things to do too. Why don't you drive Bonnie home? We'll be fine here, won't we, Laura?'

Laura lifted her head from Xavier's chest and looked up at him. 'That's a good idea. We have no idea how long we'll be. I'll give you a ring, okay?'

Xavier kissed her on the lips, stood, and stretched his arms above his head. The red rose at the edge of his tattoo poked out from the sleeve of his faded T-shirt. 'If you're sure?'

'Absolutely,' said Alice. She looked at Bonnie, who hesitated then stood, lifting her bag from the chair next to her and fiddling with the handle.

'Please ring when you hear anything.'

'Of course, we will.' Alice dragged her lips into a smile and took the seat Xavier left next to Laura. It was still warm, which made her feel a little queasy. She took Laura's hand and gave it a quick squeeze as they watched Xavier and Bonnie walk from the room.

Bonnie looked back just as they reached the automatic doors and Alice kept her cool grey eyes on her until she turned and followed Xavier out of the building, then turned her concentration to her daughter and their poorly friend.

* * *

'So, you're alright to have Jim stay in the spare room while he recovers?' Alice perched on the chair arm next to Richard, feeling girlish.

'I love how you phrase things as if they're already a done deal,' said Richard, tapping at a shaving cut under his nose with his index finger. 'Won't it be a bit awkward, having a relative stranger in the house?'

'He's not a relative stranger. It's Jim. And we owe him.'

Richard sighed. 'Are you sure he doesn't have any family who'd like to coddle him in his hour of need?'

Alice moved Richard's hand away from the red mark and put it in his lap. 'He's not as lucky as you in that respect.' She raised one eyebrow, and he nodded, reproached. 'I've spoken to his sister in Huddersfield and her husband has Alzheimer's. Her daughters are primary school teachers so they can't get away. There really is no one else.'

'Okay. You've made your point. I suppose it could be good to have another man around. Stop you two ganging up on me.' He squeezed her knee, and she caught his hand, raising it to her mouth and grazing her lips on his knuckles.

256

'It'd take more than two of you.'

'I thought as much. Does he play golf?'

Alice let go of his hand and stood, straightening her slacks. 'He's just had pneumonia, so my guess is no, he doesn't want to stand on a windy bit of grass waving a stick about.'

'Ouch.'

* * *

When Laura brought Jim home from the hospital, Alice and Richard stood at the door and greeted him like staff welcoming a special guest to a stately home. He limped up the staircase, then marvelled at the tastefully decorated room, commenting on how posh the cream duvet set was and how fancy the framed prints of Italian squares and fountains on the walls.

'I've never had one of these en suite bathrooms before, you know,' he said, touching the plush towels. 'My Lou would've loved this. It's like a five-star hotel.' He turned to Alice. 'Not that I expect waiting on, mind. You've done enough for me already.'

Alice blushed at what must look like enormous affluence. It was what she'd wanted to convey, once. Now it was just home, and she wanted so desperately to hold on to it. She'd postponed the valuation since Jim was coming to stay, but the thought of having to rearrange it buzzed in the back of her head like a wasp at a BBQ.

* * *

On Saturday, he was well enough to join the family for lunch. Alice fussed around him, pulling out the heavy dining room chair and standing over him as he sat.

'Would you like a blanket?'

Jim shook his head. 'I'm grand, thank you.'

'Leave the man alone, for goodness' sake,' said Richard, winking at Jim. 'She'll smother you with kindness if you give her half a chance.'

'I don't see you complaining,' said Alice, raising her eyebrows to make her point before adding, 'fizzy or still water?'

Laura put a piping hot pasta bake in the middle of the table and went back to the island to pick up the salad bowl.

'What's this then?' Jim asked, eyeing the dish with suspicion.

'Tuna melt,' said Laura.

'Oh, aye.' He watched Alice spoon the gloopy mixture onto his plate, strings of cheese stretching back to the dish, snapped by Alice's spoon. 'I've never 'ad that before. We ate plainly, Lou an' me.'

'If you don't fancy it, I'll warm up some of that chicken soup you like.'

Jim looked horrified. 'Don't go to any more bother on my account. This'll be just the ticket.' Alice felt for him as he took a bite of pasta, then blew out steam as he tried to chew the hot food.

'Dad,' said Laura. 'I need you to sit for me after lunch.'

'Yes, ma'am.' Richard saluted. 'It's a bit like being royalty, this portrait-sitting thing. I've never felt so important. Staying still's more difficult than you'd think though.'

Alice was reminded of how still Richard had been when he first came out of hospital, with his pale, mottled skin and laboured breathing. Every movement had been an effort and his eyes darkened with fear every time the smallest exertion caused his chest to tighten. He'd been very still then. She blinked the thought away and focused on his ruddy cheeks and bright eyes behind his glasses.

'It's a shame we couldn't keep the portrait a secret, but it's a different vibe, working from photos,' said Laura.

'I'm happy to be part of the process,' said Richard. 'I can't wait to see how it turns out.'

'You're not looking at it until your birthday.' Laura pointed her fork and Alice pressed her hand back towards the table, unable to understand how her daughter's table manners could still be so appalling after years of reminders.

'You'll tell me if she's given me horns and twelve chins, won't you, Jim?'

'I will that.' Jim chortled then turned away from the table, coughing into a handkerchief he pulled from his pocket. When he turned back, his eyes were watery. 'My Lou liked to draw a bit. Nothing like what you do, but some very pretty doodles.'

'Did you keep any of her work?'

'No. I wish I had.'

Laura speared a piece of penne and twirled it on her fork. 'I've been wondering something – and feel free to tell me to mind my own business – but why did you let us think Lou was still with you?'

Alice was surprised at the sensitive phrasing of Laura's question. She was so used to thinking of her as a clumsy child. She watched Jim finish his mouthful then put down his knife and fork. He wiped his hands on his napkin as they waited for him to speak.

'If I admitted she'd gone, then I'd be accepting I couldn't make up for what I'd done.' He paused, stroking down the bristles of his moustache. 'Or, what I hadn't done, more like.'

He sighed, keeping his eyes on his plate. 'I was always

busy, y'see. Always 'ad something I needed to get done. It wasn't until she'd passed that I realised I hadn't done any of the stuff she'd asked. The garden gate still needed a fresh coat, the bedroom door squeaked, there was still a tile missing from the splashback in the kitchen . . .'

'We're all guilty of that, Jim. There's always a list.' Richard's voice was soft.

'I know, but she didn't ask for much, Lou didn't. And it wouldn't't've killed me to do the bits and bobs, to show 'er I listened, you know.' He mopped his eyes with his hanky. 'So, after she died, I set to get the bits done, like. Only, when I'd finished what I could remember, I didn't want to stop, coz if I did, then what?'

Alice reached across and patted his hand, trying not to imagine being in the same situation if Richard was no longer there.

Jim raised his head, a weak smile lifting his moustache. 'That's where you lot came in. When it was too quiet at home, I'd come and see you at Bocks and you made me feel useful again.'

'Glad to be of service.' Laura grinned. 'Who'd have thought taking advantage of someone's good nature could be a charitable thing?'

'On that point, I have a little announcement to make.' All eyes turned to Alice. 'But first, I want to tell you, Jim, that what I'm about to say will not impact how much we all need you. Whatever the next phase of our lives brings, you will be part of it, if you wish to be.'

Colour bloomed on Jim's rough cheeks as Richard and Laura glanced at each other.

'I was looking at the progress of our planning application for the land Bocks is on.'

'For a change,' muttered Laura. Alice ignored her.

'And I'm happy to report there hasn't yet been one objection lodged.'

'There's still time, though, right?' Laura asked.

Alice couldn't understand why Laura was being difficult. Maybe she should have let her see the bank statements, poured some of the worry into her instead of almost drowning in it on her own. 'There is, but last time there were four objections by this point.' She sipped her water. 'I thought you'd be more excited about that news?'

'It's not really news, though, is it?'

'No, but if' – she paused – '*when* it is approved, you won't have to work at Bocks anymore and we'll have the money to support you to do your MA and whatever you decide to do after that. That's what you want isn't it?'

Laura twirled a strand of pink hair around her finger. 'It is, but . . .'

'But what?'

'We've only just taken Bonnie on, and she's settled in really well.'

'Bonnie?' Was that really where Laura's allegiance lay? Alice was now seriously regretting not telling Laura how close they were to losing everything. Maybe if she had, her daughter would show a little more concern for how her mother was coping, not that bloody woman. If Richard and Jim weren't at the table, she might well have let it all come out. Instead, she swallowed hard.

'That may be the case' – Alice was fairly sure it wasn't – 'but we have a choice to make, don't we? Secure our future – a stress-free life for your father and opportunities for you – or turn down a life-changing amount of capital to keep the part-time receptionist in a job.' Alice stuck her fork into a piece of cucumber and lifted it to her mouth. 'It's not much of a choice, is it?' She bit down and felt a satisfying crunch, ignoring the voice in her head that wanted to scream *for once in your life, Laura, can't you please choose me?*

Chapter Thirty-Five

Bonnie

Present Day

Sitting in her car outside the mock-Georgian frontage, with its plaster Doric columns, Bonnie resisted the urge to sneer at the crass showiness of Alice's house. The size was impressive, but inside, like the façade, was all money, no imagination or style. She tried to calculate what the house was worth. She imagined what her ideal home at that price would look like, but her mind kept wandering back to her and Stuart's sandstone villa in Scotland.

She toured her memory through forest green hallway, wood-panelled study, and the dining room, red and womb-like with multicoloured glass beads dripping from the curtain rail, sending prisms of brightness into the room. She imagined Stuart sitting alone in the huge, purple velvet armchair in the snug, under the brass floor lamp, reading one of the books about the First World War she used to tell him proved he was prematurely ageing.

Grief tightened her throat. Suddenly she wanted to push herself against Stuart's chest and have him hold her there, so tightly she couldn't distinguish between his heartbeat and hers.

She climbed from the car and huffed out three short breaths. She'd been instrumental in discovering Jim was sick, so why shouldn't she come and visit him? It was rude of Alice not to have invited her, forcing her to come unannounced. The gravel crunched under her Birkenstocks as she approached the front door. Lifting her chin in defiance, she rang the doorbell.

Thankfully, it was Laura who answered, her face brightening when she saw Bonnie. A slouchy camouflage print jumper hung off her tanned shoulder, and she looked impossibly cool. A table to the left of the door heaved with carefully placed family photos in expensive frames and Bonnie tried not to stare at the two-dimensional Lauras who gazed at her from every picture, from babyhood to graduation. All she wanted to do was pick them up and absorb every smile until she could imagine being there with her on that beach, at that wedding, through all those lost years.

Forcing herself to look away, Bonnie scanned the magnolia hallway and wondered how Laura felt about growing up in this stiflingly neutral house. She remembered the pink bathroom and nineteen seventies kitchen in her own childhood home and how she never felt like she belonged.

'Hello, stranger!'

'Hi. I hope it's okay for me to just turn up, I wanted to call in on Jim.' She pulled a Chocolate Orange from her bag. 'I brought medicine.'

'I like that flavour medicine.' Laura opened the door

wide and Bonnie stepped in. 'I might get a little sick myself if it means I can have a bit of that.'

Bonnie made a mental note to buy another to bring to work. She kicked off her sandals and put them neatly by the door.

'Follow me, the invalid's through here.'

The carpet sank under her feet as she followed Laura towards the kitchen, suddenly acutely aware of the nakedness of her feet and the metallic blue polish on her toenails.

'Bonnie's come to make sure we haven't murdered you for your money, Jim,' said Laura, and Bonnie rolled her eyes.

'There's slim pickings,' said Jim, starting to stand, but Alice, who was sitting opposite him at the table, a laptop open in front of her, flapped her arm, gesturing for him to stay seated.

'It's kind of you to come,' she said.

Bonnie felt Alice's eyes trail to her feet and wanted to curl her toes under, but kept them flat on the cold tiles, in a small act of defiance. How did this woman always manage to make her feel like she was a teacher and Bonnie was the child who'd wet themselves on the first day of term and hadn't quite been forgiven?

'Coffee?' asked Laura.

Bonnie turned away from Alice's scrutiny. 'Thanks, that'd be great.'

'Take a seat,' said Laura, and Bonnie felt obliged to move over to the table.

She sat next to Jim and nudged him with her shoulder. 'You gave us a bit of a fright, young man.'

'Sorry about that,' he said. 'I've been an old fool, haven't I?'

'Nonsense!' Alice's voice was clipped, but she put out her hand to cover Jim's, a gesture that surprised Bonnie.

'Looks like you've been well cared for.' The difference in Jim since she'd last seen him was astonishing. His skin was cheerfully ruddy, hair combed and shiny, and his teeth filled out his cheeks again.

'I couldn't have asked for better.' Jim grinned. 'But I expect I've outstayed my welcome.'

'Don't be silly,' said Laura, placing a cup on a coaster in front of Bonnie. She tapped the lid of the Chocolate Orange Bonnie had put on the table. 'And if you think you're leaving before I've had some of that, you can think again.'

'Of course, it's up to you, Jim,' said Alice, 'but I'd rather you stayed until we're certain you're one hundred per cent well, especially since we don't know how much longer we'll be seeing you at Bocks.'

She looked at Bonnie as she spoke. Her eyes sent a chill that covered Bonnie like a film of ice.

'Nothing's going to happen that quickly,' said Laura through pursed lips.

'What's happening with Bocks?' Bonnie's throat narrowed and the words squeaked a little. She coughed.

Alice closed the lid of the laptop. 'We're hopeful we'll get planning permission on the land. If we do, we'll either sell it or find a way to build on it. I'm sorry about what that will mean for your job, but I'm sure you'll agree, it's unfortunate but unavoidable.'

'Oh.' Bonnie felt the chill creep under her skin. 'Congratulations.'

'It's not a done deal,' said Laura.

'Yet,' said Alice.

'Since you're here' – Laura's voice sounded artificially

buoyant – 'would you have a look at a portrait of Dad I'm painting? He's just gone out to play golf, so I can do some work on the bits I'm struggling with. I'm not sure I've got the light right.'

Bonnie blinked quickly, trying to break her way back out of the brain freeze in her head. 'Yes, of course.' She stood too quickly and the chair toppled backwards. Jim reached out to catch it.

'Steady.'

'Sorry.' She put a hand on his warm arm. 'It's good to see you looking so well,' she managed to say, before making her feet follow Laura from the room.

The staircase curved gently and halfway up Bonnie found herself mesmerised by the huge chandelier, which dropped from the landing ceiling into the hall.

'Bit much, isn't it?' said Laura, following Bonnie's eyes. 'Mum's pride and joy.' She gave a short laugh Bonnie couldn't interpret and carried on upstairs.

Laura's room was like stepping into a different world. It was vast. An enormous bookcase, painted with a black-and-white cow print, filled the wall to the right. There was a circular rug in the middle of the floor, which gave the impression of disappearing into the ground, and a king-size bed that seemed to glow, surrounded by phosphorescent pink light. On the left, next to a tall sash window, stood an easel on a green plastic mat and a grey, paint-spattered trolley, which seemed out of place in this funky setting.

'This is' – Bonnie searched for the right word – 'fun.' What she meant was that it looked like a teenager's dream bedroom, but Laura was twenty-five, and she didn't want to give the impression she was judging her.

'I know, right?' Laura flopped onto the bed. 'That's

what happens when you come back home after university to your childhood bedroom.'

Bonnie laughed. 'So this isn't your current taste?'

'Don't get me wrong, who doesn't want neon LED lights around their bed?' Laura picked up a tiny remote control and pressed a button. The lights turned purple then blue.

'Whoa.'

'It's a trip, isn't it?'

'But I would've done something a bit different with it if I'd know I was staying this long.'

'I don't believe you,' Bonnie said.

'Rumbled.' Laura laughed, bouncing up from the bed and over to the easel. 'Have a look at this.' She bit her lip and Bonnie could see she was nervous.

The portrait was a good likeness of Richard, but the lines around his mouth and across his forehead were obviously painted. There wasn't enough tonal difference where the light from the window shone on his face.

'What do you think?'

'It's lovely. It looks like him, which is impressive. Likeness is so hard to catch.' She pointed at the forehead. 'I'd work on this area. Remember wrinkles are narrow shadows and there're gradients of shade, like everywhere else, so rather than seeing them in lines, see them in shapes, shade, and depth.'

'Can you show me?'

Laura's face was earnest as she offered the palate from the trolly to Bonnie and watched her squeeze small blobs from the tubes of acrylics onto the wooden board and mix them with a thin brush.

'Shall I use some paper to show you what I mean?'

'I'm happy for you to do it on the canvas, if that's okay

with you? If you do his forehead, I'll do the rest while you watch and tell me where I'm going wrong.'

The room fell into soft focus for Bonnie, like a dream where she and Laura were in their own private world. She showed Laura how to apply the paint deftly, how to mix the shades to get exactly the right light, how to give a cheeky glint to Richard's eye, which made it look even more like the man she'd met, whom she liked enormously, she realised.

They talked about their favourite artists while they worked, Bonnie rhapsodising about Lucien Freud and his tangible way of painting flesh, like meat on a carcass, but rich and sensuous at the same time. Laura knew a surprising amount of gossip about Freud and his relationships with his models and fellow artists, and Bonnie listened with delight as she shared snippets of the lives of Freud, Francis Bacon, and Leigh Bowery.

When Alice's clipped voice came from the doorway, it was as though the television channel had been switched from the midst of a perfect romance to the ten o'clock news. Bonnie wished she could click her heels and make a house fall on the other woman's head.

'What are you two up to? You've been a long time. I thought you came to see our patient, Bonnie?'

Bonnie wiped her hands on her linen trousers, then wished she hadn't because white paint now smeared the navy-blue material. 'Sorry, yes, we got caught up in a bit of an art lesson.'

'Oh, Laura.' Alice marched into the room. 'I thought that was *your* present to *your* dad. It won't be the same if you've let someone else tamper with it.'

Bonnie stepped back from the easel, her stomach a tight ball. 'Tamper?'

'You know what I mean.' Alice dismissed her, and she felt the ball in her stomach twist.

'No, I don't.'

Alice ignored her and addressed Laura. 'It's meant to be a special present from you.'

Laura's face contorted. 'Bonnie was helping me because I asked her to. She's only shown me how to do the wrinkles. I think you should apologise.'

Alice's nostrils flared. 'Apologise?'

Bonnie shook her head. 'I think it's time I went home.' She picked up her bag from the end of the bed.

'Don't feel you have to, Bonnie.' Laura's voice was hard. 'Mum, for goodness' sake!'

'I'll make my own way out.' Bonnie rushed from the room, down the stairs, and across the hall. She heard raised voices in Laura's bedroom and glanced up the stairs, but no one came out of the room. She shoved her feet into her sandals and opened the front door, heart pummelling her ribcage. The silver frames on the hall table glinted as though winking at her in the sunlight streaming through the open door. An overwhelming compulsion forced her arm out and her fingers to close around the cold silver of a frame with a picture of Laura as a toddler, holding an ice cream and smiling into the camera. She shoved the frame into her bag, then slammed the door behind her.

Chapter Thirty-Six

Bonnie

Present Day

Bonnie drove towards the centre of Hamblin, gripping the steering wheel until her fingers ached, her breath shuddering as she vacillated between tearfulness and fury. She didn't want to go straight home. The gaping emptiness of the flat terrified her. She surprised herself by indicating and turning into the multistorey car park, suddenly deciding she needed to be anonymous in a group of strangers, to wander and try to get her thoughts in order.

Eventually finding a parking space, she pulled the sun visor down and looked in the mirror, wiping the smudged mascara from under her eyes with a shaking finger. She looked at her face; sad green eyes surrounded by thinning skin, the eyelids puffy, blonde strands of fringe falling across the eyebrows she'd carefully shaded before going to Laura's house.

Where had the carefree girl she used to be gone? The one with a mischievous giggle who used to sketch her boyfriend with just a sheet across his groin after they'd made love? The girl who'd seen her future spread out like the most beautiful fabric, ready to be cut into any shape she imagined. She'd found herself, briefly, during the first few years with Stuart, before the anxiety crept in with the sleepless, sweaty nights and brought back all the memories and the ugly habits she thought she'd learned to control. She missed Stuart so much in that moment that it took her breath away. How could she have allowed herself to believe this charade was more important than him? She was a deluded, cruel fool.

As she climbed from the car, the frame in her bag banged against her leg. She opened the boot and gently removed the photo, averting her eyes as she lay it on the rough material of the interior, closing the boot, and plunging that pretty toddler's face into darkness. Trying to cancel out the vision of Laura, tiny and scared in the dark, she clicked the key fob, heard the car lock thunk. She walked briskly away, the sound of her sandals hitting the ground echoing around the empty space.

Tension balled her fists and shortened the muscles in her shoulders, dragging them towards her rigid neck. She trotted down the urine-stinking car park steps instead of taking the lift, almost daring someone to confront her on the gloomy stairwell. When she pushed the door open to the shopping centre, the brightness was assaulting, like stepping into Disneyland from a gulag.

The cheerful major chords spurting from the wall speakers tried and failed to lift her along with bouncy rhythms. Families walked too slowly, small children holding hands with parents who seemed heartlessly oblivious to the touch of those small fingers in theirs.

She rushed through the crowds, past Boots and the

Apple Store. She knew where she was heading now. She walked with purpose, dipping in and out of the obstructive shoppers, tutting at their lazy, pointless ambling. The automatic door swished open and the mid-August air stuck her hair to the back of her neck, muggy after the air-conditioned mall. Turning left, she waited impatiently at the pedestrian crossing as a double-decker bus rumbled by, then, as soon as the signal changed the red figure to green, she crossed the road and sped on.

Stepping through the door of Hobbycraft, anxiety fuelled her. Her short fingernails cut into her palms and she walked the aisles of the enormous art supplies shop without settling into her usual routine of mentally ticking off what she needed when searching for a specific graphite pencil or size of canvas.

She marched down the central row, passing baskets of cards for sale and multicoloured balls of wool tossed together in a jumbled rainbow, arriving at the back wall where huge trays held brightly coloured card. She turned around and walked along the side wall, passing children's supplies of fat felt tips, tubes of sparkles, and tubs of white glue.

A woman in a burgundy apron stacked boxes of masks in the shape of animal heads on a low shelf and smiled as Bonnie passed. She forced herself to slow down and focus. The image of mixing acrylics on the palette with Laura watching in admiration spurred her over to the paints.

She knew the feeling as soon as the compulsion took hold. The tightness in her jaw, the burning in her stomach, the impulse so strong there was nothing she could do to stop it. She didn't look around her to see if anyone was watching because it wouldn't have prevented her reaching out for the small metal tubes, collecting four in the palm of her hand, and moving them swiftly into the open lip of her bag.

As soon as the bag was tucked closely under her arm, she moved towards the front of the shop and the tension flowed from her. She was able to breathe into the bottom of her lungs again for the first time since Alice had walked into Laura's bedroom. She kept walking, the grey suede of the bag caressing the underside of her bare arm, out of Hobbycraft and back through the shopping centre, this time taking the lift to the third floor of the car park, where she dropped into the seat of her car with a groan.

Then the shame hit her like a fist.

* * *

She drove home on autopilot. When she arrived, it seemed the flat was twice the size it was when she'd left it. The white spaces on the walls between her paintings spread like snowdrifts. If she leaned against them, she would disappear, sink into the icy water and freeze.

The bag sat next to her on the sofa where she'd dropped it, suddenly exhausted. She stared at it, half expecting it to glow, or throb, or, better still, explode, taking its incriminating innards, and her, with it.

Minutes passed, then, suddenly, she had to see what she'd done. Tipping the bag onto the sofa, its contents cascaded onto the cushion and dropped to the floor. In the middle of the tissues, lipstick, and keys, squatted four tapered metal tubes, white except for a ring of midnight blue around the ends.

She grabbed a small canvas from her collection balanced against the wall in the spare room and the largest brush she owned. Laying the canvas on the sofa cushion, she opened the first tube and squeezed its almost black mess onto the canvas, then did the same with the next three, the smell of the paint so familiar it brought tears to her eyes.

Her vision blurred as she daubed the paint across the canvas, smearing darkness into every corner, not caring if her brush slipped and dirty scrapes appeared on the sofa. Her brushstrokes became faster, more frenetic until she was smashing at the canvas, the brush no longer a paint-brush but a weapon. She turned the brush upside down, the slippery paint sticky in her hand, as she speared the canvas with the sharp end of the brush, piercing and slitting the material until there was nothing left but a dark, dripping frame.

Chapter Thirty-Seven

Alice

Present Day

Alice rolled out the architectural drawings on the reception desk at Bocks, carefully straightening the precious sheets, then popping clean mugs from the kitchen on either side to keep them flat.

'Since it's looking so promising, come and look at what we're hoping to do.'

Polly and Jim dutifully gathered behind her.

Alice's insides had recently started to fizz with hope, and it was building every day. She still got a lump in her throat when she looked at the banking app, but now she could counter-balance it with clicking through to the planning application progress and seeing that there was only one objection. Her heart had plummeted when she'd first seen it, until she noted it was a fairly generic moan about the town's overdevelopment. Non-specific complaints weren't threatening, the architect reassured her when she rang. It was almost worth receiving his invoice for the call.

Laura sat behind the desk, tapping on the computer keyboard, stopping every so often to scratch an insect bite on her arm. It seemed to Alice she was purposely ignoring her demonstration of the building plans, which now seemed so tantalisingly close to becoming a reality. It wasn't fair because she'd waited a long time for this and should be allowed to be excited. The strain of the last few years was like a tight band around her life. Now the tie was loosening, and it felt good.

'I think it's easier to explain them like this, rather than on a screen,' she said, glancing at Jim and Polly who were dutifully focused on the complicated lines and numbers in front of them.

She pointed to the biggest block. 'This is where we are now. We plan to keep the original building and turn it into self-contained units. I think that's where we went wrong last time. The council didn't like the idea of this old red brick building being razed to the ground.'

'What's this?' Jim poked a thick finger at a smaller block to the right.

'That's the bigger of the four houses. That one will be detached, do you see?' She tapped the paper. 'Then this block here is three, two-bedroom townhouses in a cute little terrace.'

Polly raised her head and looked around the reception. 'It's weird to think this will all change.'

'It will make a lovely atrium for the flats though, don't you think? With a nice carpet and some pictures on the walls. If you decided your house was too big, Jim, there's a spacious one-bedroom flat' – she rested a manicured nail on the drawing – 'just here.'

Jim stroked his moustache, shifting from one foot to the other.

'Do you think you'd like a flat?' Alice could see Jim pottering around the communal garden, doing all the handiwork for the residents.

'That might be a bit fancy for me. Anyway, I've been talking to my sister . . . Y'know, our Gillian, who you talked to when I had the pneumonia?'

Alice nodded, remembering the concern in the woman's voice and how grateful she'd been that Alice was taking care of Jim.

'She's keen for me to go back home. She could do with the help, what with her husband being poorly, and that. And since my Lou's not here, and she were a Hamblin lass, I was thinking I might go back up north. I'll be able to buy a palace up there when I sell my house.'

Alice put her arm around him and squeezed. 'You deserve a palace. I can't pretend I won't miss you, and I'm sorry my grand plans for an onsite caretaker won't come off, but moving near your sister and nieces sounds like a good idea. As long as you promise to come back and visit.'

Jim gave her an awkward pat on the waist, and she let her arm drop from his shoulders.

'I might take that flat then,' said Laura, still looking at the screen.

'I'm not sure students can afford brand-new flats,' said Alice curtly. Laura needed to remember why they were doing this. Would it kill her to be more supportive?

The flare of irritation was extinguished when she reminded herself exactly how supportive Laura had already been over the last three years.

Laura tutted then looked up as the door buzzed open, letting in the warm air along with Bonnie in an emerald green shift dress with white stitching on oversized pockets.

'Hello, you!' Laura said.

Alice watched as Laura, Polly, and Jim all greeted Bonnie like a long-lost friend. She had darker make-up around her eyes than usual and, despite some obvious bronzer on her cheeks, she looked pale.

'I love that dress. The colour is gorgeous on you.' Alice was hurt to hear that Laura's voice had its bounce back. She was always effusive about Bonnie's clothes, as though she were Naomi Campbell or someone.

'Thanks.' Bonnie's voice was quiet in the large room, like a small child in the head teacher's office.

Alice rolled the papers and eased them back into the cardboard cylinder, clicking the plastic lid in place. 'Are you off now Bonnie's here?' she asked Laura.

'Yep.' Laura gave a final tap on the keyboard. 'Polly and I are being ladies who lunch, aren't we, Poll?'

'We certainly are. Then we might pop and see our boyfriends.' Polly swished her hair over her shoulder and pouted.

Jim laughed. 'Young 'uns today. They don't know they're born. There was no lunching when I were your age. Closest we came were a picnic in the park, won't it?'

He turned to Alice for solidarity, and she prickled at being lumped in with Jim's age group. He was twelve years older than her, and she'd had plenty of girly lunches of her own, thank you very much. In fact, that was something she could look forward to again if the plans came off. She crossed her fingers under the cylinder.

'I'd better start having a sort out if I'm going to try to sell my place,' said Jim.

'Let me know if you need any help, or a bit of moral support.' Alice imagined how hard it would be for him to sift through his wife's things. Every scarf and trinket would have a memory attached.

'Aye, will do. Thanks.' Jim's face wrinkled in a smile. He raised his hand to wave and wandered out into the sunshine.

'Is it warm out there?' asked Laura. 'It was a bit chilly when I came in this morning, but it looks glorious now.'

'It's beautiful,' said Bonnie, her voice still lacking its usual energy.

'I won't need my jacket then.' Laura stretched her arms above her head, then jumped to her feet. 'Come on, Poll. Let's do this thing.'

When the young women had left and Bonnie was behind the desk, Alice decided to sort out one of the units that had been abandoned.

'I'll be in number forty-seven if you need me. The swine hasn't paid for two years; I can't get hold of them, and I've given up hope of them ever coming back for their things so I need to work out if any of it's worth anything. Now the end is in sight for this place, it's time to get things in order.'

* * *

After an hour of boxing up files, all of which dated from at least eight years ago, Alice's back ached and she was ready for a break.

When she pushed open the door to reception, she was surprised to find the desk empty. She lifted the hatch carefully and saw the screen was still bright, as though someone had only just popped out. Her fingers were on the handle of the staffroom door when the door to the corridors that led to the storage units opened and Bonnie walked through, green dress clashing with the blood-red paint.

Her cheeks flamed when she saw Alice. 'Sorry, I was just . . .' She paused, and Alice waited. 'I was helping someone who'd lost their key.'

'Really, who?'

'I didn't get his name.'

Alice didn't believe her. Why would she look so flustered if she was just doing her job? She opened her mouth to probe further but thought better of it. Soon Bocks would be a distant memory, and this woman would be too. It wasn't worth listening to her excuses. She nodded and turned the handle, walking into the staffroom and closing the door firmly behind her.

* * *

She was dragged from the final chapter of the book she was reading by the ding of a message from Laura on her phone.

Going straight to X's after lunch. If ur still at work pls can you grab my jacket from back of sr door and take it home. Ty xxx

Alice tilted her head to look at the back of the staffroom door. The metal hook was empty. She sighed and typed.

Jacket not here. Xx

A minute later, her phone dinged again.

Must be. I had it this morning. On back of reception chair? Xx

Putting the floral bookmark Laura had bought for her inside the book and snapping it shut, Alice heaved herself from the seat and walked out through the door to reception. Bonnie was sitting in the chair facing the screen, her blonde hair, darker at the roots, just visible, but there was no jacket hanging over the back of the chair.

Alice searched her memory. She had definitely seen Laura take the denim jacket off and hang it on the hook on the back of the staffroom door this morning. She remembered because she'd noticed the insect bite on Laura's bare arm as she removed it and they'd talked about how much they hated mosquitos, reminiscing about a holiday in Italy when they'd both been covered in lumpy bites.

She also remembered Laura saying she was leaving her coat when she went for lunch because the weather had warmed up.

Bonnie raised her head from the screen as Alice lifted the hatch and stepped through. She walked around to the front of the desk so she could see her face as she spoke. 'Laura asked me to bring her coat home, but I can't find it. Have you seen it?'

She noted the pink return to Bonnie's cheeks when she said, 'I haven't, sorry.'

'She said she left it on the hook behind the door.'

Bonnie seemed to focus intently on the computer screen. 'Did she?'

'And I remember seeing her put it there and leaving for lunch without it.'

Bonnie tucked a strand of fringe behind her ear, then blew upwards to shift it when it fell back over her eye. Alice rested her elbows on the desk and leaned forwards, not moving when Bonnie glanced up then flicked her eyes away. She was hiding something.

'It's not the only thing to have gone missing recently.'

Bonnie's larynx raised and lowered. Her top lip shone with sweat. If she were innocent, surely she'd be defensive by now?

Bonnie turned to her. 'Do you want to look in my bag?' Her face had drained of colour, leaving two vivid pink blotches below her cheekbones.

Alice's voice shook as she replied, 'Yes, please.'

Bonnie leaned under the desk and brought out a grey suede slouchy bag, unzipped it, and opened it wide for Alice to look inside. No jacket.

'Thank you.' Alice felt her own colour rise and was about to make a meek apology when she remembered Bonnie emerging from the direction of the lock-up units.

'You have a unit here, don't you?'

Bonnie looked up, the pupils tiny in her suddenly frightened green eyes.

'Would you mind if I looked in your unit?'

Bonnie stood, wiping the sweat from her top lip with her hand. 'What? I would mind, actually. You have no right to go through my things.'

Alice towered over the tiny woman and spoke slowly. 'I have reason to believe you have taken things that belong to members of my family, so, I'll ask one more time, can I please see inside your unit?'

'And if I say no?'

Alice slammed the desk open and marched to where they kept the spare keys. She lifted a key from its hook. 'Number 202, right?'

Bonnie's voice was shrill. 'You can't just go into my unit. That's my private property.' She followed at Alice's heels like a snappy terrier as she charged through the red door and along the white corridors until they were standing in front of the door to unit 202.

Alice lifted the padlock and tried to insert the key. Bonnie grabbed for it, but Alice snatched it back, shoved it into the lock and turned it. As the padlock came away in her hand she was surprised to see that Bonnie was crying, but she looked away from her imploring face, pushed the door wide, and switched on the light.

She couldn't make sense of what she saw.

There, neatly lined up at the back of the space against the wall, were items she recognised. They seemed so out of place in this tiny room. Moving away from Bonnie's quiet sobs, she stepped the short distance to the wall and stood over a hairbrush, her punch glass, a packet of pastels, and Laura's mug. Then, she saw a picture of Laura as a toddler in a silver frame, which she hadn't even realised was missing from her hall table, and beside it was the faded denim jacket her daughter wore almost every day.

Face frozen in shock, she turned to Bonnie, who peeled her fingers away from her tear-stained face and said, 'I can explain.'

Chapter Thirty-Eight

Bonnie

Twenty-Five Years Ago

Bonnie woke, her mouth wide in a silent scream. She blinked, trying to recognise where she was. Then the reality of being in the narrow single bed in her childhood bedroom solidified the horror of the nightmare.

She'd dreamt she was lying next to Cahil in the hold of a plane, his body rigid with rigor mortis. She was naked and shivering as they flew back to Turkey for his burial. She didn't know why it was always that image in her dreams. Maybe it was because she hadn't wanted to burden his family with the news of their relationship after what she'd done, so she hadn't even said goodbye before they took his broken body home.

She'd stayed away from graduation, sure their mutual friends must all hate her for getting him so drunk he fell in front of that van. She hadn't opened any of the letters or cards they'd sent, asking her mum to put them straight in the bin.

She hadn't worn make-up since the night Cahil died; it would've been pointless to put mascara on her blonde eyelashes when she often found she was crying without even feeling the tears form. She didn't really feel anything anymore, which is why she was surprised to notice her heart beat more quickly and her fingers tingle when she was walking aimlessly through the aisles at the chemist on the high street, trying to fill her empty days.

Stepping more slowly through the make-up section, she appraised the spangly packages, the tiny boxes, and sparkling palettes all lined in neat rows, the first of each product rolling forwards in the plastic dispensers, asking to be taken out and held.

Her mouth suddenly dry, she could hear the sound of the cashier talking to a customer, the crackle of a plastic bag being shaken open as though it were happening next to her ear. Her heart drummed in her chest as the compulsion to look around her to make sure she was unobserved, to put out her hand and feel the hard plastic of the mascara, then lift it from the tiered stack and cup it in her palm, was irresistible. Sweat stung under her arms as she slipped it into her pocket, then walked further along the aisle, picking up an eyeshadow without even checking the colour and a thin tube of lip gloss, pocketing both while her pulse raced.

As the automatic door opened onto the street, cold air whooshed on her face. Then she felt a hand on her shoulder, almost stopping her pounding heart.

'Would you come with me, so I can look in your pockets, please?'

The woman whose hand gripped her shoulder was stocky, with a broad, blank face. Her eyelids drooped over tired, bloodshot eyes, and she looked more disappointed than angry.

'I'm sorry, what?' Bonnie's voice was weak and unconvincing. Her knees buckled, and she staggered then steadied herself, all the while feeling the weight of the woman's hand.

'Please come with me to the manager's office so I can look in your pockets. I believe you've taken items from the store without paying.' The words came out bluntly, like she was reading a script.

Bonnie didn't argue. The numbness returned. She still felt numb when her mum came to pick her up and they both stood and nodded, eyes downcast as the store manager straightened the lapels on his nylon suit and lectured them on his leniency in not calling the police . . . this time.

* * *

She didn't feel anything in the car on the way home as her mother railed about the shame and how hard it had been for her to bring a child up alone for the last fourteen years. The one thing that made it worthwhile was knowing Bonnie had turned out well and now this episode had shattered even that small consolation.

'You've let me down,' her mother said. 'And you've let yourself down. What do you think Cahil would say if he could see you now?'

* * *

Later that day those words replayed on a loop in her head as she lay in the bath, a bottle of gin balanced next to her arm, the green glass reflecting on the pink enamel, already half empty. What would Cahil say? He'd hate her, she decided. She hated herself. She picked the bottle up again and swigged, the liquid so strong its fumes burned

289

the inside of her nose. The white and pink patterned tiles she used to imagine she saw faces and figures in when she was little began to dance, their shapes distorting. She looked for the lady in the Edwardian dress she used to be able to make out in the tile by the taps, but it now looked like a roaring lion with a shaggy mane, sharp teeth bared.

She shivered and turned on the hot tap, the water sploshing onto her toes. She took another drink and lay her head back, feeling the burn as the water became too hot, scorching the skin on her feet, then her thighs, the pain satisfying even as it became unbearable.

Turning back to the gin she saw there was only a dribble left in the bottom. She squinted through the green of the bottle, watching the ancient bathroom cabinet curve through the glass, the mess of her mother's make-up bag on top made sludgy and murky.

Something else caught her eye and unease crept slowly up her spine. She shifted her head to look around the bottle to where the brown cabinet door gaped, stared at the unopened blue and white box of Tampax sitting on the top shelf. Making an ungainly effort to lift herself from the searing water, she tried to calculate when she'd last had her period, counting on her fingers. In her grief, she'd completely lost track of time, but she knew it was before her finals, before Cahil was hit by the van . . . *Shit,* at least four months ago.

The water was suddenly far too hot; she leaped up, knocking the bottle onto the tiled floor. The last thing she heard was the glass shattering as her head spun. There was a white pain then everything went dark.

* * *

Her eyelids stuck together, and her throat stung as she rose from the depths of what felt like a new nightmare. She tried to swallow, but there was sandpaper at the back of her mouth. Her tongue seemed twice the size, hugging the roof of her dry mouth. When she managed to focus, she saw a ceiling made up of polystyrene squares with a rail attached in a rectangle above her. Pale blue curtains hung from the rail and they were drawn around the bed she was lying on. Rough white sheets and a blue blanket weighed down on her. Everything hurt.

'Oh, sweetheart.'

She turned her head and her brain banged drums in her temples. Her mother was sitting next to the bed in a straight-backed chair, her head shaking from side to side very slowly, her face pale. Her cheeks were wet. 'Why didn't you tell me?'

There was a throbbing in her stomach and the image of the blue and white box tore into the back of her eyes. The horror of what she'd done jammed itself down her throat, pulling the breath from her in short gasps.

'Did you drink all that to . . .? Did you mean to . . .?'

'No.' Her voice was a hoarse whisper. 'I didn't know. I'm sorry.'

She was speaking to her mother, to Cahil, and to the new life she now realised was inside her. Oh god. Had she destroyed that too?

Chapter Thirty-Nine

Bonnie

Twenty-Five Years Ago

As the police car stopped on the pavement outside the row of terraced houses, Bonnie saw the neighbour's curtains twitching as she looked out through the car's steamed-up window. The driver's door slammed, making her jump, and the young police officer came around to her side and opened the door, offering her his hand. She shook her head, hefting herself off the back seat and onto the pavement. Her cheeks burned as he watched her turn her key in the lock.

'Keep out of trouble now, you. That little one needs its mum home and safe.' He pointed at her bulging stomach, stretching the fabric of her T-shirt, no longer disguisable, however baggy her joggers and sweatshirts.

They'd been kind at the police station, all acting as though she was stealing because she might not have enough money to take good care of the baby. But what would a newborn do with Nirvana's *In Utero* CD? The desk sergeant had cocked an eyebrow when he saw what she'd stolen, looking at her swollen stomach and smiling wryly.

'I've got to give you a caution because old man Hatton, who owns that shop, is a councillor and he'll have my guts if I let you off,' he said, but he only gave her a short lecture before the young officer was told to bring her home.

She dropped her coat on the banister in the hallway and made herself go through to the front room. Her mum was sitting on the brown velour sofa, knees tight together, hands wringing in her lap. She must've seen the police car because she was crying. Bonnie's heart contracted at the sight of her winding hands in the fading light of the winter afternoon.

'Shall I put the light on?'

'No. I don't want anyone looking in.'

'I could shut the curtains.'

'You can't close the curtains at this time. What would people think?'

Bonnie didn't like to imagine what people were thinking right now. She was twenty-two, single, pregnant, and had been brought home by the police. The curtains were the least of their worries.

She sat in the armchair nearest the door and the baby started to kick. It was as though it couldn't bear her sitting still, pointy elbows and heels demanding her attention if she ever tried to rest.

'What was it this time?'

'A CD.'

A sob escaped her mother's mouth and Bonnie envied her. She hadn't been able to cry for months. It was as though she were stuck in a nightmare, like the ones where she was chased down a dark alley and the person caught her, and she tried and tried to scream, but her voice vanished and she had to endure whatever was coming. That was her waking life now, only it was her ability to cry that had left when she needed it.

'We need to talk about that.' Her mother nodded at her stomach, the mound of it sitting higher than the arm of the chair.

'Not now, Mum.'

Her mother snarled. 'Yes. Now. It wouldn't even be here if I hadn't got you to hospital and had your stomach pumped. We've no idea what damage you've done to that poor thing. You should have had an abortion while you still could. I should have insisted, but you wouldn't listen, would you? You said you'd be alright, but you're not, are you? Not with all this business—'

She gasped, winded by the cruelty. 'You think I don't think about how I might have harmed this baby every minute of every day? You think I don't know that I was responsible for what happened to Cahil and I might have damaged his baby as well? The least I can do is give it a chance at life. That's the very least I can do.'

'How would I know what you're thinking?' She ran a hand through her thin, bleached hair. 'You're off galli-vanting around town, shoplifting, being dragged home by the bloody police. How would I know what's going on in that head of yours?' Her voice softened, and she shook her head sharply. 'But it's not fair to put that on a little baby.'

She pushed the nap of the velvet sofa one way then another, then scraped a line across the fabric with her nail. 'I know how hard it can be, bringing a kid up on your own. I thought you were going to have a different life.'

'I didn't want any of this.' Bonnie lay her head back

on the fat cushion and concentrated on the kicking in her abdomen, like the baby was knocking to be let out.

'You can start again, if you're brave enough to do what's sensible.'

Inside her head, Bonnie wailed, but no sound came. She counted her breaths in and out. When she got to five, she said, 'You think it's brave to give this baby up for adoption? Do you wish you'd given me away? Is that what you're saying?'

Her mother closed her eyes and rubbed her forehead. 'You know I'm not. But your dad was here until you were eight. We were married and I didn't know he was going to get bored and bugger off, did I? You do know Cahil's not coming back. I'm sorry, love, but that's a fact.' She tutted. 'We don't even know if he'd have wanted it if he was alive. He might've stayed in bloody Turkey.'

The baby kicked and Bonnie put her palms over her stomach, shielding it from the words. 'Don't ever say that again. You didn't know him.' They sat in silence, her mother's restless fingers dancing out of place in the stultifying air.

'This is all I've got left of him.' Bonnie's voice was strangled, squeezed by all the backed-up tears. She rubbed her hand over her stomach, her palm feeling the skin stretching and moving with her baby.

'So, it's better for it to be born to a thief, is it? To a thief and a dead dad. Who do you think's going to look after it when you're locked up because of your sticky bloody fingers? Not me, I'm telling you that. I've worked my fingers to the bone so you could go and get that fancy degree, and this is what I get in return? You have a choice, my lady. Let that baby go to a home where it will be looked after and loved. You can start again, use your education and make something of yourself.' She paused.

'Or?'

'Or find somewhere else to live.' Her voice was quiet. 'I won't do it again. It's too hard, and I know you'd end up relying on me because you've not been right since that poor lad died.' She looked across at Bonnie, tears streaming down her cheeks. 'They're crying out for babies to be adopted these days. Now girls can get abortions, there're hardly any tiny babies going to couples who are desperate.'

The streetlight came on and shed an orange light across her mother's wet face. 'You're so young. This isn't your only chance to have a family. You could give someone everything they've ever wanted and still have children when the time's right; when you've had a chance to get yourself straight and met someone who'll stick by you.'

'Cahil would've stuck by me.'

'Well, he's not here, is he?'

The room darkened, like it was filling with choking smoke, her mother fading away, her features melting into the dark apart from the orange glow, like the fires of hell, illuminating her profile.

'You honestly think I should give my baby away?'

'I do. Let it go to a good home. Then get on with your life.'

At that moment, Bonnie wished the orange glow really was a fire and that it would burn her mother to cinders for trying to persuade her to do something she knew she'd regret to the end of her days.

Chapter Forty

Alice

Present Day

'But you don't look anything like Laura. You've made a mistake.' Alice's voice trembled. She'd listened to what Bonnie said as the two women sat opposite each other on the concrete floor of Bonnie's unit, but it didn't make any sense. 'You're tiny and fair. Laura's so dark.'

'I know; she takes after her father.' She glanced up and corrected herself. 'Her biological father. He was Turkish. That's where she gets her dark eyes and lovely olive skin tone.'

How dare this woman talk about Alice's daughter's lovely skin? She knew exactly how lovely it was, since she was the one who had rubbed suntan lotion onto it every summer, kissed its cuts and bruises better when she was a tiny, helpless little girl. *Her* little girl.

'I don't believe you.'

'You don't have to believe me for it to be true.' There was a note of defiance in Bonnie's voice that made Alice shiver despite the stifling heat of the room. 'You kept Alexandra as her middle name.'

Alice put her hands on the floor, suddenly dizzy. 'That's why you bought her that bracelet? Were you leaving little clues for her to piece together?'

'No. At least, not intentionally. Does she even know she's adopted?'

'Of course she does. She's not an idiot. Even if we hadn't told her, she would've worked it out as soon as she studied biology. Two light-skinned, blue and grey eyed people don't generally make a girl who looks like Laura.'

Bonnie nodded. 'It's just, she never mentioned it.'

'Why would she?' Sweat dripped down her back. 'She's perfectly happy. She hasn't been pining for you, if that's what you're hoping.' She heard the metal in her voice, could almost taste it. 'She doesn't feel like there's a piece of her missing, like those poor creatures on *Long Lost Family*. You turning up hasn't suddenly made her life complete.'

'Good. I'm glad.'

There was a sincerity in her voice that made Alice stall. 'What do you want?'

'I don't want anything.'

Alice snorted. 'Well, that's a lie, even if the rest is true. You targeted us, inveigled your way into our business, our family. You've had an agenda from the second you came here. At least have the honesty to tell me what all this lying' – she gestured to the things lined up against the wall – 'and stealing is meant to achieve.'

Bonnie dipped her head to her knees and Alice saw her hair was sticking to the back of her neck. Her voice came out muffled. 'I don't know. That's the truth.'

The air was hot and thick. She had to open her mouth

wide to breathe at all. 'Do you want her to know who you are? Is that your next move?'

'I just wanted to make sure she was all right.'

Again, Alice heard herself laugh. 'If that were true, you'd have met her once, seen she was absolutely fine – more than fine – and scurried back to bloody Scotland with that box ticked. But you didn't, did you? So, don't pretend this was all a selfless act, that you just wanted to see the baby you gave away went to a good home.' She shifted her buttocks on the concrete. When had she last sat on the floor? Probably not since Laura was a toddler, insisting she joined in one of her sweet little games.

'She wanted for nothing.'

'I know.'

'We loved her from the minute she was put in my arms.'

'I know.'

Alice's head throbbed. She badly needed a drink. 'Then why are you still here?'

Bonnie rubbed her arms, then wiped her fringe from where it stuck to the sweat on her forehead, her gaze fixed on the photo of Laura as a toddler. 'I suppose I thought I could be a part of her life, without her knowing who I was.' She shifted her eyes to Alice. 'I didn't want to step on your toes. I know you don't believe me, but when I came here, I only wanted to get to know her, to make sure she was happy.'

'She is happy.'

'I can see that.'

Alice took a shuddering breath. 'Which is why you should leave.'

Bonnie gasped. 'But—'

'No.' Alice pointed her finger, sure of what needed to happen now. 'If you truly came here to make sure she was happy, then you have to leave now. I don't want Richard knowing about this. His health is fragile, and he doesn't need this kind of stress. We are on the brink of being in the position to allow Laura to follow her dreams, and she's happy with Xavier. This is not the time to expose yourself as some long-lost guardian and destabilise that girl. She's happy. That's what you wanted. Go home.'

Alice levered herself to standing and found her legs were shaking. Her trousers stuck to the back of her knees and she pulled the damp fabric free before stepping to the back of the unit and picking up all the things that belonged to her and Laura. 'If you leave, I won't go to the police about you stealing from us.'

The breath seemed to leave Bonnie's mouth like the air from a balloon. 'Really? You're going to hold that over me?'

She looked down, hardening herself against Bonnie's tears. 'If you can't do it for Laura, then you'll have to leave for your own sake.'

'Do you honestly think Laura would be better off without me here?'

Alice closed her eyes but couldn't stop the images of Laura laughing at something Bonnie had said or admiring one of her daring outfits playing across her vision. 'I think we all would.'

Bonnie dropped her hands to the floor. 'Okay, you win.'

Pity rose in Alice, but she bit it back. 'It's not about winning, it's about doing what's best for Laura. You may be part of her past, but we are her future, and that future is looking brighter than it has for a long time. Don't sully it by dragging up everything that led to her being here. It's not relevant. It would cause unnecessary pain.'

'Okay.'

302

'Thank you,' said Alice, putting Laura's jacket over her forearm and resisting the urge to lift it to her nose and breathe in the scent of her daughter. 'I hope I won't have to make that call.' She straightened her back and crossed into the white corridor, ignoring the quiet sobbing, which seemed to grow louder the further away she walked.

Chapter Forty-One

Alice

Present Day

Alice poured herself a large glass of white wine and sank into a dining chair. The back of her blouse was still damp with sweat as she lay her arms on the cool marble, absorbing the chill of the stone. Through the window she noticed the garden was drying to brown scrub and made a mental note to put the sprinkler on the lawn when she had the energy. For now, she was drained. She couldn't imagine ever wanting to get out of the chair again.

The sound of the front door opening and closing made her jump. Seconds later, Richard walked into the kitchen.

'Hello, I wasn't expecting you to be home,' he said, then paused, studying her. 'Wine. At this time?' He looked at his watch. 'It's only half-past three.'

'I fancied a drink.'

'Clearly. Are we celebrating something?' His forehead furrowed. 'Or commiserating?'

She dredged a smile up from somewhere deep inside. 'No, I'm just mixing it up a bit.'

Richard came closer, and she turned her head. 'The garden's getting dry.'

'It's hot today. That's why I came home from golf early, felt a bit dizzy on the ninth hole. Might have a touch of heatstroke or something.' He wrinkled his nose. 'Not feeling a hundred per cent.'

This would usually have Alice on her feet, checking his pulse, asking a million questions, but she was too tired. He was a big boy; he could tell if he was ill. She was just too tired.

'You found the glass,' he said, and she followed his eyes to the island where she'd put Bonnie's haul. 'Where was it?'

'Hm?'

'Where did you find the punch glass?' He walked to the island and picked up the mug. '*Sexy Beast*? Where's this from?'

'Oh, er. Nowhere.'

'Are you all right?' He returned to the table, bending to peer at her. 'You don't sound like yourself.'

'I'm tired. I think I might go for a lie down.'

Richard put his fingers to her forehead and the gentleness of his touch broke the shield she was trying to hold up. Tears welled, then dripped from her eyes.

'What on earth is going on?' He sat beside her. 'And don't say nothing. You're home early, drinking in the afternoon, and in tears. This isn't like you at all. Has something happened at Bocks? Shall I ring Bonnie?'

'No!'

He recoiled from the ferocity of her answer. 'What's going on?'

306

She took a mouthful of the wine. 'I don't want that woman's name mentioned in this house again.'

Beads of sweat were popping up on his forehead. He swiped them away, but more appeared.

'Why? What's she done?'

Alice put her face in her hands, the coolness from the table welcome on her hot cheeks. 'I don't want to tell you. You'll get upset.'

'I'm already upset, Alice, so spit it out, for god's sake.'

Alice took another slug of wine. 'It was Bonnie who took those things over there. She was storing them in one of the units.'

He looked over his shoulder at the sorry array of objects, his face contorted. 'Why? They're not valuable. It doesn't make any sense.'

'They're valuable to her because . . .' Her chin puckered as she tried to keep the sobs from wracking through her. 'Because she's Laura's birth mother.'

He blew out his cheeks and blinked. Alice waited for him to speak, but he stared at the things on the island, then back at her. His skin paled and his breathing seemed to quicken.

Alice scanned his face, unease pulling at her stomach. 'But it's okay. I've told her to leave. If she doesn't go, I'll call the police and have her arrested for stealing from us.'

'You did what?' His voice was hoarse, and his breath came in ragged bursts.

'She'll leave us alone, I'm sure of it.'

'You sent Laura's birth mother away, without even speaking to Laura about what she wants?'

'She's happy. It's years since she even mentioned being curious about her birth family. She's getting everything she wanted. Why introduce this upheaval when everything is going so well for her?'

'Bonnie's not upheaval. Can you even hear yourself speaking? Whether we like it or not, she's the woman who gave birth to her. She's her genetic heritage. Surely Laura has a right to know that?'

'I did it *for* Laura. She's happy and I want her to stay that way.'

'You did it for yourself.'

He stood unsteadily, then the colour vanished from his face. He reached his hand up to his neck, staggered until his knees buckled and, before Alice could reach him, he dropped to the ground.

* * *

Alice followed the instructions of the woman at the other end of the 999 call, pounding on Richard's chest, forcing herself to push so hard his ribs felt like they could crack. When the doorbell rang, she jumped to her feet, then almost fell as her head emptied of blood and her vision swam. Touching the island to steady herself, she ran through the hall, dragging the door wide, and pointing the paramedics in the direction of the kitchen through gasping tears.

She stood by the island as the green-clad man and a woman who introduced herself as Jules worked on Richard, movements brusque and urgent, attaching an oxygen mask to his face and lifting him onto a gurney while shooting questions at Alice. She told them his medical history, what medication he was on, and what had happened before he collapsed.

'We argued,' she said. 'It was my fault.'

Jules paused, like a still photograph in the midst of a

film on fast forward. 'This wasn't your fault.' She touched Alice's arm lightly before kneeling back beside Richard and wrapping a blood pressure band roughly around his arm.

Alice pressed her fingers into where the kind young woman had placed hers and pushed down until it hurt. She didn't deserve her gentle words. They meant nothing anyway because she didn't know what Alice had done.

* * *

In the ambulance, Jules kept talking to Richard. Alice willed him to respond, but his eyes stayed closed, his skin pale and sheened with moisture.

'I'm going to give you a quick shave before I put the monitors on,' said Jules before she used a plastic disposable razor to shave patches of his grey chest hair.

'These might feel a bit cold,' she said as she stuck pads onto his skin, attaching a spaghetti mass of wires to machines inside the brightly lit cavern, which sped through the streets of Hamblin, the flashing blue light visible through the windscreen and the siren blaring.

The drama of it was dream-like. An hour ago, Alice had been sitting quietly at her kitchen table, now her husband was strapped to a gurney in an ambulance being driven so quickly she had to grip the edge of the fold-down seat she was belted into as the vehicle rolled around corners and skipped to the wrong side of the road.

When the ambulance stopped, there were new blinding lights at the entrance to the hospital where people in scrubs were waiting for them. She unclipped her belt and leaped out of the way as the paramedics shouted information. She tried to grasp the words, but they bounced into her head then out again as she witnessed Richard being disentangled from the beeping machines in the ambulance's innards and the gurney gingerly pushed down a ramp. Then everything sped up and he was wheeled inside the automatic doors while people shouted over his motionless body.

She must've twisted her ankle as she jumped from the ambulance because she winced in pain as she struggled to keep up, rushing through door after door, along endless corridors, until they turned the bed into a bay and one of the women in scrubs started to drag the curtains closed, leaving her standing outside.

'Richard.' Panic rose. What if this was the last time she saw him alive, strapped to a bed, pallid and lifeless? This wasn't right. He was her husband; he was the other half of her. They couldn't just pull a flimsy curtain around him and leave her on the other side. He needed her. And she needed him.

She became aware of a man standing next to her, saying her name. 'Mrs Egerton?'

'Yes.' She looked back at the curtains. They were fully closed now. Richard had been hidden from her.

'I'm afraid we have to ask you to wait in the waiting room while we carry out some tests on your husband.'

Fear stuck her feet to the floor like suction pads. She couldn't have moved if she wanted to. 'I can't. I need to stay with Richard.'

'I promise you, we will take very good care of your husband, but some of the tests we need to do might be difficult for you to watch. It's best for both of you if you come with me.' His voice was soft with a lilting Indian accent. She looked at his face, registering for the first time there were other people in this awful situation.

'Please come with me.' His young, brown skin was

310

flawless, but the whites of his eyes were tinged with yellow and the skin bulged in incongruous bags underneath.

She nodded and forced her feet to lift to follow him, half expecting a pop as the suction sticking her down was released. Her ankle stung with every step as she passed rows of drawn curtains, arriving at a little box of a room, with huge windows on two sides, a pale blue wall with a door on another, and a TV screen facing her.

The doctor gestured for her to sit on one of the plastic seats against the back wall and took the seat next to her. She resisted the urge to tell him not to sit down, to go back and do everything he could to make Richard well. She wasn't in control here and that made things worse.

'I'll be back as soon as I can to tell you what's going on. Rest assured, your husband is in good hands.'

He stood and left Alice alone in the stark room. Through the windows she could see medics walking further along the corridor. Everyone seemed to move at an alarming pace, their faces set in grim determination. She tried not to think about what was happening to Richard behind that curtain. What did they have to do to his poor body to determine what came next? She couldn't bear the thought of his skin being punctured or sliced. She closed her eyes.

A bang made her jump. The sound came from behind the wall with the door and after a moment another bang came then another, as though someone was trying to smash their way into the room. A man's deep voice shouted something she couldn't understand, then another bang was followed by louder shouting, swearing, and repeated crashes until she wanted to curl up in the corner and hide. She wrapped her arms around herself, trying to control her trembling, and eyed the door, waiting for it to be splintered and the madman to come for her.

Instead, a quiet voice joined the swearing yells and a rhythm of conversation started, the screams followed by the measured tones of someone else, until, eventually, the shouts dropped to a rumble, then to a voice that matched the other in volume and Alice could breathe again. How did anyone work, let alone get well, in this place?

The screen on the wall was muted, but the picture flickered with the news, headlines running in a red banner along the bottom. A famous Hollywood actor had died and there was face after sad face on screen, mouths moving with what she presumed were tributes to the man who'd died.

Who would make a television tribute to Richard if this were the day his life ended? He'd lived a good life. He was kind and compassionate and loved, but there would be no red banner running along the bottom of a news programme for him.

Suddenly everything seemed pointless. Why was she pushing so hard for the planning application so she and Richard could afford to stay in a house that was far too big for the two of them? Laura would move out soon, whether Alice wanted her to or not, then she'd be left, possibly all alone, with that preposterous chandelier for company.

The young doctor appeared in the corridor and she stood as he entered the waiting room, new adrenaline surging through her. She tried to read his face. 'How is he?'

'We're going to take him down to theatre to do an angiogram to see where the blockages are. Then we'll probably do angioplasty. That means we'll be inserting a catheter with a small balloon attached into the blocked artery. We'll inflate that balloon to open up the clogged arteries and put in a mesh stent to hold the artery open permanently.'

Alice could feel her head bobbing up and down as though she were agreeing, but she wasn't taking the information in. 'Is he going to be okay?'

'We do this kind of surgery every day.'

That wasn't the commitment she wanted. 'How long until I can see him?'

'I'm afraid I can't answer that now, but it will be at least a few hours. If you want to go home and come back later, that would be okay.'

Alice almost laughed. She wasn't going anywhere. 'I'll stay. Thanks.' Then, like a parent to a teacher on a child's first day of school, she looked into his eyes and said, 'You will look after him, won't you?'

'I'll do my utmost, I give you my word.' He bobbed his head and left the room.

She needed to let Laura know what had happened. Guilt seized her by the throat. How much should she tell her about their argument? Should she tell her the truth about Bonnie? She looked at the screen of her phone. The lock screen was a picture of her little family of three in the garden on Laura's birthday, her, Richard, and Laura, all grinning at the camera. Laura had taken it as a selfie and sent a copy to Alice.

Tears dropped onto her phone as she tapped on Laura's number. She braced herself to sound strong when her daughter's bright voice answered. She couldn't tell her the truth and risk losing everything. Not now.

She told her an edited version of what had happened and listened to her child cry. She found herself promising Richard would be okay. He had to be. The alternative was too awful to contemplate.

Chapter Forty-Two

Bonnie

Present Day

The ringing on the entry bell was insistent, and Bonnie's stomach flipped as she allowed Laura into the building. She leaned against the hallway wall to steady herself and listened for footsteps outside, wondering if she might need to rush to the bathroom to throw up before Laura reached the door of the flat. She swallowed down the bile, then, steeling herself, she opened the door before Laura knocked.

Laura's bottom lip wobbled. Her eyes were slits in swollen skin. What had she done to this sweet girl? She'd messed up everything. She had been right all along; she destroyed everyone she loved. She deserved to be alone.

'I'm so sorry, Laura,' she started.

'You know?'

Bonnie's pulse jumped under her skin. 'Sorry?'

'You know about my dad? Did Mum ring?'

Bonnie closed the door, turning towards the sitting-room, her brain computing, but unable to work out the words.

'Come through. Do you want a drink?'

'No, thanks. I don't even know why I'm here. It's weird, but when Mum rang from the hospital, I just wanted to be with you.' She followed Bonnie and sank onto the sofa, rubbing her eyes with the back of her hands like a small child ready for its nap.

Blood pounded in Bonnie's ears. 'What did she say?'

'That there was no point going to the hospital because they won't let us see him until he's come round. If he comes round.' She hiccupped the words out in short sobs. 'They're operating on his heart right now.' Her voice cracked and she burst into tears.

At last her brain caught up and she could read what had happened. 'Oh god. Poor Richard.' The reprieve was blunted by the suffering on her precious child's face.

Laura's eyes continued to pool with tears. 'I'm scared.'

Bonnie sat close to her and took her hand. 'I know, sweetheart, I know.'

'I can't lose my dad.' She leaned in to Bonnie, resting her head on her shoulder.

Bonnie heard the screech of tyres, the sickening thud, and was back in the moment when Laura lost a father for the first time. Her own tears fell, dropping unseen, into Laura's hair.

They sat in silence as Bonnie stroked Laura's soft waves and made shushing sounds, all the time staring at the blue painting, wanting to curl herself around her child and protect her like the darkest blue circled around the light. Laura was the light. She brought a brightness and warmth everywhere she went, just as Bonnie had known she would, as she had painted, year after year.

Laura shifted her head and looked into Bonnie's face. 'Oh, don't cry.' She wiped Bonnie's cheeks, which brought fresh tears. After a moment, she shifted and looked up at Bonnie. 'You said you were sorry when I came in. What did you mean?'

Bonnie fought with the muscles in her face to keep them neutral. 'We don't have to talk about that now. You've got enough to deal with.'

Laura sat up straight and pulled a tissue from her sleeve, blowing her nose. 'I could do with the distraction.'

Bonnie tapped her knee when what she really wanted was to pull Laura back to her and hug her so tightly that they melded. Instead, she made herself stand. She walked to the kitchen, opened the fridge, and took out a bottle of fizzy water. Reaching into the cupboard, she picked out two glasses and filled them, watching the bubbles pelt to the surface and pop. She couldn't look at Laura when she spoke. 'I'm sorry because I'm leaving Hamblin.'

She heard Laura exhale but didn't turn around.

'It hasn't turned out the way I thought it would. I won't have a job for much longer, and . . .' She paused, looking out of the window at the clouds blowing in, threatening to cover the sun. 'I think it's time I moved on.'

'You've only been here a few months. There are other jobs. If you give it more time, the place might grow on you.'

She thought about how much the place had already grown on her. The boxy flat was now a home. She loved painting in front of the open balcony doors, with the wind fluttering the silvery curtains, watching the barges making their sedate way along the canal. She loved Jim and Polly and Angie at the life drawing classes. For a moment she allowed herself to imagine Stuart standing next to her on the balcony, his arms wrapped around her, keeping her warm as the sun went down. No. She didn't deserve him any more than she did this wonderful girl.

317

And she was wonderful. Bonnie loved Laura even more in the flesh than she had in her imagination. Her precious daughter, who had Cahil's dark eyes and strength of character, and her artistic side and sense of fun. She adored the way she spoke every thought that passed through her head and that she needed to be creative and spontaneous to feel alive.

Despite all that, she was still on an uncontrollable emotional ride, tortured by sleepless nights and compulsions she couldn't resist. Darkness shadowed every moment of joy and now she had Alice's threats pushing her like a stick in the back.

'It's not for me, I'm afraid.' She turned to face her girl, tightening the muscles in her cheeks to force a smile. 'I'm sorry.'

'But I've got used to you being around.' Laura pouted. 'And I came here when I heard about Dad. Doesn't that count for something?'

It counted for so much. Her hands shook as she took the glasses through and put them on the coffee table.

'Yes, but you've got your mum, Xavier, and Polly and Nathan. They'll be there for you.'

Laura's chin puckered. 'Don't leave until I know Dad's okay. Please. I need you.'

Not as much as I need you, thought Bonnie, but she just nodded and slid back onto the sofa beside Laura, putting her arm around her wonderful, beautiful girl.

Chapter Forty-Three

Alice

Present Day

Fussing around Richard's bedside as he watched her from behind his oxygen mask, Alice made a promise to herself she'd never take anything for granted again. She had everything she needed in her small family and, since she'd almost lost her husband and her child in the last week, she would be grateful they were both still with her and stop asking the universe for more.

She'd put the house on the market as soon as she'd heard Richard's operation had been successful. It didn't matter whether the plans worked out or not, she didn't want a big, fancy house anymore. She couldn't believe she ever had.

Laura pushed the hospital room door open with her bottom and turned around, holding up two cardboard coffee cups like trophies. 'I've found a Starbucks vending machine,' she said, handing one cup to Alice, and taking a slurp from her own. She looked down at Richard with pity, wires seemingly protruding from every inch of him. 'Now, you need to get a bit stronger, old man, and then I can get you one too.'

'He's never having a latte again,' said Alice, sitting down in the chair next to the bed. 'He's going to live on fruit, vegetables, and lean meat.'

Richard groaned from under the mask and Laura kissed his forehead. 'Don't worry, Pops, I'll sneak you in the odd treat if you pay me enough.' She turned to Alice. 'He didn't have either arrest because of his diet, though, did he?'

Alice pulled at the white covers, straightening the creases. 'Not really. They think it's hereditary because of the family history, but years of stress won't have helped.'

'Sometimes it's a blessing I'm not physically related to you two,' Laura said and laughed as Alice tutted, trying to respond normally. Laura had joked about that many times before when she was younger, but now she'd seen the characteristics she shared with Bonnie, it stung. At least she didn't look like her. That was some consolation.

'I wish it were bad diet. Then I'd be able to control it.'

Laura sat on the end of the bed. 'Sometimes you have to accept that there are things beyond even your control, Mother dearest.'

How true that was. Where had it got her, trying to manage everyone and everything?

'Don't you need to get back to work? I might try to be less controlling, but I don't want to go bankrupt before we sell the house.'

'Bonnie's covering. She said she'd work for as long as we need to look after Dad.'

Alice stiffened. 'That's nice of her.'

Laura sighed. 'Yep. Has she given in her resignation yet?'

Alice shifted to look directly at Laura, and boiling coffee spilled onto the back of her hand. She yelped and Laura jumped up and grabbed tissues from the top of Richard's bedside cabinet. 'You okay?'

She dabbed at the brown liquid, glad of the excuse to look elsewhere. 'Yes. What were you saying about Bonnie?' She took Richard's hand, and he held her fingers weakly.

Laura took the stained tissues from her and put her foot on the lever that opened the top of the bin. It bounced open, and she threw them inside. 'She said she hasn't settled in Hamblin, so she's going to move on.'

Laura let the bin lid drop, and it clanked shut. Alice was aware of Richard's tired eyes watching her from over the plastic mask. 'How do you feel about that?'

'Me?'

'Yes. You two had become close.'

Foot tapping the lever, making the bin lid open and close like a puppet's mouth, Laura scrunched her face. 'It's weird. I know you're not keen, but I like her. I felt like she, kind of, gets me. You know what I mean? It's probably because she's an artist, and we like similar sorts of things.'

Alice nodded, trying to conceal her heart being wrenched from her body and trampled on the blue linoleum floor. Was this what Richard felt like now his heart had literally been pummelled? She held his hand a little tighter.

'You can stay in touch, even if she doesn't live locally, can't you?' Richard squeezed her hand gently, and she knew he thought she was saying the right thing. He was still too weak to have a proper conversation, so she hadn't been able to ask what he thought she should do about Bonnie.

'Suppose.' Laura left the bin and sat back down. 'Seems a shame she won't be around though. I'll miss her.'

'You'll have your course to keep you busy. We'll give you the money for that, by the way. You can pay us back when you're a world-renowned artist.' Again, she felt Richard's warm hand firmer in hers. 'And it's time your dad and I got on with the rest of our lives without always waiting for things to change.' She looked at her husband and daughter, feeling some of the tension of the last few days leave her body. 'Life is short. We can't let a little thing like money stand in the way of your dreams.'

* * *

Richard was weak, but he was back home, alive, and Alice planned to keep him that way. She inspected him in his usual chair, making sure his glass of water was within reach and the blanket she'd tucked around him still covered his feet.

'Stop fussing, woman,' he said, when he glanced up and saw her leaning against the sitting-room door. 'I'm fine.'

'You won't be, if you call me *woman* again,' she said, walking to the window, her breath fogging up the glass as she watched the rain pelting down outside. When she turned back to Richard, he had his head on one side. She shivered, sensing what was coming.

'Is Laura at work?'

'Yes.'

'So, what do we tell her? How do you see all this playing out?'

Alice sat, rubbing her thumb and forefinger along the bridge of her nose. 'You're not meant to be stressed.'

'I've had my arteries hoovered and opened; I think I'll cope with a difficult conversation.'

She breathed deeply, then exhaled. 'What do you think?'

'Has she seen Bonnie recently?'

Alice lifted her hands. 'Not that I'm aware of. I know she was looking after Bocks when Laura and I were at the hospital . . .'

'Which was very good of her, considering—'

'Yes, all right,' she snapped, then dipped her head. 'Sorry.'

Richard nodded. 'She hasn't mentioned her since?'

Alice focused on the water running unpredictably down the windowpane, following one path, then shifting and joining with a different stream. 'No. She's spending all her spare time with Xavier. They seem to be getting close. He's been a godsend, to be honest; really helpful.'

'He seems like a good lad.' She felt his eyes boring into her. 'Have you come to terms with them?'

'*Them* what?'

'The two of them as an item? The fact she's at his flat more than she's here. Don't pretend it doesn't bother you.'

Alice looked at her hands resting on her knees. Blue veins protruded under her dry, criss-crossed skin. She shifted her gaze back to the window. 'I've been a fool, haven't I?'

'None of it's easy, is it? Letting go.'

'I think I'm worse at it than most. I'm trying though. I know he's good for her.'

Richard nodded and sighed. 'He is.'

They were quiet for a moment, listening to the sputtering rain swill down the gutter.

'Do we tell her about Bonnie?' Richard said, eventually. 'Is that one change too far? We need to make sure we're both saying, or not saying, the same thing.'

Alice dragged her eyes away from the mesmerising water. 'You seemed to be certain we should, before.'

Richard took off his glasses and inspected the lenses. 'I thought we should.' He breathed on the glass and rubbed at a speck of dirt. 'But she's had a lot to cope with recently.'

Alice nodded. 'And she is very happy with Xavier.'

'And she's definitely on that MA course?'

'It's all confirmed.'

'And with us moving and everything, that's going to be upheaval.'

They both turned back to the window. Alice listened to the wind thrashing the rain at the exterior wall.

'Do you think we should leave it for now, then?' he asked

'Bonnie has handed in her resignation.'

'So, there's no need, right now. And we won't stand in her way if she does want to find out more. In the future, I mean.'

'Of course.' She listened as the wind dropped for a moment and then started up again. 'Tea?'

'Lovely.'

Alice stood, patting his hand as she passed.

'We are doing the right thing, aren't we?'

She turned back and saw how tired Richard looked. He'd lost too much weight in hospital, 'I hope so. We've always tried to do what's best for our girl, haven't we?'

Richard nodded and she left the room.

* * *

When Alice popped into Bocks the following day, Laura was sitting behind the desk, looking as out of place with her pink hair and denim all-in-one as she always did.

She stood by the door, shaking the rain from her umbrella. 'All okay?'

'Yep. How's Dad?'

Alice dropped her umbrella by the door and took off her mac, laying it over the desk. 'I think he was delighted I was leaving the house. Apparently, I'm stifling him.'

'You? Overdoing it? Never!' Laura winked and Alice narrowed her eyes then laughed.

'He'll be sorry when I think he's well enough to mow the lawn. It's growing like mad in all this wet weather. I'll have to do it before that second viewing tomorrow. I think they're going to make an offer. I hope they do.' She'd watched excitement grow on the faces of the couple and their two young children as they examined every room of what had once been her cherished home and was surprised to feel like the house would be perfect for them. It didn't work for her family anymore. She was finally ready to move on.

She opened the door again to look at the rain hitting the concrete of the car park then bouncing back up, just as Jim scurried up the ramp, anorak held over his head.

'By 'eck!' he said. Alice jumped out of the way as he lowered the coat and rivulets of water dripped onto the carpet tiles. 'It was cracking the flags not long back, now we've got biblical flooding.'

'You should do the TV weather, Jim. It would be much more entertaining than all that boring isobar stuff,' said Laura.

'Might be a bit long in the tooth for all that, and I'm not sure I'd get in them tight dresses the lasses wear.' He gave a little wiggle, and they giggled at this new, playful Jim. Since his illness and his revelation about Lou, it was like a burden had lifted from him. Alice would really miss him.

'You all packed and ready for your relocation to the frozen north?'

Jim pointed his finger at Laura. 'We'll have less of that, young lady. It's none too glorious down 'ere.' He pointed outside. 'And it's not as grim up north as you soft southerners think.' He raised his chin. 'As you will see when you come and visit me in my Huddersfudlian palace.'

'Have you really bought a mansion, Jim?' Laura's eyes widened.

'Don't be daft. I've got a nice two-bedroom place in one of them new-build retirement villages. It's got all mod cons, mind, and it's no'but a mile from our Gillian's. She's tickled pink.'

'I'm sure she is,' said Alice. 'And we'd love to come and explore some of that Yorkshire countryside with you. Just say the word.'

'You'll be doing a fair bit of gadding about, now Bonnie's up and gone too.' He shoved his hand in the pocket of his coat. 'She asked me to give you this.'

Laura's face fell. 'Bonnie's gone?'

Jim put an envelope on the desk and it took all of Alice's strength to not snatch it and tear it to pieces.

'Yes. She said she'd told you she was leaving when your Richard was well enough to come home.'

Seeing Laura lift the envelope was like watching two cars speeding from opposite directions on the same side of the road. Alice felt she could see the crash about to happen, but there was nothing she could do to stop it.

Laura was speaking, but it sounded distorted. 'Yes, but

I thought she'd say goodbye properly, not just leave a note.'

She ripped open the envelope and Alice grew rigid, glued to the carpet tile she was standing on, like a child playing stuck in the mud.

The rain battered against the door as she watched her daughter reading, eyebrows knitted, waiting for the explosion, which would be louder than thunder and more painful than being struck by lightning.

'She's gone.'

A breath left Alice, and she found she was able to take another. 'And?'

'That's it, really.'

Another breath, in and out.

'She said she'd loved meeting me and she's said lovely things about me, and you, which is a bit strange because I didn't think you two hit it off.' Her voice wobbled.

Alice looked up and walked towards the desk, holding her hand out for the letter. Laura passed the paper and it flapped between them, loose and flaccid instead of the fiery bomb it could have been.

Alice wiped raindrops from the lenses of her reading glasses on the bottom of her blouse, then put them on. She started to read.

Dear Laura,

Forgive me for not saying goodbye face to face. I find endings hard. I've had a few I haven't managed to get over, which has led to me doing some pretty weird things, so I've learned it's best to walk away before I do something even more stupid than usual.

That probably won't make much sense to you, so I'll get to the bit I want you to understand: You are a very special person and I've loved spending time with you. You are a bright and beautiful soul with a huge and giving heart. You are talented, inquisitive, and you want to learn, so never stop doing that. Do your MA, paint, and sculpt, and draw. Make sense of this messy world through your art. I've always tried to, and it helps. It really does.

Enjoy every moment with Xavier. He's a lovely man. I wish I'd taken the time to get to know him better. I hope your dad continues to recover quickly, and he's back on the golf course soon. He's a wonderful father, and he adores you.

The last thing I want to say is the most important. Be kind to your mum. She is your greatest ally and your most loyal friend. She would fight any number of wars for you, and you don't know how lucky you are to have a warrior like that on your side.

Cherish her, as she cherishes you.

All the very best for the future to you and your family.

With love,
Bonnie

Tears flowed down Alice's face, dripping off her chin and onto the paper while Laura and Jim watched, exchanging concerned glances.

'You okay, Mum?'

Alice wiped her cheeks with the back of her hand. 'What a beautiful letter.'

'Yes.' Laura's chin puckered. 'I can't believe she's gone.' She looked up defiantly. 'I bet you wish you'd been nicer to her now, don't you?' she said, tactless and truthful as ever.

'She didn't make it easy,' Alice said, folding the letter and running her fingers along the creases. 'But, yes, I very much do.'

'Well, too late now.' Laura stuck out her bottom lip. 'She didn't leave a forwarding address either. I can't believe I'm not going to see her again. I thought we . . . I don't know.' She turned away.

Alice thought she'd be elated if Bonnie were no longer there, like a dagger ready to fall, but that's not how she felt at all. She sighed, putting the paper back into the envelope. Instead of relief, she felt a deep, deep sorrow.

Chapter Forty-Four

Alice

Present Day

'Let Xavier take that one,' Alice said as Richard bent down to lift a box of files from the pile in Bocks' reception. 'You'll give yourself another heart attack.'

Richard straightened and sighed. 'You were there when the doctor gave me the all-clear, and my creaky old bones let me know when I'm overdoing it, so please, let me get on with it.'

Xavier walked past Richard and picked up the box as though it were empty. 'Don't worry, old timer, I've got it.'

'Cheeky sod,' said Richard, grinning at Xavier's back as he walked down the ramp and shoved the box in the back of his van. 'And why isn't he freezing in a T-shirt in this weather?'

Laura huffed and puffed, her breath swirling in a white cloud, arms limp at her sides as she came back through the blue door. 'All I do these days is pack and unpack boxes.'

'I thought you were planning to be less of a sulky teen now you're moving in with Xavier?' Alice's hands were on her hips, but she shifted them. Laura wasn't the only one trying to be less like their old selves. 'I can't see him putting up with your strops.'

'You've met your match there,' Richard said, as they all watched Xavier shifting boxes to fit the space in the van.

'You're right, as ever. I'm going to become terribly mature and sensible.' Laura hugged Alice and pulled Richard towards her with her other arm, squeezing her parents tightly. The fur on the hood of her parka tickled Alice's nose, but she didn't move away. 'But just because I'm going to be lady of my own manor, it doesn't mean I won't still need you two legends.' She gave them both a loud kiss on their cheeks and released them.

'What do you want?' said Alice, instead of giving in to the urge to hold on to her daughter and beg her to reconsider, to live with them in the pretty little cottage they'd bought on the edge of town for all eternity.

Laura gasped. 'Nothing! I'm going to miss you two when I'm with my live-in lover.' She exaggerated the 'L's and wrinkled her nose. 'So I'm being extra nice now.'

'Well, it's very unnerving,' said Alice, proud of her ability to appear nonchalant. There was no denying Xavier was the perfect partner for Laura, but it didn't heal the wound of her little girl leaving her. 'Now come on, we need to get this stuff out of here before the end of the day.'

Xavier stood in the doorway. 'What's next?'

'My car's full of rubbish. Fancy a trip to the tip?' Richard said.

'Thought you'd never ask.'

332

'There's one more abandoned unit to clear, so I'll get on with that.' Laura gave them a little wave and disappeared through the red door as Richard and Xavier wandered down the ramp and into the car park.

Alice lifted the hatch, feeling strangely nostalgic about the squeaking hinge, and opened the door to the staffroom. She filled the kettle and leaned her back against the sink unit, wondering how Jim was settling into his new place in Huddersfield, when she heard a man's voice in reception.

'Hello? Is anyone here?'

She opened the staffroom door and popped her head around to see a tall, very thin man with dark hair and craggy lines around his mouth and nose.

'Sorry, we're closed.'

'Aye,' he said in a thick Scottish accent. 'I can see that.' He scratched his long chin. 'Are you the owner?'

Alice stepped from the doorway. 'Yes.'

'Alice Egerton?'

Cold fingers tapped their way up Alice's spine. 'Who are you?'

The man walked towards the desk and put his palms flat on it. His pale eyes were bloodshot and dark circles hung over sunken cheeks. Despite his slightly haggard appearance, he was a good-looking man and there was a softness in his voice that told Alice he wasn't a threat.

'I'm Stuart.' He scanned her face but when she didn't reply he added, 'I'm Bonnie's husband. Is she here?'

A band of tension wrapped itself around Alice's brain and tightened. 'We haven't seen Bonnie for about three months. We thought she went back to Scotland when she left here.'

'No,' he said sadly. 'I haven't seen or heard from her since she left Glasgow in March.'

'Oh. I'm sorry, but, since she didn't leave a forwarding address, I don't think I can help you.' She turned and stepped towards the staffroom, hoping he would leave.

'Can I talk to you?'

Alice stopped. She turned slowly, trying to work out her options, then realised she didn't have any. She checked the red door to the corridors was still closed, then nodded towards the staffroom. 'Come through.'

She switched on the electric fan heater in the chilly room and listened to the soft whirr of the warm air being pushed through the grille, trying to steady her trembling hands as she made them both a cup of tea.

'I don't have long. We need to clear the place for the developers. How do you think I can help?'

'I'll be as quick as I can. I know you're probably not too pleased to see me, but I'm worried about Bonnie and this is the last place I know she was at. I've only had one phone conversation with her since she left Glasgow, and it was one hell of a conversation,' he said, rubbing his hand over his face. 'I've tried ringing her, plenty of times, but she's not picking up.'

'It must've been a bad breakup, for her to disappear like that.' Alice allowed herself to hope he was only here to find Bonnie, not interfere in Laura's life.

'No.' He wrapped his hands around his mug. 'It wasn't at all. It wasn't even really like a breakup.'

'Oh?'

'It was more like, I don't know . . . a disintegration.' He glanced up, then down at his bitten nails. 'At first, she stopped sleeping properly. She was getting anxious, you know?' He looked up and Alice found she was nodding. 'Then she started acting, well, weird.'

'Weird? In what way?'

'Ach.' He sat back in his chair. 'I don't want to be disloyal.'

Alice took her reading glasses from the top of her head and nibbled on the plastic arm. 'Was she taking things?'

Stuart stiffened. 'Shit. She did that here?'

'She stole some things, mainly belonging to my daughter.'

'Your daughter's name is Laura, right?'

'Yes. Why?'

He took a drink of tea and let out a sigh. 'Right. The time I talked to Bonnie, she'd just left here. She said she'd told you' – he paused and looked in her eyes – 'who she was to that lassie.'

'She did.'

'I imagine that came as a shock to you. It did to me, I can tell you.'

'You didn't know?' Alice narrowed her eyes.

'No. But it explained a lot when she told me the full story. You haven't told her? Laura, I mean?'

Alice took a breath into her stomach. 'Bonnie was acting very strangely before she left. I can imagine it was an emotional situation for her, but that doesn't explain the stealing. I'm sorry if it doesn't sit well with you, but since Bonnie has moved on and my daughter is in a very happy and stable place in her life, I didn't see what benefit there was in telling her who her birth mother was. Not then, and not now.'

'It's not that I don't understand what you're saying, but the stealing is a symptom. It's part of her anxiety and depression. She's battled with it since Cahil died.'

Bonnie hadn't seemed particularly depressed to Alice. 'Who is Cahil and what does he have to do with Bonnie stealing from us?'

'Cahil was Bonnie's boyfriend; Laura's father.'

The band around Alice's brain tightened a notch.

'He was killed in an accident before either of them knew Bonnie was pregnant.'

Alice's stomach lurched. 'God . . . that's awful.'

'Bonnie blames herself because she encouraged him to drink and he stumbled into the road when they left the pub. The guilt has eaten away at her for nearly twenty-six years.' He rubbed his nose with his thumb knuckle, screwing up his whole face. He clearly found talking about this distressing. 'Then, before she found out she was pregnant, she almost killed herself.'

Alice gasped and Stuart put his hand out to stop her speaking. 'Not intentionally, but she'd had a lot to drink, and she collapsed, and she's always worried she might have seriously damaged the baby and ruined the wee one's life.'

'But Laura's perfectly fine. More than fine, she's clever, artistic, witty—'

'But she didn't know that, did she?' Stuart interrupted. 'Imagine what that kind of guilt does to a person? And then her mum persuaded her to give the baby up, and she did what she was told because she felt she had no right to keep her after what she thought she'd done. She believed she didn't deserve to have children after that, that she didn't deserve to be happy.'

Alice jumped as the door opened. She turned her head to see Laura standing in the doorway, mouth in a razor-blade line.

She jumped to her feet, but only got one step before Laura put her both arms out like a shield. 'Don't!' Her voice wobbled and her bottom lip trembled, chin puckering like it did when she was a tiny baby, about to wail for her bottle.

'What the fuck did I just overhear?'

'Laura.'

'Not you.' She glowered at Alice. 'You.' She pointed at Stuart. 'You're Bonnie's husband?'

Stuart stood, towering over them both. 'I am. It's good to meet you, Laura.'

She turned to Alice, who felt like she was underwater, deep down, swimming hard but unable to work out which way was up.

'You knew?'

Her voice was underwater too. She spoke, but the words came out like bubbles, popping, indistinguishable. 'I . . . erm . . . not everything.' She put her hand on the sink, feeling the ice-cold aluminium under her fingers keeping her upright.

'But you knew Bonnie was my birth mother?'

'I found out the day your dad had the heart attack.'

Laura shouted so loudly that Alice covered her ears. 'And you didn't think I might want to know?'

'I'm sorry.' Alice bent over, hands still over her ears.

'How dare you keep that from me? What the hell were you thinking?'

Stuart walked in front of Alice, and he seemed to cast a warm shadow. 'Laura, I completely understand why this is upsetting, but I'm sure your mum did what she thought was right.'

Laura's eyes flashed black. 'And how do you know? What has this got to do with you? You're not even with Bonnie anymore.'

'Bonnie is ill. I pushed too hard to try to make her get help for her anxiety and compulsive behaviour, and she decided to try to fix it her way. That's why she came to find you. She used a private investigator. She thought if she saw you were okay, then she'd be okay too.'

337

'She was okay, at least she seemed to be. I didn't see much anxiety or— What did you say?' Laura's face crumpled.

'She has some issues related to her . . .' He scratched the back of his head and grimaced. 'This is a lot to take in.'

'We got close,' Laura said, tears falling from her chin onto her top.

'And I imagine that was hard to walk away from.' Stuart smiled at Laura. When his marionette lines lifted, he looked ten years younger. 'Now, I'm really worried about her. I want to help her get better, and I need the help of both of you to do that.'

Laura's muscles slackened and Alice wanted to scoop her up. 'How?'

'Can we sit?' Stuart held his arms wide, and both women walked to the table and took a seat. Tears poured down Laura's face and pooled on the tabletop as Stuart told her what he'd told Alice. The words seemed to penetrate Alice more deeply this time and any animosity she'd felt for the small, blonde woman she'd seen as a threat, turned to pity.

When he'd answered Laura's questions, Stuart sighed. 'So, the only way I have of contacting Bonnie now is by phone. She never answers, but I text and leave voice-mails. None of her friends have heard from her and neither has her cousin, Ross, so as far as I'm aware, she's out there somewhere, alone and, possibly, quite unwell.'

'Oh god.' Alice put her hand to her mouth. 'I'm sorry.' She looked from one to the other, 'I'm so, so sorry.'

'Have you spoken to her since she left?' he asked Laura.

She wiped her face with her hand. 'No. I rang and left messages, but she never got back to me. I was hurt, to be honest, but I convinced myself I'd overestimated our connection, that it must've meant more to me than it did to her, so I left it. God, I've been so wrapped up in my masters and Xav and moving. I'm a terrible person, aren't I? How could I not realise what she needed?'

Alice covered Laura's hand with her own and her heart doubled in size when Laura didn't shake it off. 'You couldn't have known.'

'I imagine Bonnie worked hard to make sure you didn't know what she was feeling. I didn't know about you and we've been married ten years. She's had a lot of practice holding things in. She wants to protect the people she loves,' said Stuart, kindly, and Alice could imagine him and Bonnie together, him with an arm around her shoulders, her smiling up at his rugged face.

'What can we do to help?' asked Alice, her voice firmer now.

'Ideally, I want to see if I can get Bonnie to come home. If I can persuade her to come back, I can make sure she's safe and see what she needs. I won't push her – I made that mistake before – but I'm worried about her. I miss her. I need to try, for my own sanity as much as for hers.' He turned to Laura. 'Do you have your phone?'

She nodded, plucking it from the inside pocket of her coat.

'Could you text Bonnie?'

Laura brought the screen to life. 'What should I say?'

Stuart scratched his chin and grimaced 'Something like, "*I'm with Stuart and he's told me everything. Please can we talk?*"'

339

Laura nodded and began to tap on her keypad. She looked up at both of them, then pressed send. There was a whooshing sound from the phone, then they all sat quietly while the fan heater breathed out its warmth.

Ten seconds later, the phone rang.

Chapter Forty-Five

Bonnie

Present Day

Bonnie's phone vibrated in her coat. She rummaged through the pockets, pulling out tissues and keys until she finally hoisted the phone out and looked at the screen. She let out a gasp when she saw Laura's name and clicked on the message. She didn't allow herself to think before sitting on the nearest stone on the craggy hillside and pressing the call button. Laura was with Stuart. She knew everything.

Her bottom grew numb against the cold stone and her breath fogged the view of the lake, clearing to show the still, slate-grey water, then hazing over with her next ragged breath as she listened to her daughter asking if she was okay.

'I'm—' Her voice stalled in her throat.

'It's alright,' said Laura's soft voice at the other end of the line. 'You don't need to say anything now.'

'Are you alright?' It seemed like too small a question.

'Yes. It's a lot to take in, but I'm good.' Laura paused then said, 'Will you answer if Stuart calls you tonight?'

'Yes. Tell him yes,' she said, tears choking the words. 'And can we talk, when you've got your head around everything?'

'I'd like that,' said Laura and Bonnie scrunched her eyes tight and covered her mouth with her hand to stop the sobs escaping.

When she clicked off the call, she put the phone back in her pocket with trembling fingers, then struggled to stand. She tried to rub some sensation back into her buttocks before making her way down the hillside, dodging the rough tufts of grass as she descended, her heart racing.

A low mist sagged over Grasmere. Now she regretted never being able to bring herself to paint the beautiful lake, which had gone from reflecting blue skies and the low-hanging boughs of green-leaved trees when she arrived in early autumn, to the bleak, brooding waters before her now. She had planned to, when she came to a stop in the picturesque Lake District village, halfway between Hamblin and Glasgow, but however beguiling the view, she couldn't make herself capture the beauty of the place.

When she'd taken the detour off the M6, she'd just aimed to stop for a night to clear her head and decide what to do next, but the pretty slate houses and rolling hills had tempted her to put off making decisions, to stay and paint the rugged countryside and shimmering water.

She'd rented a tiny cottage and spent the early days walking, trying to fill her lungs with the sharp, fresh air. But she could never catch a satisfying breath, and when the rain came in October and soaked the village in grey – the sky, stone, and water all slicked in one miserable tone – it seemed easier to stay in bed. So, she hid under

thick blankets, smelling the peat fires from the neigh-
bouring houses and watching the smoke rise from their
chimneys through her bedroom window. Under the sill,
the paintings were stacked, their colours turned towards
the thick stone wall.

Arriving back at the front door of her rented cottage,
she fumbled with the keys, trying to master her shaking
fingers as an unfamiliar sensation nudged the corners of
her mouth upwards into a smile. She stumbled into the
house, flinging herself onto the sofa and dragging her
hiking boots off, the thick woollen socks dangling like
clown's shoes. Discarding those too, she mounted the stairs
to her bedroom.

She flicked on the light. The naked bulb spread its
yellow glow across the room. She marched to the window
and tipped the canvases towards her.

'I need to wrap you up,' she said, her voice hitching.
'It's time to go home.'

* * *

The following day, Bonnie stood on the pavement outside
the sandstone villa for the first time in eight months. Fairy
lights twinkled around the doorway, reflecting in the
stained-glass panel at the top. She walked through the
gate, past the neat privet hedge, up the path, and stood
on the doorstep for a minute, deciding whether to use her
key or knock. Taking a mammoth breath, she knocked
and waited for the shadow behind the blue and green
glass to grow larger. Stuart opened the door and his face
crinkled in a hesitant smile.

'Hello.'

'I don't want you to fix me.' She rushed out the words
she'd practised on the drive from the lakes. 'But I do want

to be with you while I get myself fixed. If that's okay with you?'

He nodded and opened the door wider, and they both pretended not to be crying as they brought in the cases and canvases from the car.

* * *

Two weeks later, Bonnie stood outside the pale stone house again, breathing in through her mouth and out through her nose, just as the counsellor had shown her. She slipped her key in the lock and entered, smelling the mulled wine scent of the diffuser that sat on the narrow table beside the wedding photo of her and Stuart, now in a new dark wood frame she'd bought from a little antique shop in town. The forest green hallway enveloped her, like a tunnel of lush branches.

'Hi,' shouted Stuart, from the kitchen at the back of the house. 'I'll put this in the oven and be through in a minute.'

She turned left into the snug, and dropped into the enormous purple armchair, allowing her vision to blur watching the intermittent flashing of the tiny bulbs on the Christmas tree in the corner.

Stuart came through wearing a checked chef's apron over his T-shirt and jeans. He handed her a cup of tea. 'How was counselling?'

She took a sip and marvelled at how he always made a perfect brew. 'Good. Yeah, it was good. She was glad I've gone on the HRT. She thinks that will help when it kicks in.'

He continued to look at her and she understood his need to know more. She'd put him through so much and, yet, here he still was, cooking her dinner, making the perfect cup of tea.

'It's different to what I thought it would be like. It's not all pouring your heart out while someone sits, silently watching you. It's more about accepting why you are the way you are, stopping beating yourself up for the past, and learning coping strategies for when things get a bit much.' He was nodding, blue eyes eager. 'The CBT is interesting. It makes sense. It's good to have something practical to help when—' She looked down at the cup. 'When the intrusive thoughts come.'

'How are you feeling about, erm . . . the intrusive thoughts?'

Bonnie smiled at his awkwardness. 'Like I'm glad I have the words to explain what goes on in my messy brain.' She tipped her head from side to side. 'Impulse control disorder, kleptomania.'

Stuart smiled. 'Yeah, you've ruined that word for me, to be honest. I can't call anyone a klepto anymore and find it funny.'

'Sorry about that.'

'I forgive you.' He shoved his hands in the pocket at the front of his apron and dipped his head, looking at her sideways. 'At the risk of undoing all that good work, can you come with me? I want to run something by you.'

She heaved her tired limbs out of the chair and followed Stuart through the hallway and into the dining room. Winter sunshine caught the glass beads hanging at the window, refracting rainbows on every surface. The crimson walls were usually hung with artwork they'd picked up at galleries over the last ten years, but now the surfaces were bare, brass picture hangers the only evidence something was missing.

Bewildered, she turned to Stuart, who pointed to the wooden floor at the side of the dining table. Following his finger, she saw three frames stacked against the legs of the dining chairs. Her heart pumped faster. The only place these pictures had ever hung was on the walls of her flat in Hamblin.

'I think it's time to stop allowing the past to be a monster,' Stuart said, picking up the blue painting and placing it carefully on the table. 'I know what these paintings signify, and I don't think you should hide them anymore. They are part of your past, and they are beautiful. You've got to let the past be, and maybe facing it and embracing it will help you to move forwards.'

Stuart hung the blue painting above the iron fireplace and Bonnie stood back, waiting to feel panic rise, but instead, the bright focus pulled her in to its warmth, reminding her of the glorious girl the centre symbolised. It felt good to be reminded of Laura, of the tiny baby she'd carried inside her. The little girl who'd grown into a wonderful, vibrant, creative, and strong woman. These paintings, on the wall of the house she shared with this generous man, could become a celebration of the intertwined lives of the two of them, not a guilty secret from her past.

'One more thing,' said Stuart, when Bonnie was straightening the last painting. He reached into the pocket of his apron and pulled out an envelope.

'What's that?'

Stuart smiled and dropped a gentle kiss on the top of her head. 'An invitation to something a bit special.'

Chapter Forty-Six

Bonnie

Present Day

The cheerful Christmas tunes on the car radio were interrupted by the sound of Bonnie's pulse in her ears. When Stuart turned the engine off and the music stopped, her heartbeat became so deafening she looked across at him, expecting him to be looking at her in wonder.

'Can you hear that?' she asked him.

'What?'

'My heartbeat.'

His nose wrinkled. 'Are you joking?'

He pulled the keys from the ignition and opened the car door, but she put her hand on his knee to stop him. 'I don't know if I can go in.'

He shut the door again. 'You might have mentioned that before I drove for six hours to get here.'

'Sorry.' She tried to swallow, but her mouth was dry.

Stuart started the car again, and she jumped. 'I don't want to leave. I'm just scared.'

He laughed. 'I was only putting the heater on. It's freezing.'

The windscreen fogged over and the blue university campus sign, lit by spotlights hidden in the bushes in front of the brick building, disappeared. The air conditioning made a clear arc on the glass and Bonnie watched as the crescent grew, the sign appearing again.

She breathed in through her mouth and out through her nose as Stuart watched, one thick eyebrow lifted.

'Ready?'

'As I'll ever be.'

He took her hand and squeezed. 'I'm so proud of you.'

'Stop it. I don't want to cry.' She flicked her fringe to the side, lifted her chin, and stepped from the car.

* * *

The lights in the building dazzled after the blackness outside. An enormous Christmas tree, gaudy with cheap tinsel and bright baubles, stood next to the turnstiles they passed through at the entrance. Bonnie blinked, looking for the signs to the exhibition room as they passed a vast library where shelves of books were lined up as far as they could see. Arrows stuck on painted walls pointed them down a corridor and soon they could hear voices buzzing.

She gripped Stuart's arm. 'I think I'm going to be sick.'

'Try to breathe evenly,' he said, and stood with his hands on her shoulders until she followed his instructions. 'She wants you here. She invited you.'

'But what if Alice is upset about that? What if she still hates me?'

The door opened and a tall woman in tailored trousers and a silk blouse stepped from the room. It was all Bonnie could do to stop herself from bolting. The woman lifted her head, and when she saw Bonnie, her eyes opened wide. But instead of the gunmetal grey Bonnie had always seen there, they were as soft and warm as the coat of a Russian Blue cat.

Bonnie froze as Alice walked towards her, her hand hovering in front of her mouth. When she reached her, Bonnie saw tears in her eyes.

'Can I give you a hug?'

Bonnie nodded, wordlessly. Alice folded her in her arms and said, 'I'm so sorry. God. I was such a . . . Thank you for coming today. Thank you.'

Alice hugged Stuart as Bonnie watched, astonished, then she straightened, dabbing at her eyes. 'Look at me,' she said, voice unsteady. 'I'm a jabbering wreck.'

'You're not alone there,' said Bonnie.

'Come on.' Alice took her elbow. 'Laura has been watching the door all evening. She can't wait to see you.'

Bonnie allowed herself to be pulled through the door, past groups of people standing in front of paintings, photographs, and sculptures, which she glimpsed in her peripheral vision as she scanned the room for Laura. They turned a corner and in the centre of a small room stood a huddle of people.

'Laura,' Alice called quietly, and Laura turned, face a flashbulb of wonder. She broke from the group and moved in what felt like slow motion to Bonnie. And then she was in front of her, arms winding around her shoulders, pulling her in.

They stayed fixed together, eyes closed, breathing in time with each other, until, eventually, Laura lifted her head and looked into Bonnie's eyes. 'Come with me for a sec.'

She took Bonnie's hand and led her back towards the door. Bonnie glanced over her shoulder at Stuart, who gave a nod and a thumbs up. They went through the door, into the corridor, then into the brightly lit ladies' toilet and stopped by a line of sinks. Laura let go of Bonnie's fingers and wrapped her arms around her again, squeezing the breath from her.

'I know I said, I'd call,' Bonnie said, into Laura's hair, 'But I couldn't find the right words. I—'

'I get it. I needed time to process everything too.' Laura said. 'I knew we had a connection,' she released Bonnie and stood back.

'I made a mess of everything. I'm so sorry.' Bonnie felt her lips twitch, halfway between a smile and a sob. Tears dripped down her cheeks and she swiped them away with her hand.

'It's okay. That's all in the past.'

'Right.'

'And we can look forward now, can't we?'

Bonnie nodded, hope tightening and releasing her heart in huge contractions.

'Breathe!' said Laura and Bonnie allowed the air to escape from her lungs in a laugh, which Laura joined in with as their eyes searched each other's faces.

'I'm so very glad you're here,' said Laura. Bonnie watched as she disappeared into a cubicle, emerging with a wad of toilet paper. 'Wipe your face. Everything is going to be okay.'

When they returned, the room was a babble of voices. Polly hugged her, Stuart was shaking hands with Richard, Xavier, and Nathan, everyone introducing each other and exchanging greetings. Then a quiet voice whispered in her ear, 'Have you seen Laura's exhibition piece?'

Bonnie turned to see Alice behind her, Laura at her side.

'Move to the side, people,' shouted Laura above the voices, and the bodies parted.

As Bonnie focused on the wall facing her, the hairs on the back of her neck lifted. Laura moved next to her, hooking one arm through hers, just as Alice did the same on the other side.

The picture on the wall could have been a mirror. In a plain white frame was a painting of three women. A perfect likeness of Alice stood on the left, and Bonnie was painted on the right-hand side. On their shoulders balanced a plinth on which sat a beautiful, glorious Laura, her pink hair waving like Botticelli's *Venus*. Her hands lay on the shoulders that carried her, and she was smiling directly out of the canvas.

Bonnie's knees buckled and the women on each side of her tightened their arms, holding her between them, moving in close so she didn't fall.

'Isn't it perfect?' said Alice.

'It is,' said Bonnie. 'It's the most beautiful thing I have ever seen.'

Acknowledgements

The process of getting this book from an idea in my head, to the book in your hands or on your e-reader, is a long and complicated one. It takes a lot of talented people to slot all the elements into place, and I'm grateful to each and every one of them.

First, my agent, Laura Williams, who is not only excellent at her job, but brilliant company too. My peerless editors, Thorne Ryan and Elisha Lundin, who waved their editorial wands and helped turn a book with potential into a novel fit to wear the Avon badge. Every person I've worked with at Avon has been enthusiastic, generous, and professional and I am honoured to be part of the gang.

Thank you to my inimitable friend, Jane Leah, who planted the seed of this story when she said, 'Lise, you wouldn't believe the weird reasons people put things in storage.'

The wise women who have helped this book along its way have my eternal gratitude: Kerry Fisher, Emma Mitchell, Suzy Oldfield and Nichola Ibe.

Thank you to my wonderful friends who read early drafts and gave me invaluable feedback: Claire McGlasson, Susie Lynes, Jodi Rilot, Emma Warburton, Heather Moore, Hannah Maynard-Slade, Emma Buxton, Katherine Bridge, Liz Penney and Tracey Cullens.

To the Writers Beers and Clitterati crew, thank you for your friendship, the most incredible retreats, and for always being at the end of a WhatsApp.

John, Eva and Isla, I know that everybody thinks their family is the best, but I'm the only one who is right.

Thanks so much for reading *Her Mother's Lies*. If you have enjoyed it, I would be so grateful if you could review and recommend.

Since you've finished reading, you'll know this book centres on a girl who was adopted and ends up with two mothers, both wonderful in different ways.

My most heartfelt thanks goes out to a woman I have never met, who gave me up for adoption soon after I was born. Like Laura, being adopted has never felt detrimental to me (thanks to being adopted by my lovely Mum and Dad, Bronwen and Kenneth. Love you both).

So, if the teen mother who gave her baby girl up in Yorkshire in 1970 ever reads this, please know you did the right thing. That girl was happy. She still is. I truly hope you are too.

If you enjoyed *Her Mother's Lies*, you'll love Lisa's debut novel *Her Daughter's Secret*.

Will her daughter's secret tear her family apart?

A gripping, heart-wrenching novel about family secrets and the price of love.

Out now!